The Rise of

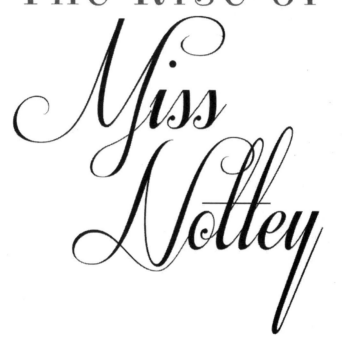

The Rise of

Miss Notley

RACHAEL
ANDERSON

Cover image credit: Lee Avison/Arcangel images

Published by HEA Publishing, LLC

ISBN-13: 978-1-941363-18-8

Oh, what a tangled web we weave
When first we practise to deceive!
—Sir Walter Scott, *Marmion*

OTHER BOOKS BY RACHAEL ANDERSON

Regency Novels
The Fall of Lord Drayson (Tanglewood 1)
Coming August 2017 . . .
The Splash of Lady Harriett (Tanglewood 3)

Contemporary Novels
Prejudice Meets Pride (Meet Your Match 1)
Rough Around the Edges Meets Refined (Meet Your Match 2)
Stick in the Mud Meets Spontaneity (Meet Your Match 3)
Not Always Happenstance (Power of the Matchmaker)
The Reluctant Bachelorette
Working it Out
Minor Adjustments
Luck of the Draw
Divinely Designed

Novellas
Righting a Wrong
Twist of Fate
The Meltdown Match

Miss Coralynn Notley stood on the steps of Langtry Park, directing a pleading glance at the stately butler. "Forgive me for arriving at such an early hour, Sims, but I must speak to Lady Harriett at once." There was a chilly bite in the morning September air, and she hugged her arms to her chest, wishing she had taken the time to don her warmer gloves. The walk had nearly frozen her fingers.

The elderly man's reply seemed to come ages later. "I am afraid she is still indisposed, Miss Notley. Perhaps you could return—"

"I will wait," blurted Cora, for she could not return home now, not when her life had turned on its end. Lady Harriett was really the only person she felt comfortable confiding in, and confide she must. "Please, Sims. This is a matter of great urgency."

Sims hesitated. His gray, almost nonexistent eyebrows cinched together tightly, making him look a bit like a prune. Cora might have laughed if it were any other morning on any other day. But she was in no mood to laugh, so she clasped her reticule tighter in her hands and implored him with her eyes. *Please do not send me away.*

"Sims, what on earth are you doing?" a feminine voice sounded behind the man. He blinked twice before turning around, using his large body to block Cora's view into the house.

"Lady Drayson," he said. "You are up and about early."

"I could not sleep," she answered. "This little one begins pounding my insides the moment the sun peeks through the windows. The only thing that quiets her is a walk around the house and a warm glass of milk."

"I see." Sims turned his head to the side and cleared his throat. His wrinkled cheeks had a pink hue to them as though embarrassed by the frank way Lady Drayson spoke of her unborn child.

"Pray tell, why must you keep the door ajar?" Lady Drayson asked. "There's a rather cold draft coming through the crack."

Sims cleared his throat again and stepped aside, revealing Cora. "We have a visitor, my lady. Miss Notley insists on speaking with Lady Harriett at once. I have told her that—"

"Heavens, Sims, let the poor girl in. She is going to catch a chill standing out there in the cold."

"Yes, my lady." He stepped aside and opened the door wider, nodding for Cora to come inside, which she did.

Cora could have hugged Lady Drayson for her kindness but settled on a grateful smile instead.

The Countess of Drayson stood at the foot of the stairs wearing a pale pink dressing gown and matching slippers. Her beautiful, long hair was woven into a braid that draped elegantly over her shoulder and a small bulge protruded from her once-small waist. Though Cora was not so well acquainted with Lady Drayson as Lady Harriett, she knew Lady Drayson to be both kind and genteel.

"Thank you, my lady," said Cora, dipping into a quick curtsy.

Lady Drayson dismissed the formality with a wave of her hand, her expression becoming concerned as she searched Cora's face. "I hope you are well, Miss Notley."

"I am," Cora rushed to say, feeling awkward for descending on the family this way. How unrefined she must appear. "That is to say, I am in body, my lady, but anxious in spirit."

Lady Drayson gave Cora's hand a comforting squeeze and smiled sympathetically. "Sims, please show Miss Notley to the drawing room. I shall undertake the task of rousing Harriett."

"Oh no," protested Cora. "I will wait for her to arise. I just . . . well, I did not wish to remain at home, is all."

"I understand," said Lady Drayson. "But Harriett will wish to be awakened, I assure you."

Cora felt a moment's relief. She had been pacing the floor of her room all night, ever since she'd overheard the conversation between her father and Sir Gowen. Even now, her stomach roiled at the memory. Cora had always known that she was of little worth in the eyes of her parents, but now she understood exactly how little that was.

"Thank you, Lady Drayson. I am most grateful to you."

Lady Drayson nodded before lifting the skirts of her dressing gown and ascending the stairs. Even in her increasing state, she appeared poised, graceful, and happy. Cora thought of the few times she had seen Lord and Lady Drayson driving or walking the grounds of their vast estate, their heads bent in conversation or smiling and laughing. They seemed so well-suited to each other. It made Cora long for the same even though she knew it could never be.

"If you'll follow me, Miss Notley," said Sims, leading the

way to the drawing room. He threw open the large, wooden doors and stood aside, allowing Cora to pass. "Please make yourself comfortable. You may have a bit of a wait as Lady Harriett is not easily roused."

Cora sank down on a chair covered in cream brocade. Her fingers fidgeted on her lap and her feet refused to remain still. She did not belong here, in this house. To call Lady Harriett her friend made Cora something of an upstart, yet Lady Harriett *was* her friend—her only friend, really. The daughter of a wealthy tradesman, Cora had often felt caught between two worlds—the world she had been born into and the world which her parents aspired to. If her Father had his way, Cora would be made to pay the price for such aspirations.

Unable to remain seated any longer, she rose and began to pace the floor, walking circles around the beautiful furniture. She did not pause to appreciate the lovely scene from the windows or admire the intricately carved marble fireplace as she had done the first time she had been shown into this room. She merely walked and waited and grew more and more angry with her fool of a father. How dare he treat her as a commodity to be traded or sold?

"Cora." Lady Harriett rushed into the room, her lavender dressing gown brushing the floor as she took hold of Cora's fisted hands. "What on earth has happened?" Her ebony hair frizzed around her face in an unruly way. Cora had never seen Lady Harriett in such an unkempt state before. It made her wonder about her own state. Was her auburn hair still secure in its bun? Now that Cora thought about it, she could feel it sway at the nape of her neck while several tendrils tickled her cheeks. How strange to not have noticed that before.

But no matter. What a silly thing to worry about at such

a moment. She clasped Lady Harriett's hands tighter. "My father struck a bargain with Sir Gowen last night. In exchange for introducing my family into society, Sir Gowen will take me as his wife, along with my dowry of twenty thousand pounds."

Lady Harriett gasped, her large, brown eyes widening in shock. "Sir Gowen? But he's twice your age and portly and . . . and the most disgusting creature in all of Essex, possibly even England." The grimace on her face showed exactly how disgusting she thought him.

"Don't forget titled," added Cora, lest Lady Harriett forget his one redeeming attribute, at least in the eyes of her parents.

"But he's only a baron—a rather disliked baron at that. No one of any sense cares a farthing for that man," Lady Harriett argued, clearly not understanding why Cora's father would have bartered for such a match.

Cora sighed. How could she understand? Not even Cora, who knew her parents well, could comprehend it. "His family name dates back several generations, and society's doors are still open to him regardless of whether or not he is well liked. Besides, what other option is there? I'm afraid no duke would have me—not even for twenty thousand pounds."

Lady Harriett's jaw hardened in determination. "You cannot marry him. I will not let you."

"Of course I will not marry him," answered Cora, for she had already determined as much. Sir Gowen looked at her—at most women, really—the way he might look at a steaming roast goose. It gave her the shivers. She would become a scullery maid before she became his wife. "My father will cut me off if I do not comply—assuming he does not strangle me first. I know I must leave, and soon, but . . . well, I really have nowhere to go. At least not yet." Feeling exhausted all of a sudden, Cora sank down on the cream brocade chair once more.

"What do you mean you have nowhere to go?" said Lady Harriett. "You will live here with us, of course." As though that would remedy everything.

Cora forced her lips into something she hoped resembled a smile. How like Lady Harriett to extend such an invitation without pausing to consider the ramifications. It reminded her of the first day they'd met, when they had both stopped in at the milliner's and simultaneously spotted a new bonnet on display.

"What a lovely creation!" they spoke in unison, only to immediately eye each other with certain misgiving.

Lady Harriett immediately pasted a smile on her face but could not hide the calculating look in her eyes. "Yes, that bit of lace is quite lovely, is it not?" She gestured to a length of lace that lay on a table near the bonnet.

Cora refused to be cowed and walked over to the display stand, lifting the bonnet for inspection. "I was not referring to the lace, but to this." It was a beautiful creation, made from tightly gathered white linen and accented with white satin ribbons. Cora had been on the hunt for just such a thing for months.

Lady Harriett took the bonnet from Cora's hands and began looking it over as well. "I am certain you were referring to the lace. This bonnet was made for my head and no other." She removed the pretty bonnet she wore and replaced it with the one on display. "See? It fits perfectly."

"Perhaps, but it pales your complexion in an alarming way. You look rather like a ghost," said Cora, unperturbed. "Perhaps a little rouge on your cheeks would help."

Lady Harriett raised her perfectly arched eyebrow. "I

find it interesting that you would say such a thing, considering we have similar coloring."

Cora lifted the hat from Lady Harriett's head and set it on her own. "Those with an untrained eye might believe that to be the case, but once they see it on my head, they would agree that it compliments my complexion most charmingly. Don't you think?"

Harriett had finally laughed. "I do, actually," she conceded, holding out her hand with a smile. "I don't believe I've had the pleasure. I am Lady Harriett Cavendish of Langtry Park."

Cora experienced a moment's alarm. *Lady* Harriett? As in the Earl of Drayson's sister? Oh dear. Cora ought not to have removed the coveted bonnet from such a distinguished head without so much as a by your leave. What must the lady think of her?

Not knowing what else to do, Cora shook hands and offered a strained smile in return. "Miss Coralynn Notley of Mooreston." Lady Harriett would surely demand to have the bonnet back now. It would be a waste for a beautiful creation to grace the head of such a lowly creature as Cora.

But Lady Harriett had surprised her. "Ah," she'd said. "You are new to the area, I believe. I have heard of Mr. Notley."

"Yes." Cora held the bonnet out to Lady Harriett. "I was only jesting before. It truly looks far better on you." She had thought that would be the end of it, for a lady of good breeding did not socialize with the daughter of a tradesman. But Cora had been wrong again. Very wrong. Not only had Lady Harriett insisted that Cora keep the bonnet, she had invited Cora and her mother to tea the very next day.

But Cora had not informed her mother about her new acquaintance. She'd merely called on Lady Harriett alone—

something she had continued to do over the next several months. To this day, her parents did not know she was a close acquaintance of Lady Harriett Cavendish's, and Cora would see that it remained that way. It was the reason she could never accept Lady Harriett's goodhearted invitation to live at Langtry Park.

"You are too kind, my friend," said Cora. "You know why I could never stay here. My father would eventually find out, and I refuse to provide any connection from your family to him. I'm hoping, instead, that you might know of someone in need of a governess, preferably somewhere far away from here where my father will never find me."

Lady Harriett's eyes constricted. "You cannot leave."

"I cannot stay."

"But—"

"Lady Harriett, please," said Cora quietly. "I have had all night to think on this, and the only solution is for me to disappear. Even though I have come of age, my father is devious and manipulative. Should I stay he will find a way to force me into matrimony."

"He won't need to," said Lady Harriett. "I will be the one to introduce your family into society. He will not need Sir Gowen's connections."

Cora had already anticipated such an offer and was ready with her response. "At what cost, Lady Harriett? You do not know my father. He will parade our family around, making us the laughingstock, and in so doing will tarnish the Cavendish good name. If you call yourself my friend, you would never subject me or your family to that. My visits to Langtry Park these past months have been a respite, a blessed escape. If you welcome my parents here as well . . ." Cora cringed at the thought, picturing her parents crossing the threshold and saying all manner of offensive and vulgar things. Cora would never wish them on anyone, least of all the Cavendish family.

"This will never do." Lady Harriett strode to the bell pull and gave it a hearty tug. When a maid appeared, she instructed the girl to fetch the rest of her family. "Please summon everyone, Molly. Even Colin."

"Lady Harriett, what are you doing?" Cora panicked. She had no wish to burden the entire family with her problems, least of all Lord and Lady Drayson. Good heavens, she should never have come.

"Relax, my friend. I'm merely summoning reinforcements," said Lady Harriett, settling herself neatly on the sofa. "Between all of us, I am entirely certain that we will come up with the perfect solution."

If only Cora could feel as confident.

THE COACH ROCKED FROM side to side as it rumbled along at a fast clip. Cora's gaze remained focused out the window, although the scenery had long since changed from trees and meadows to shadows and moonlit ponds. She could not pry her eyes away. A part of her could not wait to reach their destination while another part wished to keep riding forever.

The only other occupant—Molly, a trusted maid from Langtry Park—had fallen asleep hours before. Cora should be equally weary. It had been a long and arduous five-day journey from Danbury, and she had slept precious little of that time. Her mind refused to rest. It churned with thoughts and worries of the future and what her father would do if he ever learned that the Cavendish family had been involved with her disappearance.

They had been careful. Cora had fled her bedchamber wearing slippers that had crossed the marbled floor at Mooreston without a peep. She had taken only a small portmanteau containing another gown and some necessities, along with a reticule and a small amount of pin money. The servants' door had uttered a small creak upon opening, but no one had stirred, and Cora was able to escape into the early morning darkness without detection. Once outside, she had walked to the road, where a large and comfortable traveling coach boasting the Drayson's crest on the side awaited to steal her away.

Now here she was, five days later, rattling along somewhere in Yorkshire, getting closer and closer to Askern with each turn of the wheels and lift of the hooves. What had her parents thought when they found her gone? Had they cared? Of course they had. Who would marry Sir Gowen if not her? Cora's younger sister, Rose, was not yet seventeen and far too young and timid for the likes of him. So yes, Mr. and Mrs. Notley most assuredly cared that their eldest daughter had fled. It was not every day the sacrificial lamb went astray.

The coach lurched to a sudden stop, and Cora had to grasp Molly's arm to keep the maid from sliding to the floor. The girl startled awake and immediately cowered in the corner, tucking her thin arms tight against her chest.

"Is it a 'ighway man, Miss? Come ter take our shillin's and virtue and—"

"No, Molly," said Cora, gesturing out the window to the beautiful, glowing house beyond. "I believe it is only Knotting Tree. It seems we have finally reached our destination."

Molly's hand went to her heart and she heaved a sigh of relief. "'Twas only a dream."

A joyless smile lifted Cora's lips as she stared at the lovely house and wondered what would become of her life now. "Sometimes dreams can seem so very real, can't they, Molly?"

"That they can, Miss," agreed the maid as she righted her cap and straightened her skirt. "I ain't never felt so scared in all me life."

The door opened, allowing in a gust of chilly air, and the coachman held out his hand for Cora. She grasped it tightly and descended the steps slowly and cautiously, breathing in air that smelled woodsy and fresh. When her feet landed on the ground, she paused to gather her wits about her. Would Mr. and Mrs. Shepherd be as pleased to see her as Lady Drayson and Lady Harriett had led her to believe? It seemed unlikely.

The door of the house opened, and out came a worn and serious looking man that Cora could only assume was the butler. Behind him, an elegant man and woman emerged, peering curiously down at Cora. The woman looked too much like the Countess of Drayson not to be her mother, and the man appeared kind and intelligent, just as Lady Drayson had described him.

Mrs. Shepherd released her husband's arm, picked up her skirts, and walked quickly down the steps to meet Cora. Warmth radiated from her expression. "You must be Miss Notley. A note arrived in the post from Lucy only yesterday, and we have been anxiously awaiting your arrival ever since. I cannot tell you how pleased we are to have you here, my dear."

Whether it was the arduous journey, the lack of sleep for too many days, or the kindness in which Cora had been received by complete strangers, she couldn't say, but she felt her composure slip away as tears began to pool in her eyes. How different would her life be if she had been born to parents such as these.

For Heaven's sake, stop acting like a peagoose, she told herself sternly, quickly wiping away her tears with the tips of her gloved fingers. She had a great many things to be grateful for—the Cavendish family, for one, and now the Shepherds. Cora needed to dwell on that and not wish for something that could never be.

"Please call me Cora. And forgive me for behaving like a

silly school girl," she said to Mrs. Shepherd. "I cannot tell you how grateful I am for your kind welcome, especially considering you know nothing about me."

"I know enough," said Mrs. Shepherd. "Lucy and Harriett think the world of you, so why shouldn't we?"

Cora couldn't help but smile, and how good it felt. She could have hugged Mrs. Shepherd, but the lovely woman was already thanking Molly, the coachman, and the footmen for accompanying Cora on her long journey.

Mr. Shepherd added his thanks as well, telling the servants, "Geoffries will see that you are properly taken care of before you begin your journey home on the morrow."

"Thank you, sir," answered the coachman, dipping his hat.

Mr. Shepherd ushered his wife and Cora inside, and they adjourned to a beautiful drawing room decorated in burgundy and gold. On a circular table in front of the sofa, tea awaited them, along with a large tray filled with everything from thick slices of bread and preserves to ham and cheese and pastries. Cora's stomach rumbled in an unladylike way, reminding her that she had not eaten for hours.

"We already had our dinner, but I'm certain you must be famished," said Mrs. Shepherd. "Cook was good enough to bring up an assortment of food for you."

"It looks wonderful." Cora took a seat on a chair near the table. Her fingers itched to fill a plate, but she clasped them on her lap instead, not wishing to partake of the food in front of her hosts.

"I suddenly find that I am quite famished as well," said Mr. Shepherd, patting his stomach. "I hope you do not mind, Cora, if I fill a plate as well."

"Of course not." Cora laughed. "This is your home, after all. I am but a guest."

"A very welcome guest," he answered with a smile.

Mrs. Shepherd poured each of them some tea while Mr. Shepherd made expert work of filling a plate quite full. It was a wonder all the food remained on it.

"My goodness, you *are* hungry," said his wife.

"This plate is not for me." He looked at Cora and held out the plate. "Please be so good as to take this from me so my wife will cease teasing me."

"You'd prefer that she tease your guest, sir?" countered Cora as she accepted the plate most gratefully.

"It seems unfair, I know, but guests can get away with so much more than husbands. They can read a book whenever they wish, eat as much as they like, and refuse any and all invitations to dine elsewhere. I, on the other hand—"

"Are making me sound like quite the taskmaster," inserted Mrs. Shepherd.

"Not at all, my love," argued Mr. Shepherd. "I am only pointing out the difference in our characters. You are an exquisite butterfly who enjoys fluttering your wings about, and I prefer to remain inside my chrysalis with my books."

Mrs. Shepherd laughed and shook her head. "Chrysalis, indeed. Poor Cora. You probably had no idea you would be subjected to a lesson on the biology of insects. Please say you are not regretting your decision to come to us."

"Of course she isn't," insisted her husband. "I'll wager she couldn't find as diverting a conversation in all the drawing rooms in London."

"Considering I have never been in any London drawing room, I would have to agree." Cora sampled a small bite of a pastry as she watched her hosts. Mr. and Mrs. Shepherd reminded her of Lord and Lady Drayson, at least in the way they teased, smiled, and sat close to one another. Was this how husbands and wives behaved outside of the Notley home, or was it more of an exception than the rule? Her own parents had always bickered and found every excuse not to be in the same room as the other.

"You must prepare yourself," said Mr. Shepherd. "My wife has great plans for you, but the best part is that most of those plans involve you and not me. Really, Cora, I cannot tell you how glad I am that you have come."

Cora's gaze flew to Mrs. Shepherd's. "Plans?" she asked, suddenly anxious.

"Only as soon as you are feeling up to them," said Mrs. Shepherd. "I thought a shopping trip or two would be just the thing to start your new beginning. Lucy mentioned you would be traveling light and would be in need of some additions to your wardrobe."

Food that had looked delectable only moments before suddenly lost its allure. A shopping expedition? Did Mrs. Shepherd not know that Cora had no money for gowns or fripperies? Why would she need such things anyway?

"After that," added Mr. Shepherd, "there is sure to be afternoon teas, picnics, dinner parties, musicales, balls, and—" His wife's gentle hand on his arm quieted him.

"My dear, you appear quite pale," said Mrs. Shepherd. "Is everything all right?"

"Yes. I mean no. I mean . . ." Oh goodness, where did Cora even begin? She set her plate of food on the table and lifted anxious eyes to her hosts. "I do not know how much Lady Drayson has told you, but I did not come with the hope of being launched into local society. Rather, it is my wish that you might help me find a governess position in another household that will grant me at least a small measure of independence. I have very little money with me and do not want to be a burden on you for long."

Mrs. Shepherd leaned forward and placed her hand on

Cora's knee. "My dear girl, we do not think of you as a burden at all. When Lucy's note reached us, we were thrilled at the prospect of welcoming you into our home, especially now that we have seen for ourselves how beautiful, kind, and refined you are. It is our greatest wish to aid you in finding a suitable young man of your choosing to marry so your parents will no longer have any power over you. How can we achieve that if you do not enter society? Surely you must realize that becoming a governess will lessen your chances of making a suitable match."

"I do realize that," said Cora. "But you must understand that I am but a tradesman's daughter and have no desire to marry above my station. The polite world is not my world, and I do not want to spend the rest of my life attempting to be someone I am not. I feel like a misfit already. You see, I was raised with the luxuries the upper class enjoy—more gowns than any young lady should need, servants and more servants, a room the size of a modest farmer's cottage, and any other convenience that money can buy. Rather than attending a girl's school like others in my station, my parents enlisted a governess and tutors to train me in everything from Latin to deportment. In other words, I was brought up to be a member of the upper class, yet I am not one of them. Do you not see what a quandary I am in? I feel like a lost kitten that has been taken in by thoroughbreds."

Mrs. Shepherd's brow creased in a look of concern and she nodded slowly. "I understand why you would feel the way you do. There was a time when I felt the same."

"Truly?" Cora asked, curious to hear more. She had never before met anyone who could even begin to understand. Lady Harriett had always made a valiant attempt, but how could she truly know what it was like when she had never lived in a world other than her own?

Mrs. Shepherd patted Cora's hand before retrieving the discarded plate from the table and handing it back. "It is late and we are keeping you from eating. I propose we continue this discussion tomorrow, once we are rested and have had some time to think on the matter a little more. For now, we will leave you to enjoy your food alone. As soon as you are ready, please ring the bell, and Katy will show you to your room."

"Thank you, Mr. and Mrs. Shepherd, for opening your hearts and home to me. I am most grateful."

They nodded and stood, moving towards the door, but Mr. Shepherd paused and looked back at Cora, his expression pensive. "I want you to know, Cora, that a stray kitten can fit in quite nicely with a brood of thoroughbreds. We've had one make a home in our stables only this past week."

Cora had to smile at that. "I think you are bamming me, sir."

Humor sparkled in his eyes. "I never bam, my dear, at least not about matters of any importance. I wish you a good night."

They walked out the door, leaving Cora to her food and to her thoughts. She leaned back in her chair and looked around the spacious room, thinking how lovely it must appear in daylight. She drew in a deep breath, noting the room smelled a little stuffy, as though it did not get used much. The scent comforted her. Cora's favorite rooms had always been those not frequented by the rest of her family.

Suddenly hungry again, she retrieved her plate and ate what was left on it, enjoying the various flavors and textures of the food. When only crumbs remained, she returned the dish to the table and pulled her weary body to her feet. It only took a few moments after ringing the bell for a young girl to enter the room. Though tall, she slouched as though trying to shorten her height. Her hair was a honey color and pulled back in a severe bun with a few strands escaping. She dipped into a quick curtsy and kept her gaze trained on the carpet. "You are ready to retire, Miss Notley?"

"You must be Katy," said Cora.

The girl risked a peek at Cora and offered a timid smile. "I am, Miss. Katy Thompson, at your service."

Her sweet nature put Cora immediately at ease. "Do you enjoy working here, Katy?"

The maid seemed surprised by the question, and her answer was slow to come. "Aye, Miss. I like it very much. Mr. and Mrs. Shepherd took me on after Mr. Ludlow . . . well, took me off, I suppose you could say. They've been good ter me, givin' me a second chance so ter speak."

"Who is Mr. Ludlow?" Cora asked.

"Oh. 'E be the nearest neighbor to the east, Miss. Owner of Tanglewood. Goes through servants like me ma does flour."

Cora frowned at the description. "Is Mr. Ludlow so cantankerous that servants cannot abide working for him for long?"

"Exactin' be more like," said Katy. "But cantankerous too, for sure. There be no second chances with him. Make one mistake, and you'd better start lookin' for work somewheres else. Only yesterday, 'e sent his 'ousekeeper packin'."

"Really?" Cora found herself intrigued. It sounded like a bit of a mystery.

The maid nodded. "I 'eard it from one of the footmen meself." A light blush colored her cheeks as she smiled. "'E's rather sweet on me, you see."

"He sounds like a very intelligent footman then."

"I dunno about that." Her blush deepened, and her gaze found the carpet once more.

Cora's gaze strayed to a painting on the wall, and she took a few steps closer, noting the details on the bronze vase and the delicate brush strokes used to create the flower petals. What sort of person painted this? It could have been anyone—an accomplished lady or a lowly artist. How interesting the art of painting was. For the upper class, it was a pastime—an accepted way for a lady to fritter away her time. For the lower class, it was a means of survival.

Which person placed more value in the skill? Cora wondered, thinking about her own skills and how useful they were, especially if she did not belong in society. Perhaps that was the crux of the matter. If she could only find something truly useful to do with her life, she might finally find her place in this world.

She turned around and faced the maid. "Tell me, Katy, how would one go about seeking a housekeeper position?"

Katy's brows drew together in a look of confusion. "You'd 'ave to apply to the butler, I suppose. But why would you want ter know such a thin'?"

Cora hesitated, realizing Katy would not understand. Very few could, she imagined. Not even her sister, Rose, seemed to find fault with the upstart ways of their parents. She didn't seem to find fault with anything. "I'm only curious, is all. I've never sought a position of any kind. You simply made me wonder how one went about it, is all."

"Be grateful you 'aven't 'ad ter do it, Miss. There ain't nothin' grand about workin'."

"Perhaps not, Katy. But I must say that I am grateful to you for showing me to my room. It has been a long and weary day for the both of us, I imagine."

"Of course, Miss." Katy curtsied once more. She took a few steps towards the door before adding, "What a lovely room it is, Miss. Mr. and Mrs. Shepherd wanted you to 'ave one of the grandest rooms in all the house."

Cora forced a smile to her lips, even though a heavy feeling of guilt weighed on her. She certainly didn't deserve a grand room anymore than she deserved to waltz into local society. Mr. Shepherd could say all he liked about kittens and thoroughbreds, but no matter how well they might get on in his stables, one was still a feline and the other a horse. There was no changing that.

"CORA, SURELY YOU'RE NOT SERIOUS." Mrs. Shepherd clutched her fork as she gaped at Cora from across the table during breakfast. "A housekeeper?"

Cora feigned a calmness she did not feel. Last night, when she had made the decision to pursue this course, it had felt right. But now, in light of day and with Mrs. Shepherd looking at her as though she'd gone mad, her confidence waned. "Yes, a housekeeper."

"But . . . why?"

"I understand that the neighboring estate—Tanglewood, I believe?—is in need of such a person, and as I am in need of a position, I thought the news providential."

"You are a *tradesman's* daughter, not a farmer's daughter. And an heiress at that," stated Mrs. Shepherd firmly. "Only think of what this could do to your reputation."

Cora *had* thought of that. Late into the night, as she'd mulled everything over in her mind, the likelihood of a ruined reputation had most certainly surfaced. In fact, Mrs. Shepherd had landed on the very thing that had convinced Cora to move ahead with this plan.

23

"I realize that it will likely ruin my reputation, but that does not sway me," answered Cora.

Mrs. Shepherd's eyes widened in astonishment. She glanced at her husband briefly, but he seemed absorbed in reading a letter he'd just received, so Mrs. Shepherd turned back to Cora. "You seem . . . pleased by the prospect. I cannot understand it."

"Can you not?" Mr. Shepherd finally spoke, setting his correspondence aside and turning his attention to his wife. "Should Mr. Notley discover the whereabouts of his eldest daughter, do you think Sir Gowen will be inclined to wed a girl who ran off to become a housekeeper rather than marry him? I'm certain even his pride has its limits. A daughter of a tradesman is one thing; a housekeeper quite another."

"Which is precisely the point I am attempting to make," answered Mrs. Shepherd. "My dear, if you follow through with this plan, no door in polite society will ever be open to you again."

"I understand." Cora refrained from adding that no door was open to her now.

Mrs. Shepherd pressed her lips together and carefully set down her fork. When she lifted her eyes to Cora's once more, they were filled with worry. "Do you also understand that it won't only be Sir Gowen you will discourage? It will be every other possible suitor?"

Cora nodded. "Yes. But sadly, the only type of suitor who will not be discouraged by my low connections will be those who want my father's wealth more than me. I do not wish for such a marriage." Especially not now that she had seen firsthand that happy unions existed.

"But not all men are like that," Mrs. Shepherd pressed. "I was once a seamstress, you know, and . . . well, I am not a seamstress any longer."

Cora's smile softened. "If only I could be as fortunate."

"You can be." Mrs. Shepherd directed a pleading look at her husband, who was now chewing on a thick slice of bacon as though nothing at all was amiss. When he caught his wife's look, he swallowed, set down his fork, and cleared his throat.

"I think it's a brilliant idea."

"What?" Mrs. Shepherd gaped at her husband, but he paid her no mind.

"Tell me, Cora," he said. "How much do you know about drying and pounding herbs?"

"Herbs?" Cora frowned. What did herbs have to do with anything?

"Do you know how to make preserves? Pastries? Do you enjoy distilling waters?"

"I, er . . ."

"What about maintaining household accounts, managing the maids and the cook, and provisioning everything from candles to linens?"

Cora could now see that he was pointing out her sorry lack of qualifications. Although his line of questioning unnerved her, she refused to let him dissuade her. She lifted her chin. "I have always had a firm grasp of numbers, sir, and as to the rest . . . well, I am a fast learner. I believe I shall get along nicely."

"Then we are agreed," he said, picking up his correspondence once more. "You will make an admirable housekeeper, I am certain. Mrs. Shepherd and I wish you very well indeed."

Not sure how to reply, Cora glanced at Mrs. Shepherd, noting that she did not appear quite so frantic any longer. The worry lines had vanished, along with any and all arguments. She settled back into her seat and picked up her fork to resume her eating.

Feeling suddenly out of charity with her hosts, Cora stabbed at the eggs on her plate and took a frustrated bite. With or without their confidence, she would apply to the butler at Tanglewood this very afternoon for the housekeeping position. If he found her as unqualified as he likely would, she would beg for a job in the scullery instead.

Before Cora lost her nerve, she raised her fist and rapped loudly on the door of the service entrance. While she waited for it to open, she rubbed her tender knuckles and looked around. Both the house and the grounds had an aged beauty about them, but in contrast to the warm and welcoming feeling that had surrounded Knotting Tree, the feeling at Tanglewood was decidedly unwelcoming. She couldn't explain why, exactly. Perhaps it was the gardeners who had barely flicked a glance at her, the maid who refused to look up when she passed by only moments before, or the way her knock had echoed hollowly from inside, as though the walls of the house were nothing but a cavernous shell. Whatever it was, Cora didn't care for it.

The door opened with a creak, and a woman a few years older and several inches taller answered. She wore a white cap, a gray dress, and a once-white apron that had become a dingy gray. Her red hair was neatly tucked back into a tight bun, and her cold, gray eyes narrowed as she inspected the newcomer. "You be needin' somethin'?"

Did no one smile on this property? thought Cora as she forced a cheerful reply. "I should like to apply to the butler for the position of housekeeper, if you please."

The woman's eyes widened slightly before her lips

curled into a sneer. She barked out a laugh. "You? A 'ouse-keeper?" Another grating laugh sounded.

Cora was grateful for the maid's reaction. It annoyed her enough to reaffirm her resolve, and she found it easy to meet the woman's gaze squarely. "If you would be so kind as to tell the butler that Miss Notley is here to see him, I would be most grateful." Cora wished she had thought to ask Katy the name of the butler.

"If I'd be so kind," mimicked the maid in a mocking tone. She chortled as she left Cora standing on the step while she went in search of the butler, or at least Cora hoped that's where she'd gone. She sighed and took a step back from the house, glancing up at the gray stone walls. What sort of people worked and lived inside? For most of her life, the only people who had ever been kind to Cora were her family's servants. Her governess, especially. They had been the ones to show Cora the difference between coarseness and refinement, disinterest and genuine concern, tolerance and love. She had assumed all servants were as kind. Apparently, that was not the case. Would the butler laugh at her as well?

Cora was left to simmer for what felt like an eternity. When the maid finally reappeared, her mocking expression had been replaced with a sour glare. Cora found the change intriguing.

"Mr. Ludlow wants ter speak with you right away." The maid turned on her heel, leaving Cora in a state of shock. *Mr. Ludlow?* As in the owner of this cavernous house—the employer Katy described as exacting and cantankerous? Heavens. To think she had been worried about the butler laughing her out of the house. What would Mr. Ludlow say or do? A job as a scullery maid seemed highly unlikely now.

Left with no other options, Cora drew in a deep breath and forced her feet forward. At least she would have a good tale to tell when she returned to Knotting Tree sufficiently humbled.

JONATHAN STARED AT THE charcoal ashes in the large
fireplace as he rested his hand on the polished stone mantle.
It glistened from the afternoon light coming through the two
large windows on the western side of the house. Letting his
arm drop to his side, he wandered over to the nearest
window and peered out over his vast estate. The views from
this spot made his study one of his favorite rooms in the
house. The pristine pond, the untamed wilderness, the
immaculate gardens—it could all be seen from this prime
vantage point. He found the sight most inspiring, especially
when he thought back to the wretched state Tanglewood had
been in only fifteen months prior. Now look at it. It was
breathtaking and magnificent, just as he had hoped it would
one day become.

If only his servants could inspire as much hope in him.

Jonathan clasped his hands behind his back and
frowned. In the short fifteen months that he had owned
Tanglewood, he had already been through several stablehands, a few footmen, and a handful of maids—not to mention three housekeepers. Three! He could not understand it.
Had the overall integrity of people decayed so regrettably

that no one could be trusted these days? If not for his butler, steward, and valet, Jonathan would have no faith left in humanity.

"Sir, Miss Notley's 'ere to see you."

"Thank you, Sally. You may send her in." Sally seemed like a good enough girl. She had a surliness about her that he didn't care for, but she was a hard and dependable worker. For that he was grateful.

Jonathan turned from the window as a woman walked into the room—a *young* woman, far younger than any housekeeper he had ever hired. She couldn't be more than twenty. Even more perplexing was her gown. Though simple, it was well made and finer than most in her station. The bonnet she carried appeared finer still.

Rather than drop her gaze to the ground and offer him a quick curtsy as most would have done, she met his gaze with lovely blue eyes. Honest eyes. Telling eyes. Eyes that told of her anxiety and determination, along with her surprise. Apparently Jonathon wasn't what she had expected either. Perhaps she had pictured him older, uglier, or stodgier, as he had pictured her.

He gestured to an armchair adjacent to the fireplace. "Would you care to take a seat, Miss Notley?"

"I would. Thank you, Mr. Ludlow." Her cultured speech further surprised him. She moved gracefully towards the chair and sat down on the edge of her seat. The light from the windows glinted off her hair. He could see now that the color was a rich auburn rather than the dark brown he had first supposed. Smooth and shiny, it had obviously been well cared for.

Who was this woman, and where had she come from? Jonathan had never laid eyes on her before. He was certain that if he'd caught even a glimpse of her, he would have remembered those blue eyes, high cheekbones, and full lips. She was quite beautiful.

"I have been told you are here to inquire after the housekeeping position," he said for clarification. Perhaps he had misunderstood Sally. He felt as though he should be offering her some refreshment, not interviewing her for a position.

Miss Notley pressed her lips together for a moment before squaring her shoulders. "That is correct, sir."

He continued to watch her, wondering about the circumstances that had brought her to this point. "You are not from around here, are you?" he asked.

"I have come from Essex."

"Essex is a far cry from Yorkshire. What has brought you this far north?"

She swallowed and seemed to choose her words carefully. "I was in need of a change, sir."

"A change of scenery?" he inquired.

She hesitated a moment. "A change in circumstances."

Jonathan waited for her to continue but she did not. What did that mean, exactly? Surely a housekeeping position was not a change most people would desire. Unless . . . Was she running away from something? Or, more likely, *someone*?

"You are not in some sort of trouble with the law, are you?"

"No." Her shoulders relaxed somewhat. "I have committed no wrongs in the eyes of the law, I assure you. I am a person of integrity."

Jonathan had no reason to continue to pry into her personal matters, but her cryptic answers intrigued him. What had brought her here and why did she wish to be his housekeeper? Was Miss Notley even her real name? She claimed to be a person of integrity, but was she truly?

Jonathan had dismissed his previous housekeeper only two days before, so Miss Notley must have already been in Askern. Where was she staying? At the inn? "Might I enquire as to how you came to hear about the housekeeping position?"

"Of course. Katy Thompson is . . . an acquaintance of mine. I believe she once worked as a maid in this house and is currently employed at Knotting Tree."

Knotting Tree, mused Jonathan, mentally adding another piece to the riddle that was Miss Notley. Were the Shepherds acquaintances of hers as well? No, how could they be? If she was a guest at Knotting Tree, she wouldn't be here looking for work. Perhaps she was a relative of Katy's, though he found that unlikely as well.

"I remember Katy Thompson," mused Jonathan. The chit had flirted outrageously with any male servant, causing a great deal of mischief in his household. Jonathan had put up with it until he caught her kissing one of his stablehands during working hours. Having no tolerance for any sort of dishonesty, they had both been dismissed immediately.

Jonathan took a seat across from Miss Notley and studied her for a moment. "Forgive my bluntness, but you seem very . . . young to be seeking such a position."

She raised her chin a notch. "I am not quite two and twenty, sir, but whether that is young, old, or exactly right is a matter of opinion. To the elderly, I may seem very young indeed, but to a babe, I would appear quite ancient. The question you must answer for yourself is whether I am the right person for the position or not."

Jonathan found her frankness refreshing and even smiled a little. "*Are* you the right person for the position?" he asked.

"That is for you to determine. Not I."

"Ah." His smile widened as he settled back in his chair and pressed his fingertips together. "Well, Miss Notley, you should be glad to know you have passed the first test."

Her brows drew together in confusion. "What test was that, sir?"

"That you recognize me as the commanding figure in this household. I must admit that you strike me as the sort of person who might be prone to overstepping the bounds of my authority."

Her gaze dropped to her lap for a moment before meeting his once more. "I cannot deny that I may overstep, as you put it, but if I do, you may feel free to set me firmly back in my place. I shall go without complaint, I assure you."

Her reply elicited a chuckle from him. Jonathan could not remember ever having such an interesting interview before. "Tell me of your qualifications," he said.

Panic appeared on her face, and she quickly averted her gaze to her lap. "Yes, of course. My qualifications . . ." her voice trailed off and her forehead furrowed.

Jonathan brushed his chin with his index finger, enjoying the way she fidgeted and squirmed. "It must be an extensive list if you cannot know where to begin," he said dryly.

She drew her lower lip into her mouth for a moment before allowing it to go free. The look she finally directed towards him was one of chagrin. "Actually, sir, the list is not so extensive as that."

Trying to hide his mirth, he asked, "Can you tell me at least one thing that might recommend you?"

She cast her eyes about the room as though looking for inspiration. When her gaze landed on his desk, she brightened. "I have a solid head for numbers, sir."

"My steward manages most of the accounts."

"Oh." She bit her lip again and frowned before brightening once more. "I am an adequate manager of people."

"Only adequate?" Jonathan couldn't help the chuckle that erupted with the words. Her forehead creased again, and he could practically see her mind churning. She was probably thinking over every encounter she ever had, attempting to judge if that made her more than adequate with people or not.

"Tell me this, Miss Notley," Jonathan said, feeling an unaccountable desire to rescue her. "Could you see to it the maids perform their duties with precision and in a timely way?"

"Certainly."

"Could you dismiss a maid if she fails to accomplish what is expected and search out a suitable replacement?"

"Of course."

"Could you handle the marketing of household and grocery items and work in conjunction with my cook, Mrs. Caddy, to make sure that the pantry and larder are well stocked at all times?"

Miss Notley was a little slower to answer that question. "I believe so."

Jonathan leaned forward, resting his elbows on his knees. "A housekeeper must account for all linens, silverware, soaps, candles, and the like. In other words, the store room would be entirely under your management as well." He allowed her to mull over those duties for a moment before adding, "You say you have a solid head for numbers, so I'm assuming the responsibilities of inventory and provisioning should not be a problem for you."

"No, sir." Based on the way her back straightened slightly, she seemed to take at least a little confidence from that.

"When I have dinner guests," Jonathan continued, "Mrs. Caddy prepares the food, but the housekeeper sees to it that it is served in a pleasing, organized, and timely fashion. Is that something you would feel comfortable overseeing?"

"Certainly," she said, though the word sounded a bit strangled as though she had to force it out.

"Lastly, there's the matter of the still room, which is also managed by the housekeeper. We have a maid specific to that room who will be at your disposal, but a housekeeper must know how to do everything from pounding sugars and drying herbs to pickling vegetables, making preserves and vinegars, distilling waters, and even brewing a soothing tea whenever I feel a headache coming on."

Eyes large and round, Miss Notley stared at him with something akin to horror. Jonathan could barely refrain from laughing. He pressed his lips together to keep them from twitching and waited patiently for her answer.

She finally cleared her throat, and when she spoke, her voice was strong and confident. "I can read a recipe card and follow its directions with precision. I am also handy with the needle."

"My valet and the laundry maid typically do the mending."

She let out a breath, and her shoulders slumped as though she had finally recognized the futility of this interview. "Of course."

Jonathan steepled his fingers under his chin and considered her, wondering what to do. She was grossly unqualified, that much was certain, and he would be a fool to hire such a person. Yet there was something about her that gave him pause. Her frank honesty, perhaps? Her obvious vulnerability? Her show of inner strength? Could she, as she implied, learn how to be a decent housekeeper if given the opportunity?

"Might I see your references?" he asked, grasping for a reason—any reason—to retain her.

Surprisingly enough, her lips began to twitch, and she uttered what sounded like a snicker. When her telling blue eyes met his they were filled with humor. "Mr. Ludlow, surely you must know by now that I haven't any references. As my obvious lack of experience can attest, all I can truly offer is a willing heart and a desire to learn, which is clearly not enough. Please forgive me for taking up so much of your time. I will see myself out."

She took her bonnet by the ribbons, and Jonathan watched her rise with mixed feelings. Offering her the position would undoubtedly cause an uproar in his household—he could already hear Mrs. Caddy grumbling about the woman's many ineptitudes. But he had never met anyone who had spoken with such honesty. It was a rare quality indeed and one he was not anxious to let slip through his fingers. She seemed intelligent enough. Perhaps she *could* catch on quickly. She also seemed the genuine sort who could win over and possibly unite the rest of his staff. Was it possible, once she learned her duties and settled in, that she could become the housekeeper he had been searching for?

Jonathan did not know. But she inspired a hope in him that he had never felt from another candidate.

She was almost out the door when his voice stopped her. "I feel it necessary to point out that you are overstepping the bounds, Mrs. Notley. I have not yet dismissed you."

Her body froze, and she slowly turned around. The look she gave him was one of bewilderment. "You mean *Miss* Notley, not Mrs. Notley, do you not?"

He rose from his chair and stepped towards her, clasping his fingers behind his back. "Married or unmarried, all housekeepers are called Mrs. as a show of respect."

Her mouth parted slightly before she snapped it closed. "You mean to say that—"

"Welcome to Tanglewood, Mrs. Notley." Jonathan had to resist the strangest urge to bow. "I pray you will be as good at managing the female staff as you have been at managing me."

Cora returned to Knotting Tree with a lightness in her gait. In her jubilee, the distance between the two estates felt like a short jaunt away, rather than the long walk it had seemed only an hour before. She had done what she had set out to do—what the Shepherds and the saucy maid, Sally, had led her to believe she would not be able to do. She had been offered the position of housekeeper at Tanglewood. How it had come to pass, she could not say, only that it had.

Her feet skipped up the steps, and when Geoffries answered the door and led her down the long hallway to the library, her feet practically trotted across the marble floor as well. The grandness of the room, with its rows and rows of books, barely registered in Cora's mind as she sought out her host and hostess. Seated in a large wingback chair, Mr. Shepherd read from a book while Mrs. Shepherd sat at a small desk not far away, penning what appeared to be a letter. Both looked up when Cora entered. She quickly wiped the smile from her face, knowing they would not find her news nearly as pleasing as she did.

Mr. Shepherd closed his book and set it on a small table before standing and gesturing for Cora to take a seat. Mrs. Shepherd stood as well, coming to sit beside Cora on the settee.

"You appear conflicted, Cora," said Mr. Shepherd. "It has me rather intrigued. What news do you have for us?"

Rachael Anderson

Cora clasped her fingers together to keep them from fidgeting. "I am conflicted, sir. While I believe the news to be most wonderful, I worry that you and Mrs. Shepherd will find it distressing."

He watched her for a moment, showing neither surprise nor concern. Mrs. Shepherd, on the other hand, could not hide her worry.

"You were offered the position," she said.

"Yes." Cora answered, almost cringing as she did so. How odd that she had known the Shepherds for less than a day and yet she desired their good opinion far more than she had ever desired it from her own mother and father.

"I see," Mr. Shepherd finally said, his expression still impassive. Cora had no idea what he was thinking and wished he could not mask his emotions so easily. She had never been able to hide how she felt.

"Stephen, surely we can't allow—"

"We can't *not* allow it, my love," he corrected his wife gently, looking at Cora. "Are you certain you have thought this through, Miss Notley?"

"I have, sir, and I am determined. I will report tomorrow morning for my first day." She paused, choosing her next words with caution. "I know you think I am about to commit a monumental folly, but it is my folly to make, is it not?"

His lips lifted slightly at that. "It is."

Mrs. Shepherd cast a warning glance at her husband. "Yes, but you are under our care now, and it is therefore our duty to make certain that you understand the consequences of your choice. Please consider carefully before you move forward with this."

"Tanglewood feels so hollow." Cora blurted, needing them to understand. "When I first entered its walls, it seemed

38

to be missing its heart and I didn't much care for the place at all. But after I had spoken with Mr. Ludlow, I felt . . . differently. I no longer believe Tanglewood has no heart. I believe it's merely broken and in need of fixing."

Cora pressed her lips together, trying to form her emotions into words. "I should very much like for my life to serve a purpose—to do something good, something of value, something that will make me feel useful and needed. This afternoon I have been offered such an opportunity, and I would like to take it. My decision is no longer about running away or making myself appear less desirable to the likes of Sir Gowen. It is about discovering what capabilities I have outside of the drawing room and exploring any and all possibilities. Tarnishing my reputation is merely a perk."

Mr. Shepherd smiled a little. "I believe you are the only young lady of my acquaintance who views a tarnished reputation as a perk."

An answering smile lifted Cora's mouth. "If you ever have the unlucky experience of meeting Sir Gowen, I daresay you would consider it a positive as well."

"I hope never to have such an opportunity."

Mrs. Shepherd's brow remained creased. "Tell me, Cora, what was your opinion of Mr. Ludlow?"

"Mr. Ludlow?" Cora thought back to the moment she had laid eyes on the man. She had noticed his height immediately and had been surprised by how young he looked. He couldn't be much more than thirty. He was also handsome, but not in the usual way of gentlemen. He had allowed his hair to grow longer than was fashionable and kept it a bit unruly. But it seemed to fit him, as though he was a bit unruly or even untamed. He moved and spoke with an air of intelligence and confidence, and his striking green eyes had made her feel transparent. When he smiled, a charming dimple had appeared on his left cheek. The sight of it had the most perplexing effect on her stomach—almost like a tickle, but not quite.

Cora nearly touched her stomach at the memory, but quickly chided herself for such silliness. Goodness, she was about to be the man's housekeeper, not his partner for the next dance. She needed to remember her place and not allow her mind to dwell on Mr. Ludlow despite his pleasing appearance and mysterious ways.

Cora forced her mind to other things she had noticed— his kindness, professionalism, and candor—and finally gave Mrs. Shepherd an answer. "I thought him intelligent, eloquent, and fair. I made my inexperience known, he stated his expectations, and . . . well, he seemed pleased enough with my answers to offer me a chance."

"You were perfectly clear about your . . . er, abilities?" Mrs. Shepherd pressed.

"Or lack thereof?" Cora smiled. If she had made anything perfectly clear, it had been that. "Yes, I most certainly did."

She frowned. "And he still offered you the position."

"Yes."

"I see." Mrs. Shepherd lapsed into a thoughtful silence, saying nothing more. Cora found herself wondering what the woman saw that she didn't. Had Mr. Ludlow been wrong to offer her the position? Did Mrs. Shepherd believe he'd taken leave of his senses?

Perhaps he had, thought Cora with a frown of her own.

When Mrs. Shepherd spoke again, she seemed to choose her words carefully. "While I cannot condone this plan, I do agree with Mr. Shepherd that we are in no position to tell you what you may or may not do with your life. If you truly mean to go through with this, all I can offer you is my hope that the experience is everything you want it to be. But if it is not, or if you find yourself in a situation that you no longer wish to be in, please know that you always have a place here with us."

"Yes," agreed Mr. Shepherd. "And we would very much like for you to pay us a visit on the first afternoon you have free. We will be most anxious for news."

Cora nodded as a feeling of nervousness settled around her. The tension in the air made it seem as though the Shepherds foresaw something she didn't. But what?

"Thank you for your kindness to me," said Cora. "If you truly will not mind having a housekeeper call on you, I will most certainly visit."

"You can come as a scullery maid and we would welcome you with open arms," said Mr. Shepherd.

Cora's heart warmed at his words. "That is good to hear. I'm very much afraid that once Mr. Ludlow realizes the full extent of my incompetence, he will surely reduce me to the scullery."

The comment produced a smile from Mrs. Shepherd. It was only a small one that didn't quite reach her eyes, but it was a smile nonetheless. Cora would have to content herself with that.

"You will probably be given a few uniforms for your work," said Mrs. Shepherd. "But I should think that you will want something more than what you brought with you to wear on your afternoons off. Since you have denied me the opportunity to take you on a shopping excursion, would you allow me to outfit you with a few of my older gowns instead? We seem to be of a similar height and size. I'm certain we can find a few things that will fit you nicely."

Cora would never admit it out loud, but one of the most difficult things about leaving Danbury—aside from saying goodbye to Lady Harriett—was walking away from her extensive wardrobe. Her father had insisted that she be as well dressed as any of the gentry, and Cora had never fought him on that score. What woman didn't enjoy having lovely clothes to wear? It was one of the blessings of wealth she would miss most.

She looked gratefully at Mrs. Shepherd. "I should like that very much."

"I am glad to hear it. Why don't you go up to your room, and I will meet you there in a short while?"

Cora nodded and rose slowly, feeling strangely hesitant to leave. As she walked down the hall and up the grand staircase, she thought of how drastically her life was about to change. Today, she was a welcomed and honored guest returning to her lavish bedchamber. On the morrow, she would take on the role of a servant—one who would be required to look for dust and discrepancies rather than be at liberty to enjoy the beauty surrounding her.

Once she reached the landing, Cora realized she had left her favorite bonnet on the settee. Turning around, she quickened her steps down the stairs. Geoffries was nowhere to be seen, so Cora lifted her hand to knock on the library door, only to be stopped by the voices of Mr. and Mrs. Shepherd coming through a small crack.

"But we know so little about him," Mrs. Shepherd was saying. "He may seem charming and kind at social engagements, but he has never been forthcoming with personal information and is still a mystery to everyone in town. We don't even know what brought him to Askern, let alone where he came from. What if he is no gentleman at all? Surely he could see that Cora has been well educated and brought up in a situation of some wealth. One look at her gown and bonnet would make that much obvious, to say nothing of her refined speech. I cannot help but wonder at his reasons for hiring a beautiful young woman who is not skilled at all in housekeeping. I own, I am fearful for her safety."

"My dear, you must calm yourself," urged Mr. Shepherd in that tranquil way he seemed to approach every situation. "Mr. Ludlow has always behaved as a gentleman, and until proven otherwise, he must remain a gentleman. That said, I do think it is past time that we further our acquaintance with our nearest neighbor, wouldn't you agree?"

"Yes," Mrs. Shepherd said. "I have a great many questions I should like him to answer."

Mr. Shepherd chuckled. "You mean to interview him as he has interviewed our Cora?"

"I think it only fair I should be allowed to do so," she said.

He laughed. "And we shall, together. But not overtly, of course. Rather, we will probe and question in a subtle, neighborly way so that Mr. Ludlow will be none the wiser."

"And should we detect even the smallest amount of indecency in him, you must promise that you will remove Cora from Tanglewood immediately."

"Of course." A moment of silence followed before Mr. Shepherd's voice sounded again. "Something is still bothering you. What is it?"

"I feel as though we are sending our kitten to the wolves. Perhaps I worry too much."

"It does you credit, my love. But off you go now. Cora is surely awaiting your arrival with the promised gowns."

Cora quickly spun around, lifted her skirts, and raced back up the stairs and into her room. She closed the door and let her breath come out in heavy spurts. Only moments before she had felt like a confident woman ready to take on the world, but now she felt young and naïve, like a fanciful schoolgirl who had no notion of what the real world was like. Her heart pounded in the most unnerving way, and for the first time since accepting the position, Cora experienced doubt.

"IT'S ABOUT TIME YOU got 'ere." Mrs. Caddy was a short, round woman with frizzy gray curls held down by a white cap. She stood bent over a large mound of dough, kneading it with strong hands. When she glanced up, her expression looked haggard and cross, as though Cora's appearance came as an annoyance rather than a relief. "The maids 'ave been up for 'ours."

Cora tightened her hold on her bag and reminded herself that she answered to Mr. Ludlow and not to Mrs. Caddy. "Mr. Ludlow said that I should come in the morning. He did not specify a time, and I did not think you would like me to arrive during the frenzy of breakfast preparations, so I have come now instead."

"Of course you did. Why come earlier, when you could leave me ter arrange the trays meself?" Mrs. Caddy said with a huff.

She used the plural form of tray as though a regiment of soldiers resided here and not one man. Cora lifted a brow. "Is Mr. Ludlow entertaining guests at the moment, or did you mean to say I left you with his tray to arrange?" Cora attempted to soften her words with a smile.

Unfortunately, the smile did not serve its purpose. Cora was awarded a solid glare before Mrs. Caddy began pounding away at the ball of dough. Cora supposed she should be grateful the woman took to abusing the dough and not her.

"Could you direct me to my room, Mrs. Caddy?" Cora asked, not sure where to go. The maid who had answered the door had led her to the kitchen then left without a word.

"Up the stairs, first room on the right."

"Thank you."

"Be warned that mine's the second room, and I'm told me snore can wake the dead."

"Of course it can," Cora muttered under her breath as she lugged her bags towards the stairs. With all the new gowns Mrs. Shepherd had provided her, Cora had needed additional luggage. She felt the burden of it now.

A gangly footman with a mop of blond curls and freckles stopped her progress by reaching for her bag. "I'd be 'appy to 'elp if you like. My name's 'Arry. I take it you're ter be the new 'ousekeeper? Mrs. Notley, is it?"

"Yes, and I would be grateful—"

"You'll be doin' nothin' of the kind, 'Arry," called the cook. "You'd best finish polishin' that silver or Watts'll be polishin' your backside."

Harry rolled his eyes. "Lest you be forgettin', Mrs. Caddy, I take my orders from Watts and not you."

"Don't be gormless. That's what I said—that Watts'd be polishin' your backside, not me."

Harry chose to ignore the comment and winked at Cora. "Let me be the first ter give you a proper welcome ter Tanglewood, Mrs. Notley. In case you 'aven't noticed, people 'ere are a bit tangled too—Mrs. Caddy bein' the worst of the lot. 'Appen you're here ter sort us all out."

"Sort you out, more like," Mrs. Caddy said.

"Never mind 'er," said Harry loud enough for Mrs. Caddy to hear. "She's just a crotchety old 'ag who don't like no one or nothin'."

Based on her brief interaction with the woman, Cora could not disagree with Harry's assessment. She followed him up the stairs, grateful for at least one friendly face. Harry deposited her bag just inside the door before winking at her again. "You be needin' anythin' else, Mrs. Notley?"

"No, thank you, Harry. It seems I am in your debt."

His smile turned devilish, and his eyes perused her person. He leaned a shoulder against the wall. "'Ow grateful are you, exactly?"

Not appreciating his tone or insinuation, Cora frowned at him and folded her arms. "If you are expecting more from me than a thank you, Harry, you will be disappointed. I am a housekeeper, not a trollop."

Harry's face reddened, and his gaze dropped to the floor. "My apologies, Mrs. Notley. I was just 'avin' a little fun is all. Didn't mean nothin' by it, I swear."

Cora sighed, not wanting to make enemies with the one person who had been kind to her. "Fun is all well and good, Harry," she said. "But not at the expense of a person's reputation. I will gladly accept your apology if you will accept my offer of friendship and only friendship."

His smile returned, along with an approving glint in his eyes. He shoved away from the wall. "I think you're goin' ter get on fine 'ere, Mrs. Notley. Truth be told, I'd be glad ter call you friend. Good ones are 'ard ter come by round 'ere."

"Friends it is then," she replied, grateful he had not taken offense at her words. "Thank you again for your help with my bag."

"If'n you ever need anythin', just give me a holler, and

I'll come runnin'." He brushed past her and trotted down the stairs, his slightly too-long arms dangling awkwardly at his sides. He looked to be a few years older than Cora but seemed younger somehow.

She released a deep breath and stepped into her new room. Compared to what she was used to, this space was small and plain, but it also happened to be larger than she had expected, likely because it was the housekeeper's room. It contained a bed, a wardrobe, and even a comfortable looking chair. Above the bed, a small window looked out over the wilderness area at the side of the house and let in a fair amount of light. Cora smiled at the sight, knowing any free time she might have could be pleasantly spent right here.

Cora hurried to unpack her few things, including the three extra gowns Mrs. Shepherd insisted on giving her. They were lovely creations of pink, peach, and blue muslin that complemented Cora's darker complexion, adding some cheerful color to her plain and pitiful wardrobe. On top of the chest she found four light gray dresses, white aprons, and a few caps. She touched them gingerly, trying not to compare their drabness to the gowns she had recently unpacked.

Once settled, she changed into her new uniform, tied the apron around her waist, and placed the cap on her head. The small looking glass above the bed afforded her only a glimpse of her head. She turned her face from one side to the other, examining her new look. Not too terrible, she thought, even if it did make her look a mite pale.

Knowing Mrs. Caddy was likely working herself into an even greater state of petulance, Cora gave the room one last glance before returning downstairs to where Mrs. Caddy was now rolling out the beaten dough on the table. Cora approached with caution.

"Do you know where I might find Mr. Ludlow?" she asked.

"He's assessin' the estate with the land steward," came the cook's reply. She continued to roll the dough, not bothering to say anything more.

"Oh." Cora glanced around the kitchen, at a loss as to what to do or where to go. Mr. Ludlow knew that she would arrive this morning. Surely he hadn't thought she could assume her duties with what little information they'd discussed during their initial meeting. Cora needed at least some direction, and from the coolness of Mrs. Caddy's reception, it would not come from her.

Sally chose that moment to enter the kitchen. She took one look at Cora, and her eyes narrowed. "I suppose I'm ter report ter you now."

"Yes," Cora answered, struggling to feign a confidence she did not feel. The woman was at least five years her senior and taller to boot. It was obvious she despised the idea of reporting to someone younger and less experienced. If Cora did not tread carefully, things between them could get sticky. She needed to find a way to "manage" Sally in a way that would not make her feel managed.

"It's Sally, is it not?"

"Aye, *Mrs. Notley*." Sally sounded more demeaning than respectful.

Cora pushed aside her irritation and mustered a cheery tone. "Considering it is my first day and I am unfamiliar with Tanglewood, I was hoping you would be willing to show me around."

Sally immediately bristled and appeared ready to give Cora a set down, but she seemed to rethink her reaction, and her scorn was replaced with a calculating look. The smile she offered Cora was anything but genuine.

"I'd be 'appy to show you 'round, Mrs. Notley."

Cora suddenly wished she could withdraw the request,

but now that it had been extended and accepted, all she could do was say, "Thank you, Sally."

"'Ow about we start off in the still room?" Sally gestured to a doorway on the other side of the kitchen and started towards it, not waiting for Cora's answer.

Cora followed at a slower pace, half expecting to be assaulted the moment she stepped in the room, but the maid stayed several paces away. Cora did not know what to think of the woman. Perhaps this was her way of attempting to be nice? As the housekeeper, Cora did have the power to dismiss her, after all.

Cora glanced around the room, seeing that it did, indeed, look still. And cramped. A massive wooden table stood in the middle, holding all sorts of interesting gadgets and instruments. She had never seen most of them before and could only imagine what they were used for. Drying herbs hung from a string across one wall, and two other walls were lined with shelves filled with bottles, jars, and pots of all different sizes and shapes. The last wall contained a stove that heated a large pot of something. The steam rising from the top made the room stuffy and hot. Already, Cora was beginning to perspire. She looked around, trying not to be dismayed at the prospect of needing to frequent this room. If not for the small window in the back corner and the light it allowed into the room, she might have considered dismissing herself and making a dash back to Knotting Tree.

Sally began rattling off everything that took place in the still room—what each gadget was used for, where the recipes were kept, what herbs were currently hanging on the line. Then she went on to explain the extensive variety of foodstuffs that were made in the room. She used words Cora had never heard before and spoke so quickly that it sounded like a different language. It didn't take long for Cora's mind to whirl, wonder, and worry. Was that cloth used to roll sugars or was it a cleaning rag? What was distillation, exactly? Had Sally said "cask"? If so, what was it used for and how? Would Cora really be required to know how to restore flat wines and make pastries? Surely that responsibility fell to the cook, did it not? She couldn't remember Mr. Ludlow mentioning anything about pastries.

The more Sally prattled, the more smug and arrogant she became, as though she took great satisfaction from overwhelming the new housekeeper. It wasn't long before Cora began to wonder if the wooden mallet could also be used to strike the housemaid.

When Sally finally finished her speech, she had the audacity to approach Cora with a swing in her hips and a challenge in her eyes. "You know nothin' about 'ousekeepin', do you? 'Appen the only reason you got the position over me is because you's younger and prettier. Watch and see. As soon as Mr. Ludlow 'as 'is fun with you, you'll be out on your backside quicker than Katy Thompson."

She purposefully bumped into Cora's shoulder on her way out of the room, and Cora let her leave without comment. No good would come from sparring with Sally now, not when the woman was in such a foul mood. Cora's father and his quick temper had taught her that much. But it irked her that she had to stand by and keep her mouth shut when she had a great deal she wanted to say to the maid.

What sort of household was this? And what had Sally meant about Katy Thompson? Was Mr. Ludlow the reason Katy had left? Had he trifled with her then tossed her out once he'd tired of her? Was that why he'd been through so many servants and why the Shepherds seemed so concerned? Cora couldn't think of another explanation.

She frowned and clenched her jaw as anger took a self-righteous hold on her spirit. Apparently Harry wasn't the only person who needed clarification on boundaries.

"Has Mrs. Notley arrived yet, Mrs. Caddy?" a deep, reverberating voice echoed from the kitchen, sounding like a soft rumble of thunder.

"Only just," snipped Mrs. Caddy.

Before the cook could say anything more, Cora strode purposefully from the still room. She nearly ran into a small, timid-looking girl, who ducked past her. *The still room maid?* Cora wondered briefly before pushing the thought aside and focusing on the man in front of her. Tall and large, with the broadest shoulders she'd ever seen, the man's upper body resembled the shape of a box. Cora couldn't help but wonder how his long, lean legs managed the weight. He appeared so out of balance. Even his aged face was more square than oval, with deep grooves surrounding his mouth and eyes.

This must be Watts, she thought.

"Hello," said Cora. "I am Mrs. Notley."

"So you have come at last," he said.

Cora refrained from informing him that she had arrived an hour earlier. "I apologize if I have kept anyone waiting."

"Your timing is most convenient," he said in a formal manner, not sounding upset at all. "I have been instructed to broaden your understanding of Tanglewood and your duties, and have only now been able to make myself free enough to do so. If you had arrived earlier, you would have been made to wait. I am Watts, the butler here at Tanglewood."

Sorely tempted to arch an eyebrow at Mrs. Caddy with a look that said, *Hear that? My timing is convenient,* Cora instead focused her attention on the butler. "It is good to meet you, Watts. I will appreciate whatever help you can give me."

"Shall we begin upstairs?" he asked. "As the housekeeper, you will need to understand the exacting standards the maids are expected to maintain. If a job is not properly done, both you and the maid will be held responsible as you are her direct supervisor."

"Of course." Cora prayed the list of expectations for the upstairs rooms would be shorter and less foreign to her than that of the still room.

Watts walked from the kitchen with long and fast strides, and Cora had to be quick on her feet to maintain pace with him. They arrived in the great hall just as the front door opened. Mr. Ludlow strode inside, looking as impeccably dressed and handsome as he had in their first meeting. He nodded to Watts and Cora before stripping off his riding gloves and handing them to an accompanying valet or a footman—Cora couldn't be sure which. The servant merely accepted the gloves and disappeared down a hall.

"Good day, Mr. Ludlow." Watts's voice boomed through the vast space, filling it with a richness that Cora found oddly comforting.

"Good day, Watts." Mr. Ludlow's gaze slipped to Cora. "And you as well, Mrs. Notley. I hope you have been made to feel welcome and have not been too overwhelmed on your first day here. Your dress seems to fit all right."

"Yes," said Cora stiffly. Was that appreciation she spied in his gaze? The thought further rankled her, and she determined to speak with him as soon as possible. "Sir, there is a small matter I wish to discuss with you when you have a moment."

Mr. Ludlow looked a bit surprised, and Watt's immediately came to his rescue. "Is it something I might be able to help you with, Mrs. Notley? Mr. Ludlow is a busy man."

"I understand," said Cora. "But I'm afraid this is a matter

only Mr. Ludlow can clarify for me—not an urgent one, by any means. Any spare moment will suffice."

After a brief hesitation, Mr. Ludlow gestured to a lovely room located at the side of the great hall. "I have a few moments now, Mrs. Notley. Would you care to join me in the parlor?"

"Oh, I did not mean . . ." Cora cast a concerned look at the butler. She had not expected an immediate interview with her employer. "Watts was about to show me—"

"If now is convenient for Mr. Ludlow, it is convenient for me," said Watts. "You will find me in the kitchen once you have finished your conversation."

Cora nodded and followed Mr. Ludlow into the parlor. He closed the doors and stood in front of them with his arms folded, looking far more intimidating than he had during their last meeting. He said nothing, merely lifted an inquiring eyebrow and waited.

Caught unprepared, Cora stared at him, trying to organize her thoughts into words. After a few moments of awkward silence, he lost patience. "What is it you wished to speak with me about, Mrs. Notley? Or are we to stand here staring at each other all afternoon?"

Not knowing how else to begin, Cora blurted, "Why have you hired me, sir?"

He blinked a few times before frowning. "I believe I have made that perfectly clear. You are to be the housekeeper, are you not?"

This was going to be more difficult than she had imagined. "Yes, of course, but there has been some talk about, or rather concerns expressed . . ." How did one put this delicately?

"About . . .?" he prodded, obviously not thrilled that his morning regime had been waylaid.

"About the reasons I have been offered the position," she quickly said, hoping that would be enough to make him understand her meaning.

Unfortunately, his brows drew together in confusion. "What are you saying, Mrs. Notley? I have hired you to do certain duties that will hopefully make my household run more smoothly. What other reason could I possibly have for offering you the position?"

"You have hired me to do a job I am untrained to do," she said. "While I am grateful for the opportunity, I also find it necessary to clarify that I have come here to be a house-keeper and only a housekeeper. Even though I am young and . . ." Her voice drifted off. Had she almost referred to herself as pretty? Goodness, this was proving to be very awkward indeed.

"Beautiful?" he finally guessed, not looking at all pleased with the direction the conversation was taking.

"I was going to say not repulsive," she fibbed.

"Very well," he said. "Even though you are young and not repulsive . . ." He moved his hand in a circular gesture, urging her to finish her thought.

Cora straightened her shoulders and forced herself to continue. "I am not the sort of girl who would ever . . . fraternize with her employer." Her face infused with heat, but she forced her gaze to remain steady.

"I see." He walked slowly towards her, rubbing his chin with his hand. A few steps away, he stopped and eyed her quizzically. "Have I made any improper advances towards you?"

"No, sir."

"Have I spoken to you in an unprofessional manner?"

"No."

"Have I *looked* at you in a way that has made you feel uncomfortable?"

"No." Cora thought of how he'd noticed her dress fit well, but it would be ridiculous to mention something so inconsequential. She suddenly wished she had not felt the need to clarify anything. He made her feel as though she had put the cart before the horse when what she had been trying to do was see that the cart and horse simply stayed in their proper places. Was that so wrong?

"Might I ask who, exactly, has led you to believe that I am the sort of man capable of, how did you put it? *Fraternizing* with my help?"

"I, er, would rather not say, sir." Though Cora felt no loyalty towards Sally, she refused to bring Mr. and Mrs. Shepherd's names into the conversation. "I did not mean to besmirch your name or cause any offense, Mr. Ludlow. I merely wanted to make my feelings on the matter clear."

"And you have."

"Good." Cora dropped into a quick curtsy, anxious to get away. "I shall go and find Watts now."

She was almost to the door when his voice stopped her. "Once again, you are attempting to scuttle away before we have completed our conversation."

Slowly, she turned around and lifted her eyes to his. "I never scuttle, sir."

"What would you call that rapid walk of yours?"

"A rapid walk," she said quickly, making him chuckle. "And I apologize. I had thought our conversation finished."

"No," he said. "You merely wished for it to be finished."

"And you do not?" How could he not wish to put this awkward business behind them?

"I think it only fair that I be given the opportunity to explain my thoughts on the matter."

Cora clasped her fingers together and did her best not to fidget.

Mr. Ludlow's gaze dropped to the carpet, and he began a slow and steady walk around her person as though deep in thought. Once he had circled all the way around, he stopped in front of her and looked directly into her eyes. "Mrs. Notley, I would like you to know that your youth, inexperience, and . . . non-repulsiveness"—His lips twitched a little at that—" did not weigh at all in your favor. In fact, they weighed against you. What impressed me most was your integrity. That is not a trait a person can learn, the way one might learn to carve a ham or arrange a platter. Rather, it is a quality that comes from within and one I happen to value far greater than experience, age, or . . . beauty." He smiled, revealing that charming dimple.

Cora suddenly felt as though her heart would dash right out of her chest. It pounded and thudded, echoing loudly in her ears. No one had ever looked at her with such warmth or complimented her with such plain speaking. She couldn't help but feel drawn to him in a way that was not appropriate at all to her new station. She immediately broke eye contact.

"Thank you for explaining that to me, Mr. Ludlow. It relieves my mind greatly. I shall strive to not disappoint the trust you have bestowed upon me."

"I'm sure you shall."

She refused to look at him, worried he'd see her attraction written plainly across her face. If only she could find *him* a little repulsive. "Am I excused now, sir?"

"You may go."

"Thank you." She dipped into a quick curtsy and did her absolute best not to scuttle from the room.

"MR. LUDLOW IS REQUESTIN' ter see you in the drawin' room, Mrs. Notley." The gleeful way Sally spoke told Cora that whatever her employer wished to speak to her about would not be good.

Cora set aside the mallet she was using to pound sugar and opened and closed her hands, trying to relieve the soreness in her palms and fingers. Already calluses were beginning to form. Her weary body ached in places she did not think it could ache, and it had taken every ounce of strength she possessed to pull herself from her bed that morning. It was a good kind of weary—the kind that made her too tired to fear what was to come.

Her one thought of *What have I done now?* was more lackluster than concerned.

Cora's first week of work had been disastrous. It seemed she was destined to learn the proper way of things by doing them completely wrong. On the day she'd gone to market, she had made what she thought was an excellent bargain on a particularly tender cut of beef, but upon returning to Tanglewood, Mrs. Caddy had taken one look at the parcel and tossed it into the trash. She proceeded to give Cora an earful about wasting good shillings on meat not fit for even the animals. She did not explain why it was unfit for humans or animals, merely berated Cora for several minutes, as though a sound lecture would keep her from purchasing bad meat again. It was Watts who had pulled her aside in the end, offering a kind tutorial about the color and qualities she needed to look for in fresh meat and how one negotiated a fair price for it. Cora's esteem for Watts grew a great deal after that.

Not quite a day later, a once-white tablecloth she had taken upon herself to wash had emerged from the water with a decidedly lavender hue to it. *Lavender*, in a bachelor's household! When Cora turned to Watts for help, he'd reached into the tub and fished out a handful of soggy flower petals, holding them out for her inspection.

"The petals might give the cloth a pleasing scent, but surely you know that the color will bleed off the petals and dye the cloth permanently. I'm afraid it will be impossible to return this to its former white now."

Cora had found it necessary to defend herself. "I may be inexperienced, Watts, but I am not a widgeon. I know how cloth is dyed and I did not add those petals to the wash basin. I merely mixed in soap and a bit of that powdery substance in that jar, like the laundry maid taught me to do."

"Perhaps next time you should make sure there are no petals in the basin before you begin."

Cora had almost told him the tub had been clean as well—she had made sure of it—but then she recalled that she had not shaken out the cloth before adding it to the water. Some of the purple chrysanthemums she had used as table decorations the night before must have been carried away with it, so it was her doing after all.

Cora stared down at the soggy and ruined cloth.

Perhaps Mr. Ludlow would come to enjoy this particular shade of lavender? The sympathetic look on Watts's face had not given her much hope.

Unfortunately, that was not the end of her misfortunes. She had also burned her first attempt at pastries and filled the kitchen with an awful-smelling smoke that lingered in the air the remainder of the day, and, according to Mrs. Caddy, gave every meal a pungent flavor. After that, there had been the broken vase, the kitchen curtain that had caught fire when she placed a burning candle too close to it, and her first attempt at a restorative tea gone very wrong. Mr. Ludlow had sent the tea back directly, along with a note for Cora that read:

> *The tea may not have helped the ache in my head but it certainly restored my stamina. I have never scuttled from my bed so quickly.*

Cora wasn't sure what to think of such a missive—at least not until Harry had taken it upon himself to sample the tea. He immediately ran to the sink and spit it out.

That is what he meant by scuttle, Cora thought dismally.

"What the blimey did you put in that?" he gasped, downing a mug of ale to ward off the flavor.

Cora had later discovered she'd added cayenne and not cinnamon as the recipe had called for. But in her defense, the two bottles had been shelved incorrectly, and they looked so much alike that she had not realized the difference until she had dipped her finger into the tea and tasted it herself. The heat that burned her tongue told her something other than cinnamon had been added.

That had been yesterday, and now, only hours before her first afternoon off, Cora was being summoned for yet another problem. Why else would Mr. Ludlow be requesting an audience with her at this time of morning? If everything was running as it should, he would leave her to it.

Outside Mr. Ludlow's study, Cora squared her shoulders and walked in, mustering all the energy she still possessed.

Mr. Ludlow was seated in a large wingback chair, staring at a tray of sweet rolls that Mrs. Caddy had made earlier.

"Do have a seat, Mrs. Notley," he said, gesturing to the armchair across from him.

Cora sank down slowly, eyeing him with apprehension. He didn't seem angry or annoyed, merely thoughtful. Was that good or bad? Perhaps he only wanted to discuss upcoming plans with her.

He picked up a plate containing one of the sweet rolls and held it out to Cora. "Might I offer you some refreshment?"

She shook her head slowly, thinking how very odd of him to say such a thing to his housekeeper. Mrs. Caddy had made those for visitors, not housekeepers. "No thank you, sir. I am not hungry."

"Mrs. Caddy is quite famous for her sweet rolls in these parts. You really ought to at least try one."

Thus persuaded, Cora accepted the plate and took a small bite of the roll. The bread was light and wonderful, but the blueberry preserves—the ones Cora had made only two days prior—gave it an overpowering salty flavor that caused her to wince and almost choke. She had to force herself to swallow the bite and immediately wished for a cup of something to wash it down.

Mr. Ludlow offered her some tea, which she accepted gratefully.

"Those preserves are dreadful," she finally spluttered, her face heating in shame.

He leaned against the back of his chair and rested his hands on the arms. "I'm glad we are in agreement on that. I might have thought it was only me, but my recent visitor, Mr. Shepherd, seemed to have similar thoughts about the roll, considering one bite was all he took as well."

Cora straightened at the news. It felt like ages since she had seen the Shepherds, and the mere mention of their name made her yearn for more.

"Mr. Shepherd was here?" she asked, belatedly realizing how odd her question must have sounded.

Mr. Ludlow lifted his brow. "Do you know him?"

Cora hesitated with her answer, choosing her words carefully. "I know he is well liked by his servants." Katy had rambled on about her employers and how dear they were to all in the household. In the short duration Cora had known the Shepherds, they had become dear to her as well. "Sir, I am truly sorry about the preserves. I do not know what happened."

"I would venture a guess that you mistook the salt for sugar," he said.

"Yes, I had gathered as much as well," said Cora. What she didn't understand was how the salt came to be in the sugar jar, for she was certain she had read the label correctly—or, at least she thought she had. Apparently she could never be certain about anything anymore. It only served to get her into trouble.

Would this be the end of it, then? Had Mr. Ludlow finally had enough of her, and after only one week? Cora sat with her fingers clasped on her lap, waiting for him to tell her as much. But he continued to gaze at the tray of sweet rolls while rubbing his chin in thought.

Finally, his eyes looked her way, and he quirked an eyebrow. "What, no preemptive leaving this time?"

"I have not been dismissed, sir," she said.

The edges of his mouth raised slightly—not enough for his dimple to appear, but enough for Cora to notice that he approved of her answer. "So you can be taught," he said.

"Eventually," she answered.

He emitted a small chuckle. "Glad to hear it. I have invited a few business associates to Tanglewood on Friday next and would very much like everything to run as smoothly as possible. They will be here the entire weekend."

She blinked at him a few times before his words registered, and she realized she was not being relieved of her duties—at least not at this moment.

"I understand, sir." Cora swallowed, also realizing the pressure she would be under to see that everything went well for his guests. Had he said an entire weekend? "I will be sure to sample all of the food before it is served to you and your guests."

"I would appreciate that," he said.

Cora nodded, waiting for him to say that she could leave.

As though reading her thoughts, he added, "You may go, Mrs. Notley."

She immediately stood and made for the door, but he called her back as soon as her fingers touched the knob.

"Mrs. Notley, would you be so kind as to take this tray of sweet rolls with you?"

Her face suffused with heat. She should have thought of that herself. "Certainly, Mr. Ludlow."

"It would probably be wise for you to not give Mrs. Caddy an opportunity to taste those as well."

"I had already drawn that conclusion, sir," said Cora as she took the tray. "I thought the pigs might enjoy them."

He smiled. "I'm sure Mrs. Caddy would be gratified to know that her morning's labors went to such worthy creatures."

"I will not tell her if you will not." Cora worried she was overstepping the bounds by saying as much, but from the glint of humor in his eyes, he did not think her remark out of line.

"And if the pigs should decide they want sweet—or rather, salty—rolls every morning?" he asked.

"Considering I made a dozen jars of these particular preserves, that should not be a problem." Cora frowned at the reminder, wondering how she would remove all traces of the salty fruit without Mrs. Caddy noticing.

Mr. Ludlow barked out a laugh. His dimple appeared, causing her stomach to twist into pleasurable knots. He was so very handsome. "Perhaps when the pigs go to slaughter, the meat will already contain enough salt for preservation."

"Sir, you should not say such vulgar things in front of a lady," she teased, enjoying the banter far more than she should. The moment his expression became quizzical, she realized her slip of the tongue.

"*Are* you a lady, Mrs. Notley?"

She had not meant to imply such a thing, nor had she meant to strike up what he might consider a flirtation. She blamed her wayward tongue on her exhaustion and knew she would need to guard herself better in the future.

"I am a housekeeper, sir. That is all." With the tray balanced between her arms, she turned and quit the room. Thankfully, he did not call her back.

When Cora returned to the kitchen after feeding all

traces of the salty rolls to the pigs, she spotted a maid placing what remained of the rolls into a basket with Watts overseeing her progress. He caught Cora's eye and gave her a hint of a knowing smile.

"Mrs. Notley," he said. "I am glad you are here at last. Mr. Ludlow would like these rolls, along with your . . . flavorful preserves, to be taken to those who might have more need of them than we."

Cora was more than happy to approve this plan and made a mental note to thank Mr. Ludlow for his thoughtfulness the next time she saw him.

"I don't know why they all need ter go," grumbled Mrs. Caddy. She cast a longing look at the basket and added, "Mr. Ludlow usually gives us what's left."

"He is sorry that he cannot do so with this lot," said Watts. "But if it is not too much trouble, Mrs. Caddy, he has asked that you make some of your wonderful Banbury cakes to share with the staff as a replacement, so long as you remember to use cinnamon and cloves and not cayenne." Watts gave Cora a subtle wink, and she found herself stifling a conspiratorial smile. He had come to her aid more than once in his kind, fatherly way, and she could not deny that she was growing vastly fond of him.

Mrs. Caddy did not recognize the comment as a rib and immediately bristled. "I've never mistaken cayenne for cinnamon!"

"Are those the sweet rolls made with Mrs. Notley's blackberry preserves?" Sally ask when she entered the room. Normally, the mere sound of her voice grated on Cora's nerves, but this time it was a welcome interruption—at least until Sally snatched one of the rolls from the basket.

"I think I'll have a taste." She took a small bite and immediately spit it out, uttering a sort of snorting noise that sounded most unladylike. Cora might have laughed if not for the sour look on Sally's face. "Gads, what did you do ter those blackberries? Drown them in salt?"

Cora thought the comment rather tame for her. "They'll last a great deal longer now, will they not?"

Sally glowered. "I thought even simple folk know the difference between salt and sugar."

Cora sighed, wondering if Sally had any sense of humor at all. How dreary life would be if one could not see the comedy in situations such as these. For just a moment, she found herself pitying Sally.

"What are you talking about?" Mrs. Caddy's short legs strode over. "What's wrong with me rolls?"

"Nothin' at all, I'm sure." Sally directed a look of triumph at Cora. "It's Mrs. Notley's preserves that's the problem."

Mrs. Caddy took a bite, and her mouth immediately twisted in revulsion, looking a bit like a mound of dough that had been punched down in the middle.

She glared at Cora. "You knew, and you were goin' ter stand there and let Watts deliver these rolls—*my* rolls—to the villagers so they'll think me cookin's gone to pots?"

"Of course not," said Watts. "These are going to the goats, not the villagers."

"Goats!" Mrs. Caddy cried, her face going red.

Cora cringed, wondering what Mrs. Caddy would say if she discovered the first offerings had already been given to the pigs.

"Goats will eat anything," said Watts good-naturedly. "But if you consider that too wasteful, perhaps you have a better suggestion?"

Mrs. Caddy's pudgy fingers formed fists as she glared at the butler. "I think Mrs. Notley should be made ter eat every last crumb. 'Appen then she'll learn ter make preserves."

Watts did not appear to like the comment. His eyes narrowed, and his voice became hard and firm. "I find it rather interesting, Mrs. Caddy, that you did not taste the preserves before this moment. You usually help yourself to quite a few samples of the food as you're preparing it. One might think you sent those sweet rolls up to Mr. Ludlow and his guest knowing what they were."

"How dare you be accusin' me of such things!" Mrs. Caddy seethed, her face becoming an unnatural shade of purple.

"And how dare you expect perfection from a woman who is not as experienced as you. I'll wager your first attempts at making sweet rolls did not go so well either. Perhaps if you remembered that, and realized that Mrs. Notley is doing her best, you would be kinder and more helpful so that she might learn her duties better instead of being made to feel worse at every turn."

Mrs. Caddy had nothing to say to this. She clenched her jaw and stormed back to work, chopping the vegetables with gusto. Cora resisted the urge to break into applause and throw her arms around Watts. He had quieted the ruckus with a handful of sentences, and even Sally seemed to think it best to skulk away. Cora hoped that meant the subject of salty blackberry preserves would be forever put to rest.

She sent Watts a smile, mouthed "thank you," and grabbed a bucket off the counter with the intent to pick more blackberries. Even though she would be free to leave in another hour, Cora wanted to try to right her latest wrong. If she had to spend a few hours of her afternoon off making more blackberry preserves, so be it. With any luck, all would go well and she could still pop in at Knotting Tree for a quick visit with the Shepherds. After this week, she needed to see their kind faces again.

From the corner of her eye, she spotted Alice, the still room maid, scrubbing a pot at the sink. Cora hesitated at the door, not sure what to make of the girl. It was apparent she was a hard worker, but she spoke only when spoken to and had always been timid in her replies. Not wishing to cause her undue distress, Cora had mostly left her to her duties while she tried to learn hers, but watching the girl hunch over the sink, Cora wondered if Alice also felt like an outsider.

"Alice," Cora called, making the poor girl jump and spin around. She had an anxious look about her as though she feared being scolded for scrubbing pots.

Cora picked up another bucket and held it out to her. "I am wondering if you might venture out with me to pick some more blackberries. It's a lovely day, and I think the outdoors will do us both some good. I could also use your help making more preserves, if you'd be so kind. Something tells me that you know a great deal more about the difference between salt and sugar than I."

The girl's expression relaxed a little, and she cautiously accepted the bucket. Cora took it as a good sign and smiled as she led the girl outside. Perhaps today would not be the culmination of a dreadful week after all. Rather, it would be a happy new beginning.

"MRS. NOTLEY!" MRS. CADDY'S shrill voice sounded from the still room, making Cora want to ignore it and run back upstairs where she had been inspecting the bedchambers for the three guests due to arrive any moment.

She drew in a breath and followed Mrs. Caddy's voice, hoping the woman's mood would be cheerier than it sounded, even though she knew better. The set down Watts had given the cook had quieted the issue of the salty preserves, but it did nothing to better the relations between her and Mrs. Caddy. Cora continued to feel like the grime under the woman's nails.

Her second week had gone little better than the first, and only because Cora had learned to rely more on the talents of Alice. The girl was a wonder. The new batches of blackberry preserves had been greatly improved and she was teaching Cora the most efficient methods of drying and bottling herbs, along with how to make a proper dough for pastries.

Outside the still room, however, Cora had plated the Chateaubriand Steak improperly, she'd spilled vinegar down the front of her only clean dress, and she had been late to market, resulting in less-than-fresh lemons for the lemon cream dessert. Mrs. Caddy had not been at all happy about that and had wasted no time voicing her disapproval to Mr. Ludlow.

Now she expected Cora to come running when she called, which was precisely why Cora wanted to ignore her and go the other way.

She mustered up a cheerful tone and entered the still room. "You bellowed, Mrs. Caddy?"

The cook's movements were frantic as she rummaged through the jars of spices. "Where's the thyme? I need it for the ragout." She picked up bottle after bottle, setting each down with a clank.

Cora approached the jars with a frown, frustrated that the once-neat rows were neat no longer. "It is here somewhere. If you had not shuffled everything around, I could have found it directly. I keep the thyme here next to the turmeric."

"Well, it's not there now, is it? And I've not shuffled anythin'."

It would be pointless to argue with Mrs. Caddy, so Cora ignored the comment and went through each and every bottle, sure she'd spot the jar soon enough. But, as Mrs. Caddy insisted, the thyme was not to be found.

Cora studied the lineup. "I do not understand. Where else could it be if not here?"

"If anyone should know, 'tis you."

With a sigh, Cora began looking through cupboards and drawers for the errant jar. Had Alice misplaced it somewhere? She was out in the garden harvesting carrots or Cora would have asked—not that it would do any good. Alice always put everything back in its proper place.

"How much thyme do you need, Mrs. Caddy?" Cora finally said when she could not find the missing herb. "I shall go pluck some from the garden right away."

"I don't want it fresh! It needs ter be dried! 'Tis the only way I've ever made it, and I can't try somethin' new, not when Mr. Ludlow's ter 'ave important guests tonight."

Cora was not knowledgeable enough in culinary matters to know if fresh herbs made an adequate substitution for dried. It seemed like they should, but she would have to take Mrs. Caddy's word that the two were not interchangeable. "Let me ask Alice if she knows where the jar has gone."

"But I need it now!" Mrs. Caddy said. "The broth needs ter sit for at least four hours if it's ter 'ave any flavor at all."

"I understand," said Cora. "And we shall do our best to see that you have your thyme as soon as possible."

Mrs. Caddy stormed off, and Cora strode out to the gardens where she learned, much to her regret, that Alice had no notion of where the herb had gone. Together, they returned to the still room and went through every jar on every shelf, once again with no luck.

By that point, Mrs. Caddy was wringing her hands as she strode anxiously around the kitchen. "What am I ter do? I can't very well make ragout without thyme!"

Not knowing where else to look, Cora could think of only one solution. "I will go straightaway to Knotting Tree and ask to borrow some from the cook there," she offered.

This had a perplexing effect on Mrs. Caddy. Rather than appear relieved, she raised her wooden spoon and shook it angrily at Cora. "I'll never borrow nothin' from the likes of that woman! Thinks she's the Queen of England, she does! I'll serve ragout without thyme before I go beggin' 'elp from 'er."

"Wonderful," said Cora. "Let's go without the thyme then."

Mrs. Caddy's face contorted into a look of pure outrage. "Are you daft? I can't be doin' that or the ragout will 'ave no flavor at'll!"

Cora felt her patience begin to slip away. There was obviously no pacifying the woman when she was in this state. Perhaps Cora could make up a cup of tea laced with laudanum and coerce Mrs. Caddy to drink it. She could put the cook to bed and attempt to make the ragout herself using fresh thyme. Surely fresh would taste better anyway, would it not? Cora really did not know.

"Well, Mrs. Caddy, the dried thyme cannot be found at this moment, so if you are unwilling to use the fresh thyme or even borrow some from the neighboring estate, the only other option is for you to switch today's menu with tomorrow's and make the roast pork and apples tonight instead. Alice and I will find you some dried thyme for tomorrow night."

"But Mr. Ludlow said it's ter be ragout tonight and pork tomorrow," argued Mrs. Caddy.

Cora barely refrained from raising her voice. "What difference will it make if they are switched? I daresay Mr. Ludlow will not even remember."

Mrs. Caddy opened her mouth to protest but seemed to think better of it and pinched her lips together in a frown. "'Appen you might be right."

Cora had never been more surprised in her life. She almost asked Mrs. Caddy to repeat the words just to be sure. "Wonderful. Now that we've settled that, is there anything I can do to help with tonight's dinner preparations?"

Expecting a snide comment about not needing the sort of help the housekeeper offered, Cora was once again stunned when Mrs. Caddy dropped a bushel of apples on the table in front of her.

"I need apples peeled quick as a wink. Think you're up ter it?"

Cora couldn't help but smile. "I may not be so quick as that, but I shall do my best."

Mrs. Caddy grunted, handed Cora a knife, and bustled off to prepare the pork. Feeling oddly victorious—or, at least hopeful that victory would one day come—Cora picked up an apple and began to peel it.

The dinner plates were returned not five minutes after they had been sent up, as full as they had been when they'd left. Cora frowned as two footmen carried the trays back into the kitchen and set them on the table. Mr. Ludlow was not far behind, passing her with barely a glance. He did not look at all happy, which caused a nervous pulse to beat about the room. Cora saw it in the tremble of hands, the intakes of breaths, and the sudden quiet that descended.

"Mrs. Caddy," he said, his deep voice sounding stern.

Mrs. Caddy pressed the palms of her hands together in an anxious way. "Is somethin' the matter, Mr. Ludlow?"

"Is there a reason the pork and apples were served tonight instead of the ragout as we discussed earlier this week?"

Mrs. Caddy cast an anxious glance at Cora before returning her gaze to their employer. "The thyme went missin', sir, and ragout can't be made without it. Mrs. Notley suggested we switch the menus, and I didn't see no 'arm in it." Her voice shook as she spoke, as though she feared the wrath of Mr. Ludlow—the likes of which Cora had never seen. She found it odd that all the servants seemed to live in fear of the man when he had been nothing but kind to her.

"How, exactly, did the thyme go missing?" His voice remained calm despite the fact that he was obviously upset with the switch, though Cora could not understand why.

Since it was her job to manage the spices, she stepped forward to answer. "Sir, it was on the shelf yesterday, and today it was not. Perhaps the jar sprouted wings and flew away."

His usual sense of humor did not emerge, and when his jaw hardened, Cora immediately wished her flippancy back. "Forgive me. I did not mean to make light of a serious matter."

"I'm sorry, sir!" Mrs. Caddy said, her voice rising. "I should've asked you first. It all 'appened so fast. I did not think . . ." Her voice trailed off, and her eyes became watery. "Am I ter be dismissed?"

Mr. Ludlow did not answer immediately, and Cora did not know why. Surely he would not dismiss Mrs. Caddy for such an innocent mistake, not when he had allowed Cora to remain after many more serious blunders.

She walked around the table to stand at Mrs. Caddy's side. It was only fair that she bear most of the blame. "Sir, as Mrs. Caddy said, it was my suggestion to switch the menus. If anyone should be held accountable, it is I. But, pray tell, is there a reason the pork will not suffice for tonight?"

Mr. Ludlow flicked a glance at Cora before returning his attention to Mrs. Caddy. "Under normal circumstances it would not matter in the slightest. But we have a guest with us tonight who will be leaving tomorrow morning—a Mr. Thomas, who happens to have a vicious allergy to cinnamon, which is an ingredient in the apple glaze, correct?"

Mrs. Caddy appeared horrified. "You mean ter say if 'e'd eaten—"

"He would have been rendered unable to breathe, and

76

we would not have been able to get the doctor here in time to resuscitate him. He made his allergy very clear to me when he accepted my invitation, and I assured him that no dish containing cinnamon would be served. He was about to eat a bite when I put two and two together and put a stop to it."

"Great Jehoshaphat," Mrs. Caddy whispered, leaning heavily on the counter. "I about killed a man." Cora never would have imagined her capable of such vulnerability.

Feeling it necessary to intercede once more, Cora put a hand on Mrs. Caddy's shoulder. "But you did not," she said kindly. "Mr. Thomas is alive and well, is he not, sir?"

"Alive, well, and vastly hungry, as are the rest of my guests. Which leads us to the next problem. What are we to serve in place of the pork and glaze?"

Mrs. Caddy's eyes widened in shock, as though she hadn't realized the full extent of the situation until now. "I do not know, sir. All we have is the turtle soup I made for the servant's table."

"Turtle soup," Mr. Ludlow repeated slowly, as though Mrs. Caddy had proposed feeding the men table scraps instead of a hearty and tasty soup. He sighed in frustration and planted both palms on the table. "These are men I hope to do business with at some point, and you are saying that all I can offer them after a near-death experience is turtle soup?"

"Do you not like turtle soup, sir?" Cora asked, wondering at his strong reaction.

"I do not, as Mrs. Caddy well knows."

The cook burst into tears and cowered against the counter, her body trembling in anguish. "I'm sorry, sir! 'Tis all me fault."

For whatever reason, it bothered Cora to see the prideful Mrs. Caddy brought so low. Her heart went out to the woman. She eyed the dinner plates, wondering how the situation could be salvaged.

"Mr. Ludlow," Cora asked. "It is only Mr. Thomas who is allergic, is that right?"

"Yes."

"What if I were to slice him some fresh pork and serve it to him without the glaze?"

"The pork is not cooked with the glaze already on it?" he asked.

"No. They are made separately and the meat glazed just before it is taken up."

"Will it not taste dry without the sauce?"

The conversation served to bolster Mrs. Caddy's spirits. Tears forgotten, she ran to the larder and brought out a jar of applesauce. "There's no cinnamon in this. I'll warm this and serve it on Mr. Thomas's plate. It won't taste as pleasin', but it'll give the pork some flavor and keep it from bein' too dry."

Mr. Ludlow considered her a moment before nodding his agreement. "Very well. But you must make certain Mr. Thomas receives the plate without the cinnamon. I will do my best to explain what has happened and pray that they, like Mrs. Notley, can find some humor in the situation."

Unfortunately, Mr. Ludlow did not seem to find any. He appeared weary, as though his patience was wearing thin with a staff that couldn't see to things properly. He began to walk away, and Cora rushed forward to lay a hand on his arm. When he stopped abruptly and looked down, she immediately pulled it away, realizing she had greatly over-stepped this time.

"Forgive me, sir," she said. "I merely wanted to point out that I am responsible for the spices. It was under my watch that the thyme went missing."

"I realize that, Mrs. Notley," was all he said before walking out of the kitchen and leaving behind a housekeeper who had finally gotten a glimpse of the employer the others viewed as formidable.

Cora drew in a deep breath and turned back to Mrs. Caddy, clapping her hands in a forced show of cheeriness. "Shall we get to work, then? If you heat up that sauce, Mrs. Caddy, I will make some new plates with meat hot from the oven. It is not necessarily a bad thing to starve guests a little before feeding them. They will likely be so ravenous that anything will taste like heaven, especially the delectable custard you made for dessert. Mark my words, Mrs. Caddy, all will be forgiven in no time."

Mrs. Caddy nodded, her formerly take-charge attitude renewed. "Thank you, Mrs. Notley. You're a good lass, you are." She gave Cora's arm a firm pat and got to work.

Cora couldn't help the smile that came to her lips as she re-plated the pork. For an upside-down day, it had righted well enough. Hopefully Mr. Ludlow would come to that conclusion as well. But even if he didn't, Cora would leave Tanglewood with the knowledge that she had done what she did not think could be done. She had formed at least a tentative friendship with Mrs. Caddy.

Sometimes miracles did happen.

JONATHAN SAT IN HIS favorite chair in his study, his attention claimed by the lively flames dancing in the fireplace. The transfixing display of reds and oranges flashed and crackled before him as though laughing and mocking his fiasco of an evening. As the memories returned, burning like flames inside his head, his jaw clenched, and he threw his half drained glass of brandy at the fire, experiencing a moment of satisfaction as the glass shattered and what remained of the drink roared into flames.

The afternoon had begun most promising. Everyone had arrived in a timely fashion, and once Jonathan proposed his idea of repurposing the northern section of Tanglewood for an agricultural venture, all seemed intrigued and interested. They had entered the dining room in like minds, anxious to continue their discussions and move forward with definitive plans.

That's when everything began to go awry.

Not only was Mr. Thomas nearly suffocated by his allergy, but he returned to his room to find it filled with smoke. He immediately called fire, sending the entire house into upheaval, even though it was not a fire at all, merely inadequate ventilation caused by a closed damper. Still, every item in the man's room smelled of smoke, and he refused to abide another moment in a house that seemed intent on killing him. Not even the charming Mrs. Notley, with her smiles, apologies, and quick wit could convince him to remain.

Soon after, Mr. Kent entered his bedchamber, only to run out again because of a putrid smell. While Mrs. Notley and a few maids searched the room for the cause of it, Mr. Hervey discovered a live snake under his bed covers. His frantic shouts caused another ruckus, and it wasn't long before the two remaining men took their leave as well, informing Jonathan that he must learn to manage an orderly household before they believed him capable of managing a business.

Jonathan let them go without argument because he had no argument to give. Had the situation been reversed, he would have thought the same and likely left as well. But that didn't make it any less maddening. Jonathan had spent months researching and polishing his proposal and had tracked down men with both experience and large enough pocketbooks to invest. And now his efforts had come to naught, all because he'd chosen to hire an honest, beautiful, and inept housekeeper.

He leaned forward and dropped his head to his palms, raking his fingers through his hair and wondering what the devil must be done. Mrs. Notley may have proven that she could keep a cool head and cheerful disposition in the midst of adversity, but her lack of experience was proving to be an obstacle that could not be overcome. Jonathan had been a fool to believe otherwise, and now he was left with the unhappy task of having to explain to a kind and virtuous woman that her talents—or lack thereof—were no longer needed.

He should ring the bell and summon her now, but he could not bring himself to do it. Why? He had never before felt such dread at the prospect of dismissing a servant, and he couldn't account for it. Why did it feel as though he'd be sending away a friend that, oddly enough, he'd greatly miss? For whatever reason, his relationship with Mrs. Notley seemed more personal, somehow, even though it was not and never could be.

That alone should be reason enough to dismiss her, and yet . . . Jonathan frowned at the bell pull, telling himself that she had left him no choice this time. Mrs. Notley truly must go and he must begin the process of hiring yet another housekeeper. Good gads. Did a woman exist who could do the job properly? Other households didn't seem to have such a difficult time filling positions and retaining servants. Why was he? If only Watts would take a wife. A man with his exacting standards would surely pick a woman who would be capable of working alongside him in the role of housekeeper.

Jonathan looked around for another glass to throw at the fire but a quiet knock interrupted his perusal.

He drew in a deep breath and straightened. "Enter," he called, expecting to see Watts.

To his surprise, Mrs. Caddy walked in, looking as skittish as a newborn kitten. Clutched in her hand was a glass bottle containing some sort of dark substance.

What the deuce is wrong now? Jonathan thought in frustration. He needed a long night of rest before he was ready to deal with anything more.

Mrs. Caddy held the bottle out for his inspection. "The missin' thyme, sir."

He frowned as he studied the contents of the jar, wondering why it had suddenly appeared now and not at a more convenient time. "It's not missing any longer, I see."

"No, sir."

"Where did you find it?"

Mrs. Caddy hesitated, and her hands shook as she clutched the bottle to her abdomen. "Sally's room."

"What?" Jonathan's frown deepened. He had expected her to say the bottom of a drawer or at the back of a cupboard, not in a maid's room—a maid who had served him faithfully since he had come to Tanglewood. How the devil had it come to be in Sally's room, and what had prompted Mrs. Caddy to look for it there?

Tears welled up in the cook's eyes, and Jonathan had to stifle his annoyance. He used to think the woman incapable of dissembling, but now he was beginning to wonder if she had lost her senses and would never return to her former brusque self. He prayed this was a momentary lapse on her part and that tomorrow all would be right once again so that he would not be made to search for a new housekeeper *and* cook. What a ludicrous joke that would be.

"I know I shouldn't 'ave done it, sir, but she was actin' a might strange when I 'appened upon her in the still room earlier, makin' excuses about bein' there and such. It wasn't till later that I gave the matter some thought and wondered if it was 'er who'd done somethin' with the missin' 'erb. I waited for 'er to go out walkin' like she does every night, and when I searched 'er room, I found this tucked under 'er pillow."

Mrs. Caddy paused, still fidgeting. "The worst bit is, I don't think that's all she's done, neither. Only yesterday, Roddy, the stableboy, was talkin' about findin' a snake in the outbuildin', and Sally asked ter see it. I also saw 'er pickin' purple mums the day Mrs. Notley dyed your best cloth the same color, and I spotted Sally in the still room before Mrs. Notley made 'er first batch of preserves. I can't prove nothin' except the 'erbs, but 'tis no secret Sally don't like Mrs. Notley much."

Jonathan leaned forward in his chair, trying to make sense of the woman's ramblings. "I was under the assumption that you didn't care much for Mrs. Notley either."

This had a humbling effect on Mrs. Caddy, for she bowed her head in shame. "Not at first, I suppose. She don't know nothin' about 'ousekeepin'. But she's a good sort of girl who don't deserve to be dismissed for somethin' she didn't do."

Jonathan clasped his fingers under his chin as he considered all that Mrs. Caddy had revealed. It was mostly conjecture, and he had a difficult time believing Sally was responsible for every misadventure that had happened to Mrs. Notley. But the cook had a jar of herbs that had come from Sally's room. That alone made him angry. Had she been trying to sabotage the housekeeper? If so, it should be Sally who left and not Mrs. Notley.

This thought had a perplexing effect on Jonathan. Most employers would be vexed at the prospect of dismissing a well-trained and hardworking housemaid over an incompetent housekeeper, but it felt as though a great burden had been lifted from his shoulders. How odd. Even without Sally about, Mrs. Notley would still be prone to errors, and yet Jonathan found himself more relieved than worried. It was as though he wanted the mayhem to continue.

No. That wasn't it. The truth was far more troubling. Deep down, Jonathan knew what he wanted most was to keep seeing Mrs. Notley around the house. Her smiles, her lovely face, her laughter, her warmth. She made Tanglewood feel like a home, and he wanted that feeling to remain. As loathe as he was to admit it, Jonathan wasn't ready to let her walk out of his home, or his life, just yet.

And now, thanks to Mrs. Caddy's recent revelations, perhaps he wouldn't have to.

The cook was still wringing her hands and swaying

anxiously back and forth as though awaiting a trial of some sort. Jonathan could not figure the woman out. She had done nothing wrong. "Thank you for bringing this to my attention, Mrs. Caddy. If you will be kind enough to leave the herbs on that table there, I will handle things from here."

Ever so slowly, she bent to do as he bid, but when she rose, tears again welled in her eyes.

What the deuce? Jonathan would never understand a woman's emotions. A headache began to creep into his forehead, and he began rubbing his temples to keep it at bay.

"Am I ter be dismissed, sir?" she blurted. "Please tell me now, so I don't keep worryin' and wonderin'."

"Why on earth would I dismiss you, Mrs. Caddy?" Jonathan asked, baffled as to why she would be concerned about such an outcome. Indeed, he felt like increasing her wages. If only she'd cease crying, he might offer to do exactly that.

"I almost killed a man!" she exclaimed with a trembling voice that bespoke even more tears—the gushing sort that made him most uncomfortable.

Jonathan increased the pressure on his temples and mustered as much patience as he could. "You did not almost kill a man, Mrs. Caddy, and I am sorry you have been made to bear such a burden tonight. I ought to have told you about the allergy when we discussed the menu, but I did not. So if anyone is to blame, it is I. Please do not trouble yourself further about the incident. Mr. Thomas is alive and well and now happily ensconced at the inn, where he will stay until tomorrow's coach back to London. You are an excellent cook, and I would not dream of replacing you because of something that was not your fault."

Mrs. Caddy's hand flew to her mouth as tears continued to run from her eyes. At least they were happy tears now, which was a slight improvement. "I don't know what ter say except thank you, sir! Thank you, thank you, thank you!"

"Goodnight, Mrs. Caddy," said Jonathan, anxious to be done with tears of all kinds.

"G'night, sir." She swept from the room, her mood the antithesis of what it had been only minutes before. And at last, peace was restored in the kitchens.

He hoped.

Jonathan watched her go with a hint of a smile, but when his thoughts drifted to what must be done now, his smile faded. With a deep breath, he rose to ring the bell that would summon Watts.

The butler soon appeared. "Is there something I can do for you, Mr. Ludlow?"

"Unfortunately, yes," said Jonathan. "When Sally returns from her walk, would you tell her that I would like a word?"

If Watts was surprised by the request, he hid it well. He bowed politely and said, "Of course, sir. I will notify her right away."

"Thank you."

Jonathan sat back in his chair, mentally preparing himself for another interchange with a servant that would likely not end nearly as well as the last one had. He only prayed that Sally would refrain from weeping.

Cora had only just finished hanging some thyme to dry when an anguished sob sounded from the kitchen. She wiped her hands on her apron and stepped down from the stool before peeking out of the still room to investigate. Sally sat hunched over the table, her shoulders shuddering as sobs wracked her body.

Everyone else had gone to bed, and the haunting sound echoed through the room. The combination of the full moon coming through the window and a small candle casting vague shadows on the walls only added to the eeriness. Cora hesitated on the threshold between the two rooms, not sure what to do. Sally would certainly not appreciate any interference from her, yet Cora could not leave the woman to face such despair alone.

She approached tentatively. "Sally? Are you well?" The question was a silly one considering the housemaid was certainly not well, but Cora could not think of a kinder way to intrude.

Sally's shoulders froze for a moment before her head slowly lifted. Tears had stained her cheeks a bright pink, and her red hair splayed around her face in an untidy mess of tangles. She looked utterly wretched and not at all happy that she had been caught in such a state, especially by Cora.

Her eyes narrowed into a venomous rage. "'Tis all your doin'." She jabbed a finger at Cora. "You've wrecked everythin', and now me and me lad's ter be tossed ter the streets. I wish you'd never come ter Tanglewood!"

Sally flung herself from the stool and ran up the stairs. A few moments later, a door slammed and Cora flinched at the coldness of it. She wrapped her arms to her chest and shivered.

What have I done now? she thought as weariness took a vicious hold on her. She sank down on a stool and combed through her mind for anything she might have said or done to cause Sally harm—or her lad. What had she meant by that, anyway? Could Sally possibly be a mother? If so, where was the child, and why was Sally so worried about being tossed to the streets? If anyone should be concerned with such a fate, it was Cora.

After all that had occurred, she was certain her next meeting with Mr. Ludlow would not go nearly as well as the others. In less than a day, she had spoiled whatever business prospects he might have had with his guests—or rather, former guests. Cora had not thought to check all the dampers, she had not considered looking under the bed sheets for slithering reptiles, and she still had no idea what had caused that dreadful odor. It had begun to dissipate as they searched the room, and they had not been able to locate the source. It seemed to come from everywhere and then nowhere. In the end, the fault for everything lay entirely at Cora's door. Coupled with all the days before, her list of blunders had grown to an overwhelming number—far too many for Mr. Ludlow to forgive any longer.

Cora rested her arms on the table, wishing she could go off to bed and forget this day had ever happened, but sleep would undoubtedly elude her, and the view of the moon was so much nicer from here. So she remained perched on the stool, staring out the large window into the beautiful night. How serene and lovely it looked. If only she could borrow some of that peace and wrap it around her like a quilt. Perhaps then she could fall asleep and feel better equipped to face whatever the morning brought.

Cora wasn't sure how long she sat in the dark. She only knew her eyelids were beginning to droop when a rustling sound stirred her awake once more. Something with tiny, prickly feet scampered over the tops of her slippers, causing the hairs on her arms to rise. With a squeal, she crawled onto the table and stood, stomping her feet while shaking out her dress. Years ago, a mouse ran up her skirts, and she had never been able to forget the awful sensation of it. The memory alone made her shake her skirts with even more vigor.

"What the devil are you doing?" came Mr. Ludlow's deep voice from the doorway.

Cora froze as her face grew very warm. Of all the people to happen by at such a moment, why did it have to be him? Was the dreadfulness of this night doomed to never end?

The candle he held highlighted his handsome face in a mysterious, almost romantic way, and Cora shivered for completely different reasons. His hair appeared more unruly than usual, flying this way and that, and he no longer wore a jacket—merely an untucked shirt, trousers, and stockings. She had never seen him so unkempt, and she realized she probably didn't look much different. Worse actually, for she was standing on top of the table. Mrs. Caddy would undoubtedly swat her with a rolling pin if she caught her there.

Cora cleared her throat and tried to regain some dignity by pointing at the floor. "There was a mouse, I believe. It ran across my foot, and I was afraid it had climbed up my skirts, so I . . ." He appeared to be fighting back a smile, so she finished her explanation with an annoyed, "Oh, never mind. It's obviously gone now, whatever it was."

"Are you certain it is not hiding in your apron pocket, waiting for the dancing to stop so that it might make its escape?"

Cora frowned at her apron, giving it one final shake just to be sure. When Mr. Ludlow began chuckling, she redirected her frown at him. "I was not dancing and do stop laughing. The creature gave me quite a fright, and it is unkind of you to find the situation humorous."

"How can I not find it humorous when I so clearly witnessed you scuttle onto the table—you, who claims to never scuttle."

"I don't," she defended. "I merely crawled . . . quickly."

"I'm quite certain that you scuttled."

"Truly, you must stop laughing at once. I have had a trying day, and this is not helping at all."

Mr. Ludlow was good enough to mold his mouth into an obedient line, though his eyes still sparkled with mirth. He set down his candle and walked over to her, extending his hand. "Do you wish to join me on the floor, Mrs. Notley, or would you prefer to finish your dance?"

She glared before taking his hand and stepping down. The moment her feet made contact with the floor, she withdrew her fingers and cast a wary glance around to make sure the mouse was nowhere to be seen. When she lifted her eyes to his and realized how close they stood to each other, she took a step back.

"I, er . . . was just about to retire for the night." She paused. "That is, if I may have your leave to do so, sir?"

He dismissed the question with a wave of his hand. "Chance encounters do not require such formality, but now that I have caught you here, I wonder if I might have a word with you."

Right now? Cora felt suddenly anxious. Why had she not gone to bed with the rest of the staff? Could this conversation not wait until morning, when Cora felt at least a little more rested and prepared? Or would she ever feel prepared? Cora frowned at the thought. Perhaps it would be better to be done with it now, when the darkness of night would help to stifle the awkward embarrassment of it all.

She relaxed her shoulders and sighed, accepting the inevitable. "I know what you wish to say to me, sir, and I will not make you say it aloud. If you will allow me to stay the night, I promise to pack my things and be gone before you arise in the morning. You have put your trust in me, and I . . ." Her lips lifted into a sad, humorless smile. "Well, I have bungled things completely, haven't I? I do not know how else to make amends other than to tell you how truly sorry I am and show myself the door. I wish I knew of someone who could serve as a proper replacement, but I'm afraid I do not."

He did not look at all saddened at the prospect of saying goodbye. If anything, he appeared entertained. It rankled her. Though she had not expected him to mourn her loss, a little sadness or concern would have been appreciated.

"Where will you go?" he asked.

"Somewhere other than here."

"And where is that?" He brushed something off the front of his shirt as though he was only making polite conversation and did not care about her answer in the least.

"Forgive my impertinence, sir, but I do not see how that information is any business of yours. I am no longer employed by you, after all."

"Are you not?"

Cora scowled at him. "Are you quite awake, sir? I have already explained to you that I will be leaving first thing in the morning. Were you not attending?"

His lips twitched into a grin, and his eyes continued sparkling with mirth. "I find myself ravenous at the moment, so I'm afraid my stomach is claiming much of my attention. If I can scrounge up some bread and cheese, will you not join me for a midnight snack, Mrs. Notley?"

Not waiting for a response, he walked into the larder and began rummaging around, leaving Cora to stare after him in stunned silence. He was acting quite addled.

"My name is *Miss* Notley now, sir, and I'm afraid I cannot join you. I am going to bed."

He continued with his search, opening a canister to sniff its contents, only to put it back on the counter with a grimace. "Does that particular bed happen to be in the servants' quarters in this house?"

"Er . . . yes?"

"Then it is still Mrs. Notley. Ah, here we are." He found a loaf of bread under a cloth napkin and a bottle of blackberry preserves on a shelf. "Please say you'll join me. It is bad manners to eat in front of another person and I would rather not have any more accusations thrown at me tonight."

"I have no intention of accusing you of anything, sir, and you will not be eating in front of me if I go to bed."

"I wish you would not." He moved past her and sat on one of the stools, cutting off two slices of bread and slathering preserves over the top of both. He held one out to her. "I have it on good authority that these preserves have been approved for human consumption. Would you care for a taste?"

His hunger was obviously affecting his good sense. It would not be at all wise for her to eat with him, especially at this hour, and so she remained standing, determined to stand her ground even though the snack did tantalize her stomach. It had been hours since she'd partaken of food.

"Mr. Ludlow, you know it would be improper for me to share an informal meal with you. I'm afraid I cannot."

He took a bite of the bread and cocked his head, studying her as he chewed and swallowed. The dark depths of his eyes caused her stomach to rise and fall like waves in an ocean during a storm.

"You are making me behave most ungentlemanly, Mrs. Notley, and I cannot understand it," he finally said. "We are in a public room and you are my servant. I share a drink with Watts on occasion, and I do not see how this is any different. That aside, our conversation is not yet finished. So if you have a care at all for my sensibilities, and I cannot believe you would be so callous as to not, will you do me the honor of taking a seat, eating a slice of bread, and listening to what I have to say?"

Cora put a hand on her stomach to quiet it, but it continued to toss and turn. He had a way of unsettling her in a volatile way, and sitting next to him felt dangerous somehow. Perhaps it was not improper for a housekeeper to share a slice of bread in the kitchen with her employer, but when the housekeeper was young, vulnerable, and fiercely attracted to that particular employer, she'd be a fool to let him sway her.

When she said nothing, he shook his head in capitulation. "If you will not sit, I suppose I must stand as well. How very cruel you are."

Good gracious he was a stubborn man, Cora thought with annoyance.

"Very well, sir, but only for a moment." She glanced around to make sure they were truly alone before taking a seat on the stool beside him and keeping as far to the left as possible. She shot him a glare as she snatched a slice of bread from his hand and popped it into her mouth. With any luck, the food would settle her stomach.

He grinned. "Ah, see? I knew you could not be so cruel as that."

Cora refused to be charmed by his dimple or the way his hair fell across his forehead. She turned her gaze out the window, forced the bread down her throat, and kept her voice as even as she could. "Sir, please tell me what it is you have to say."

"Very well." He shifted towards her and his elbow brushed against her arm, causing it to erupt in gooseflesh. She slid a little more to the left and focused on the moonlit shrubs outside the window.

"I have dismissed Sally," he said.

Shrubs forgotten, Cora gaped at him in astonishment. "I beg your pardon?"

"The missing thyme was found in her room, and once I questioned her further, I also discovered that she switched out the sugar with salt, added purple flowers to your wash basin, closed the damper in Mr. Thomas's bedchamber, and hid a snake under Mr. Hervey's bed sheets. The smell in Mr. Kent's room was a rotten egg that Sally covertly retrieved during your search and tossed out the window."

Cora stared at Mr. Ludlow, disbelieving. Why would Sally do such things? The housemaid had made her dislike of the new housekeeper quite clear, but to go to such great lengths to see her gone? Cora could scarce believe it.

"She wanted the housekeeper position," Mr. Ludlow went on to explain. "She thought that if she found a way to be rid of you, I would be desperate enough to offer her the job instead."

"Oh," was all Cora could think to say. Her mind reeled with all these revelations. She thought of every cruel word Sally had ever said, every look of derision, and every mean prank she had played with the hope of seeing Cora sacked. In the end, it was all for naught. Mr. Ludlow had sacked Sally instead. No wonder she had been sobbing earlier. Her plan had backfired most abominably.

Cora's initial instinct was to be glad of Sally's fate. The woman deserved what she got for being so unkind and manipulative. But the image of Sally crumpled over the table in such a wretched state made Cora pity her and her son, if she indeed had one.

With so much to lose, why had Sally put her job at risk? Was it so detestable to answer to a younger, less experienced woman, or was there more to the equation? Had Sally also been thinking of her child and how a larger salary would ease the burden of providing for him? Or perhaps the "lad" she'd mentioned was a pet dog, and the woman was simply mean-spirited.

Cora's head spun with questions. They poked and pestered, seeking answers and understanding but finding nothing. She peered at Mr. Ludlow. "Did she explain why becoming the housekeeper was so important to her?"

"I did not ask," he answered. "Once she had revealed her actions to me, I informed her that I could not allow such deceit to go unpunished. She was dismissed immediately and will be leaving in the morning."

"Without a reference, I suppose," Cora murmured, more to herself than to him.

"Of course without a reference. She behaved deceitfully, and I could not, in good conscience, recommend her to anyone."

"Of course not." Cora stared at her hands. Despite all that had happened, her heart mourned a little for Sally. If anyone knew what it felt like to face a bleak and uncertain future, it was Cora.

"She readily admitted to everything?" she asked, not quite believing it.

Mr. Ludlow glanced down at the remaining bread on the platter and pushed it away, as though he'd lost his appetite. "Not at first. It wasn't until I pointed out a few gaping holes in her denials that she crumbled and revealed all. But was it the entire truth? I cannot know because she has broken my trust, and a servant I cannot trust is a servant I cannot employ."

It was an understandable sentiment, but it troubled Cora that he had come to that decision without attempting to understand the complexities of Sally's mind or circumstances. Was there a reason he had not involved his housekeeper in his decision? Surely, as the manager of the housemaids and the object of Sally's deceit, Cora ought to have been consulted, or at the very least informed, on what was to be done with Sally *before* it was done. Was that not the proper way of things?

Cora bit down on her lower lip and chose her next words with caution. "As your housekeeper, is it not my responsibility to manage the housemaids?"

"In most circumstances, yes."

"Is there a reason why you did not discuss the matter with me before you dismissed Sally?" Cora asked, hoping he wouldn't find the question impertinent.

He lifted a brow. "What would have been the point? Involving you would have only complicated matters, and I wanted it finished. A few hours ago, I was informed of Sally's trickery by another servant and took it upon myself to handle the situation, which I have done. And now you have been informed as well." He paused, scrutinizing her. "Your position is now secure and a certain housemaid who has brought you nothing but grief will no longer be employed here. I would have thought such news would be cause for celebration, and yet you do not strike me as relieved or happy by the turn of events tonight."

Cora could understand his confusion. Even *she* did not comprehend her emotions at the moment. She only knew that something still troubled her, like a nagging, forgotten memory. It prodded and poked, pressing her to understand the situation better.

She turned to face Mr. Ludlow, and in so doing pressed her knee against his. A jolt of something warm and sweet ran through her body, muddling her mind further. She drew back a little but held his gaze as she attempted to gather her loose thoughts and weave them together with a little more clarity.

"I know how much you value honesty, Mr. Ludlow, and I hope you feel as though you can be equally honest with me as well." She paused, searching his face. "Did you not involve me in this decision because you thought me incapable of dealing with Sally on my own?"

His mouth remained straight and his eyes guarded, giving away nothing. "I have had a great deal more experience in these matters, Mrs. Notley. But pray tell, if I had passed the responsibility to you, how would you have handled the situation?"

"I do not know," she answered. "I have never been faced with such a circumstance. But now that you have taken it upon yourself to set things to rights, I suppose I will never know, will I?" Cora's brow furrowed. He spoke so passionately about the importance of trust, and yet he did not trust her—at least not in the way she wanted him to. That knowledge hurt worse than any cruel comment Sally had ever made. Cora could not say why Mr. Ludlow's good opinion meant so much to her, only that it did, and she felt a great desire to prove her worthiness.

As a housekeeper, she quickly amended, knowing she was coming dangerously close to forgetting the reason she should care.

When Mr. Ludlow finally spoke, his voice was quiet and firm. "As your employer, I am not required to ask your permission or seek your advice as to whether or not I should dismiss a deceitful housemaid."

Cora chilled and stiffened, telling herself she should be grateful for the set down. It put her firmly back in her place and reminded her that she had no right to question his decisions or ask anything of him. Would she never learn?

Her gaze dropped to the floor and she nodded. "Pray forgive my impertinence, Mr. Ludlow, and accept my heartfelt gratitude for discovering what Sally was about. It is a great relief to know I am still employed."

He sighed, slid off his stool, and stood, holding out his hand to her. She tentatively placed her fingers in his, and a delightful sensation bubbled up her arm and down her spine as he pulled her to her feet. He kept hold of her hand as he said, "There is nothing to forgive, Mrs. Notley. I suppose I should have discussed the matter with you before speaking with Sally, but I cannot turn the clock back now and alter the events of this night no matter how much you or I might wish it. I can, however, attempt to make amends by staying out of matters from this point on and allowing you to choose Sally's replacement. Does that sound like a fair compromise?"

Cora felt a great urgency to put some space between her and the man who was causing her heart to pound in a most alarming way—partly because of his nearness and partly because of the task he'd just given her. She gently pulled her fingers from his grasp so she could give the matter some more thought.

Was he truly trying to make amends or was this his way of ridding himself of a responsibility he'd rather not bear? From the glint of humor in his eyes, it was likely the latter, and Cora had played neatly into his hands. He knew very well that she would have no idea how to go about hiring a replacement for Sally, and yet he'd just placed her in a position where her only response could be gratitude.

"You've played your hand well, sir," Cora finally said with a hint of a smile. "Touché."

His lips quirked into an answering grin. "You did imply that you wanted to prove how capable you are, did you not?"

She laughed. "I believe my tongue gets the better of me at times."

"Only sometimes?"

"Perhaps more often than not."

He chuckled and lifted his hand as if to touch her cheek,

thought better of it, and let it fall back to his side. He cleared his throat and withdrew a step. "A few hours ago, I worried that it was you I would have to dismiss. But now . . . well, let's just say that I am very glad it did not come to that."

The warmth in his gaze set her heart to pounding yet again, and Cora felt an urgent need to lighten the heaviness his words had created.

"I knew the lavender cloth would grow on you in time. Or was it the cayenne in your tea? Or perhaps you've a fondness for the, er . . . crispy pastries I made yesterday? Yes, I can certainly see why you are glad I shall remain."

He grinned. "Life is certainly not dull with you here, is it?"

"That is a kind way of phrasing it, but I'm certain you wish it would be a little duller at times, such as today with your guests, perhaps?"

Cora wished her words back immediately. She disliked the creases that appeared on his forehead and the firm set in his jaw. Seconds ago, his dimple had made an appearance, only to be scared away by the reminder of a ruined evening.

"The fault for today lay at Sally's door and not yours," he said.

"If it is any consolation," said Cora, "men who flee at the sight of a reptile, a little smoke, and a horrid stench are obviously people who crumple under pressure fairly easily. Are those really the sort of men you wish to do business with? Like it or not, perhaps Sally did you a favor."

Amazingly enough, the creases smoothed from his forehead and the worry cleared from his eyes. Though his dimple did not return, his jaw relaxed, and a hint of a smile tipped the edges of his lips. "You are quite right, Mrs. Notley, though I still cannot forgive Sally."

"I pity her then. To lose your good opinion would be a sorry plight indeed. I certainly would not wish it."

"And why is that?" He peered at her in earnest and moved a smidge closer, making the air feel thicker and harder to breathe.

Cora wanted to move nearer as well, but the knowledge frightened her into retreating a step. She made her voice sound as flippant as possible. "If I lost your good opinion, I would be out of a job, would I not? And likely without a reference, too." The reminder of Sally made her frown, and she found herself thinking once more about the maid.

"Do you pity her?" he asked, his tone curious.

"I do," Cora answered. "It is a dreadful thing to have to endure the consequences of one's own making."

He nodded. "I agree, but I still cannot pity her. Perhaps I lack your kindness and empathy."

"Some would consider it a weakness."

"And others an asset." His eyebrow quirked as though challenging her to refute the praise.

She shifted uncomfortably, wishing she could flee to her room—or even scuttle, for that matter. The late hour, the moonlight glistening across the brown waves of his hair, the way he spoke in dulcet tones—Cora's emotions had never experienced so much upheaval in such a short time. She could only pray that tomorrow would bring a return of normalcy and, with any luck, dullness, so she could go about her duties without the constant need of his intervention. It was the only way she could ever find peace at Tanglewood.

"I can see you are tired," he finally said. "How ill-mannered of me to keep you from your bed. I wish you a good night, Mrs. Notley."

"Thank you, sir." Cora did not hesitate in quitting the room. She stole up the stairs, changed into her nightclothes, and dropped down on her bed. Only then did she allow herself to think about her employer and wonder if she would have been better off if Sally had not been discovered and Mr. Ludlow had dismissed her instead.

CORA DID NOT SLEEP a wink that night. Besides Mrs. Caddy's louder-than-usual snoring, her mind would not be still. In the early hours of the morning, when the sky began to change from inky black to murky gray, Cora heard the sound of a door opening and closing. Shuffling followed, and she knew without cracking her door that Sally was making her departure before the other servants awoke.

When Cora could no longer hear footsteps, she rolled from her bed, pulled on a robe and slid her feet into some slippers. She left her room, trod quickly down the stairs, and went outside. The early morning chill assaulted her body, and she drew her wrap tighter about her. Through the gloom of early morning, she squinted, searching for movement, finally spotting a dark form up ahead.

"Sally!" Cora called, quickening her steps.

The maid—or rather, former maid—turned around. As Cora neared, she could see hatred and distrust written plainly across Sally's face. Cora stopped several paces away, wondering why she had felt the need to follow. Sally loathed her. What good did she think she could do?

"I, er . . ." Cora wasn't sure how to begin. "Where are you going?"

Sally scoffed and lifted her hands—both of which carried small bags. "Where does it look like I'm goin'? Ter a ball, of course."

All things considered, it had been a ridiculous question to ask, but Sally's impolite tone did not help matters. Cora let out a breath and tried again. "What I meant to say was . . . Do you have somewhere *to* go?"

The question seemed to catch Sally off guard. She looked momentarily perplexed before her jaw tightened and her chin lifted in defiance. "Ain't no business of yours."

Cora was tempted to agree and wish Sally to the devil, and she might have done exactly that if not for the vulnerability and fear she spied in her eyes. It was plain to see the woman did not know where she was going or what she would do.

"Why did you do it?" Cora asked, needing to know. "Do you find the notion of answering to a woman younger and less experienced than you so intolerable? Or is that only a part of the reason?"

Sally pressed her lips together, refusing to answer.

"Do you have a son, Sally?" Cora pressed, gentler this time.

The maid's jaw clenched and she turned away. Cora thought she caught a glimmer of moisture in her eyes, but Sally blinked, and when she looked back at Cora, all that remained was a fierce look of pride. "Aye, I 'ave a lad. 'Ad a husband too before he succumbed ter the fever and died. Now it's just Jimmy and me. 'E's not quite three and livin' with the McCoard's yonder. I pay what I can ter keep 'im fed and cared for, but they say they need more and . . . well, I've got no more ter give." She sniffed and shook her head, allowing the tears to come without blinking them away. "I used ter think I could get ahead. If I worked 'ard enough I could one day . . ." She shook her head angrily. "I don't know what I was thinkin'. People like me don't get ahead."

Surprised by Sally's admission, Cora did not respond immediately. It had likely cost the woman a great deal to reveal as much, and yet she had. She had also confessed her misdeeds to Mr. Ludlow. Though Cora could never condone Sally's actions, her anger and frustration softened. She no longer viewed Sally as mean-spirited. She saw her as a young mother who had allowed her circumstances to make her bitter, cruel, and miserable. Perhaps all Sally truly needed was a show of kindness. Cora could offer her that much, at least.

"Sally, I should like for you to return to Tanglewood and resume your position as housemaid." The words flew out before Cora could rethink them, and although they felt like the right thing to say, a part of her hoped Sally would refuse the offer.

The maid's eyes widened in shock. She pulled her bags in front of her and clasped the handles together with both hands. Her expression was uncertain, distrustful, and perhaps even confused, but the derision had vanished. Cora experienced a measure of relief at that.

"Mr. Ludlow has given me leave to offer the position to whomever I deem fit to do the job. You have proven yourself to be a hard worker, and you are knowledgeable in the operations of Tanglewood—far more knowledgeable than I am at the moment. But if you choose to return, you must accept the fact that I am the housekeeper and you are a housemaid. I do not harbor any delusions that we will become great friends, but I do expect an appropriate level of respect from you."

Cora paused in her speech, but when Sally remained silent, she forged on. "Perhaps we might even strike a bargain, if you're willing. I believe the reason you were passed over for the position of housekeeper is because you lack education and a certain air of decorum in manner and speech. Housekeepers are often called upon to interact with guests in a dignified manner, and if you are to ever be considered for such a position, you must learn how to comport yourself in that way. That is something I can teach you. So here is my proposition: I will instruct you in proper speech and decorum if you will instruct me in the proper ways of housekeeping—and by instruct, I mean without the aid of snakes, rotten eggs, flower petals, or closed dampers."

Cora directed a stern look at Sally, wanting her to understand the extent of her folly. "I was not the only one you injured, you know."

Sally appeared stricken before she lowered her eyes to the ground in a show of humility. She nodded and swallowed. "I ain't proud of what I've done, Mrs. Notley, make no mistake about that. I ain't deservin' of your sympathy neither. But there's no denyin' I need the wages, and Tanglewood's the closest estate to me lad. I also want ter learn 'ow to speak proper-like, so . . . I suppose I accept your bargain."

Cora arched an eyebrow. "Without snakes, rotten eggs, or salt in the sugar jar?"

"Nor frogs, neither." Sally actually smiled—smiled! It looked so foreign and yet lovely at the same time. A rush of joy filled Cora from the inside out, furthering her belief in the power of kindness. It was a feeling that invigorated her like a sound night's sleep never could. Cora decided she really must get Sally to smile more often.

"A truce then?" she asked, extending her hand.

Sally set one bag down to shake hands. As soon as they had sealed their bargain, Cora picked up the bag. It was much heavier than it looked and took all of Cora's strength and both of her frigid hands to carry the thing back inside, where she gratefully handed it to a not-quite-awake Harry, asking if he would be so kind as to return it to Sally's room.

"You did *what*?" Jonathan gaped at Cora. He had been enjoying a nice, peaceful morning in his study when Watts had entered to ask if Mrs. Notley could have a word with him. Not opposed to seeing his housekeeper again so soon, Jonathan had agreed, but he had not been prepared for the news she had just imparted to him. He had supposed the matter of Sally finished. She had been dismissed—by *him*—and should be long departed. But now Mrs. Notley had taken it upon herself to *un*-dismiss the woman? Could he possibly have heard correctly?

"You did tell me I could offer the position to whomever I chose, did you not?" Mrs. Notley appeared innocent as though she could not understand his surprise and vexation.

Jonathan was not normally a man without words, but he had no response to this. One would think it obvious that the position of housemaid could be extended to any woman *except* the girl he had sacked only yesterday. Good gads, did he really need to clarify this? Surely, even the inexperienced Mrs. Notley should know he would be opposed to rehiring the chit. Mrs. Notley should be opposed as well! What the deuce had she been thinking?

Jonathan slowly pushed himself from his chair and stood, planting his palms on his desk as he leaned forward to examine his housekeeper. "You cannot be serious."

"I am." She had the temerity to seat herself in one of his armchairs and clasp her fingers in her lap as though she planned to stay for a cozy chat. "Perhaps you would like to know my reasons for doing as I have done?" she asked.

"The only reason that you could possibly have for behaving so irrationally is that you have lost your mind."

Her answer was a grin. It parted her beautiful lips, caused her eyes to sparkle, and made him feel as though he was the one going mad and not the other way around. "I may very well have," she said. "It does go missing every now and again."

Jonathan could only stare and wonder if he was not in the middle of some very strange dream. "Perhaps you could find where yours has gone, retrieve it, and undo what you have done," he said. "I thought I made it perfectly clear that I will not employ a servant I cannot trust."

His speech seemed to have little effect, if any, on his housekeeper. She remained impervious. "It was I who employed her, not you."

"But it is *I* who employ *you*." Was this not obvious?

"I realize that," she said. "But you did grant me leave to hire whomever I wished, and that is what I have done. Would you like to know why?"

"No," he said curtly. "What I'd like is for you to tell Sally that she must pack her things and leave this house once and for all. I believed you to be a woman of integrity, Mrs. Notley, and yet you have undermined my authority. I can scarce believe it, let alone understand it."

"You would understand, if you would only listen."

Jonathan was through listening. He had never felt more trampled upon and by someone he had come to trust and even admire. Mrs. Notley may have her reasons for doing what she had done, but she had obviously not spared a thought for him or how this would reflect upon his position as master of this household. He was the overseer, and if he made a decision, like it or not, she must abide by it. Did she think this a great joke?

"Mrs. Notley," he said, attempting to control his brewing anger. "The way I see it, you have two options before you. You can either return to Sally and explain that you have made a mistake, or you can return to your room and pack your own bags. I will not countenance such utter disregard for my feelings on this matter. Is that clear?"

All humor drained from her features, leaving behind a pale complexion with glittering blue eyes and rosy cheeks. Her jaw hardened, and she slowly stood, lifting her chin in a defiant way he both admired and despised.

"If those are my only options, sir, I must choose the latter because I refuse to tell a mother she will no longer have the means to care for her child. You may not wish to know my reasons, but I will tell you anyway because you should know them. Sally's a hard worker and a good maid. Her animosity towards me was only a small part of the reason she wished to take my place as housekeeper. The larger part—the one that drove her to behave so desperately and foolishly— was her son. She's a widow and has a child. Did you know that? Did you also know that if she cannot find a way to pay his caregivers more than she has paid in the past, the boy will be turned out at month's end? Until this morning, I did not know any of this. But I do now, and so do you."

Mrs. Notley pressed her lips together and looked briefly down at the floor before meeting his gaze once again. The underlying sadness he saw in her expression pierced his heart. "I assure you, Mr. Ludlow, it was not my intention to disregard your feelings or undermine your authority in any way. You instructed me to hire a housemaid of my choosing, and I opted to grant Sally what I considered to be a much-needed second chance. She may have done very wrong, and I do not condone her actions in the slightest, but she is sorry for them and anxious to make amends."

Cora paused, appearing to weigh her next words, and when she spoke again it was with conviction. "Sometimes a person has a good reason for behaving badly, and it is my belief that forgiveness and understanding can put a stop to the bad and inspire the good. I hope you will come to believe that as well and allow her to stay. But, as you have made very plain, you are the master here, and that choice is up to you. I wish you good day, sir."

Mrs. Notley did not wait for a response. She turned around and walked briskly out the door. Jonathan watched her go, saying nothing to stop her.

He dropped slowly down to his chair, thinking about all she had said. Mrs. Notley had most certainly overstepped the bounds this time, but he could no longer fault her for it. Rather, he faulted himself. He'd behaved like a tyrannical cad, and she had every right to despise him. But at the same time, she had taken a situation that had been clear in its resolution and had muddied it in the most frustrating way. Jonathan did not believe in second chances and he abhorred the thought of employing a maid he could not trust. But now that he was aware that an innocent child's welfare was at stake, how could he not? He felt cornered without any way to defend himself, and it was maddening.

This was exactly the reason an employer should never take a personal interest in one's servants. It complicated matters in the extreme and made Jonathan wish that he had never taken a personal interest in his housekeeper. Perhaps then his world would not be so askew at the moment.

10

By the time Jonathan had come to terms with Sally's reinstatement and went in search of Mrs. Notley, she had already gone. Her room had been cleared of all personal effects and only Mrs. Caddy and Alice knew of her absence. Apparently, she had asked them to convey her goodbyes to the rest of the staff before slipping out the door.

"Where has she gone?" Jonathan demanded of Mrs. Caddy, annoyed that Mrs. Notley had taken herself off so quickly. Surely she had known that he would come around eventually.

"She wouldn't say, sir," said the cook as she pounded out a large piece of beef with some sort of mallet. "She only said that inexperience finally got the better of 'er and it was time ter go." She set the mallet down and wiped the back of her arm across her perspiring forehead. "Is that true, sir? I thought, after last night, that—"

"No, it is not true," interrupted Jonathan. "We had a bit of a . . . misunderstanding is all. Which is why I must learn where she has gone."

Mrs. Caddy harrumphed, a sure sign that she had returned to her usual self. Though Jonathan was glad to see it, her seeming indifference annoyed him. Only last night the woman had made an argument on behalf of Mrs. Notley, and now she didn't seem to care a fig that the housekeeper had gone.

"Will she be comin' back then?" Mrs. Caddy asked as she rubbed the meat with some sort of seasoning.

"It is my hope that she will."

"Glad to 'ear it," said the cook to Jonathan's surprise. Apparently he'd obviously been too hasty in believing the worst of the woman, just as he'd done with Mrs. Notley and Sally.

"Truth be told, I was sorry to see 'er go," added Mrs. Caddy.

Not as sorry as I, Jonathan thought with a sigh. He had a great many things to do today, but now all would have to be put on hold so that he could seek out his elusive housekeeper. How was it possible that she could pack her things and leave so quickly? Every task she attempted to complete typically took twice the amount of time it should.

He glanced at the timid still room maid and gave it one last try. "Alice, can you think of anywhere she might be?"

Alice stared at the floor, and in a voice so quiet he could hardly hear, said, "She seemed ter know some folks at Knottin' Tree. 'Appen she went lookin' for work there?"

Of course! Why hadn't Jonathan thought of that himself? Knotting Tree was the obvious place to begin his search. Mrs. Notley had mentioned she knew Katy and even seemed to be acquainted with Mr. Shepherd as well. Surely someone there would know something more about Mrs. Notley.

"Thank you, Alice," he said. Not wasting another moment, he pushed through the service door and strode towards the stables. With any luck, he would be able to track down his housekeeper and return to Tanglewood within the hour.

Jonathan followed the elderly butler into the drawing room at Knotting Tree, where, much to his astonishment, he discovered Mrs. Notley enjoying a cup of tea with Mr. and Mrs. Shepherd. Only hours before, she had been wearing a gray dress and white apron, appearing every inch a young and attractive housekeeper. Now she wore a lovely peach gown that complimented her figure and made her eyes sparkle in the most captivating way. Jonathan could scarce refrain from staring at her. She looked beautiful, refined, and stately, as though she belonged in this very setting. It brought him back to their first meeting, and not for the first time he wondered about her past.

When the butler announced his presence, Mrs. Notley watched him warily.

Before either of them spoke, Mr. Shepherd came to his feet and cleared his throat. "Mr. Ludlow, how good of you to call. Please join us and forgive our informality. I must say that we were not expecting visitors at this early hour."

"And I was not expecting to find my housekeeper in your drawing room," answered Jonathan, his eyes still on Mrs. Notley. The question in his words weighed heavily between them, bringing with it an awkwardness that caused her to shift uncomfortably. She obviously knew what had brought her here. It was he who did not.

"I am your housekeeper no longer, sir," she finally said, casting a pleading look at Mr. Shepherd, who wasted no time coming to her aid.

"Cora has been telling us about the recent happenings at Tanglewood." Though he spoke with an air of nonchalance, there was an underlying sternness in his tone. "Mrs.

Shepherd and I are quite captivated by the tale, are we not, my dear?"

"Quite," she agreed, gesturing to the tea tray. "Would you care for some refreshment, Mr. Ludlow? As you can see, our cook has sent up enough to feed an entire regiment."

Jonathan wasn't the least bit hungry, but he took a seat beside Mrs. Notley—or was it Miss Notley? Cora? He no longer knew what to call the woman. And what, exactly, had she been telling the Shepherds?

As though perceiving his thoughts, she said, "You have rather good timing, Mr. Ludlow. I had just arrived at the moment in the story where you bestowed upon me your ultimatum to either send Sally away or leave myself. Perhaps you would care to take it from there?"

She appeared so calm and collected and perfectly comfortable in this home. He could not make sense of it. How had she come to be Tanglewood's housekeeper if she was in a position to take tea with his nearest, and most distinguished, neighbor? Had this all been a great lark to her—a way to pass the time? Had she thought it would be great fun to play at housekeeping for a few weeks, stir up trouble, and return with the most entertaining of tales?

In Jonathan's confused and cluttered mind, it was the only explanation that made a modicum of sense. The thought did nothing to improve his disposition. It had the opposite effect, in fact.

"Yes, I would very much like to continue the tale," he said, his jaw tightening. "Only this morning, Mrs. Notley—" He glanced pointedly at her, his eyes cold and hard. "Or is that not your true name?" For all he knew, she could be Miss Spencer, Lady Arabella, or an illegitimate daughter of Mr. Shepherd's who made a living as an actress. If so, she should never be cast as a housekeeper. She was deplorable at it.

"No, it is not my true name," she confirmed.

Jonathan felt his nostrils flare as a rush of anger filled him. If there was something he detested more than anything, it was being deceived and taken for a fool, and he was beginning to feel very taken.

"As I said before," she continued. "It is *Miss* Notley now. Miss Coralynn Eliza Notley, to be precise."

Jonathan's jaw clenched. Why must she be so aggravating at times? What game was she playing at, and why did he suddenly feel like a pawn? Did she keep him in suspense for her own amusement?

"And who is Miss Coralynn Eliza Notley?" he demanded.

"You need not answer that," said Mr. Shepherd in a calm, but firm way. "Mr. Ludlow has no right to demand anything of you any longer."

Miss Notley sighed and relaxed against the back of her chair, smoothing her hands over the fabric of the armrests. After a few moments, she said, "Perhaps he does not have the right, Mr. Shepherd, but after the many kindnesses he has shown me during the past few weeks, I believe he deserves an explanation."

"Very well," said Mr. Shepherd, settling back in his chair with his arms folded. He obviously had no intention of leaving the room. It was apparent he did not trust Mr. Ludlow to behave like a gentleman.

Mrs. Shepherd must have perceived the situation differently, for she laid a hand on her husband's arm. "I am certain Mr. Ludlow and Cora have much to discuss. Perhaps they would prefer to do so without an audience?"

Mr. Shepherd didn't seem overly keen on this idea, but he raised a questioning eyebrow at Miss Notley. When she gave a slight nod, he answered with a curt nod of his own, then rose to his feet and extended a hand to his wife.

"Please ring should you need anything, Cora," he said before he and Mrs. Shepherd took their leave. As soon as the door had closed behind them, Jonathan twisted towards Miss Notley, wondering what sort of explanation she would give him.

She glanced briefly his way before drawing in a long breath and exhaling slowly. When she was ready, she began spinning an intriguing and sad tale of a young tradesman's daughter who had been raised in a life of luxury by unfeeling parents, only to be bartered off to the first titled gentleman who came along. It did not matter that he was twice her age and the most disagreeable man she'd ever met. All that mattered was his title.

"If I had been a good daughter, I would have agreed to the marriage, but alas, I was too headstrong and obstinate to go along with such a plan," she continued. "My friend, Lady Harriett Cavendish, and her family are connected to the Shepherds. It was she and Lady Drayson who arranged for me to travel to Yorkshire and stay here at Knotting Tree. When I first arrived, the Shepherds wanted to take me in and introduce me into local society with the hope of finding me a good match. But it was my wish to seek employment so that I might have the freedom to choose the direction my life should take. You were good enough to offer me such an opportunity, at least for a short time."

A hint of a smile touched her lips. "And so here we are, with me once again at the mercy of others and you . . . well, I'm not certain why you have come, sir."

As he listened, Jonathan's frustration ebbed. He knew how it felt to leave a comfortable life and travel to an unknown place with the hope of beginning anew. But Jonathan had done so with the means and ability to take care of himself. How much more difficult would it have been to set out with nothing as Miss Notley had done?

"So," Jonathan finally spoke, "you have sought your independence by entering into service."

She laughed lightly. "You make me sound like a widgeon when you phrase it that way."

Jonathan would miss hearing that laugh. He'd miss her gentle voice, her lovely blue eyes, and the way she frowned and bit her lower lip whenever he'd called her to task. No other servant had ever been as candid and direct with him, and he realized how much he'd enjoyed it.

When Jonathan had first come to Askern, he'd immersed himself into society. There had been a time he had attended each and every social function and had hosted many of his own. But as time passed, and mothers and daughters began suffocating him with various matchmaking antics, he'd sought relief by withdrawing and focusing on his estate instead. At first it had been the distraction he'd needed, but Miss Notley's presence—or rather, her absence— had served to remind him exactly how lonely he'd allowed his life to become.

Perhaps it was time to change that.

"Might I ask what you have decided to do about Sally?" Miss Notley's question pulled Jonathan's wayward thoughts back to the present.

He cleared his throat and frowned at the unhappy reminder of this morning's events. He still did not care for the outcome, but it was done now. "She will stay for the time being, but only on a trial basis. One more incident and, child or no, she will no longer be welcome at Tanglewood."

The instant approval in Miss Notley's eyes, the lovely smile that touched her lips, and the warmth in which she gazed at him made Jonathan feel as though everything would turn out all right in the end. He had to wonder at the effect she had on his disposition. From the first time he'd laid eyes on her, she'd been able to make him feel things he hadn't in a long time—both good and bad. It was as though she'd stumbled upon the key to his locked emotions and had wasted no time in freeing them.

"Is that why you have come?" she asked. "To tell me about Sally?"

"No," he answered, conflicted. The reason he had come was no longer valid.

When he said nothing more, Miss Notley leaned forward in her seat. "Mr. Ludlow." She paused, her fingers twisting together the way they did every time she grew nervous about something. Any moment, she would draw her lower lip into her mouth and—ahh, just like that.

Jonathan held back a smile. "Yes?" he prompted.

She released her lip and raised her gaze to his. "I wonder if . . . well . . . if you will not grant me another chance at Tanglewood as well? If I promise to never again retain a servant that you have recently sacked?"

He tried his best not to grin. "How long is recently, exactly? Do you mean to wait a fortnight before retaining said servant?"

Her lips twitched. "Let me rephrase. I promise to never again retain a servant that you wish to remain sacked. Is that better?"

"It's clearer," he conceded, settling back in his chair as he wondered what to do from here. Only this morning he had left Tanglewood for the express purpose of returning his housekeeper to her rightful position, but now that he was aware of her situation, he felt hesitant to follow through with that plan. Why did she wish for such a thing, anyway? Did she truly believe that a servant's life was a freer life? A better life? Why was she so opposed to entering into society? And why did he suddenly wish that she would?

The truth of the matter was that he no longer wanted her to return to Tanglewood. He wanted her to do as Mr. and Mrs. Shepherd wished and take her place where she truly belonged. He wanted to be able to stand up with her at dances, play whist with her at soirées, accompany her into dinners, and pay court to her.

If she returned to housekeeping, an imaginary line would come between them—one that the rules of society dictated he could not cross, at least not in the way he now wished to cross. She would be his servant and he, her master, and never the twain shall meet for Jonathan was not one to take certain liberties with anyone on his staff.

"If I say no," Jonathan hedged, "what would become of Miss Notley?"

She straightened her shoulders and lifted her chin. "I would seek employment elsewhere, of course."

"You would not allow Mr. and Mrs. Shepherd to take you about in society?"

"Certainly not. I would never wish for such a thing."

"Why?"

"I do not belong in that world."

"Nonsense," he said. "We are not in London. This is Askern, where several respectable families are involved in some sort of trade. You would fit in quite nicely."

Miss Notley frowned at her hands. After a moment or two, she said, "What I meant to say was I have no desire to belong in that world."

In other words, she had no desire to belong in Jonathan's world. The thought injured him. "Why is that?"

"Because, sir, it is a world in which men hold all the power and women hold none. The life a servant may be rigorous and demanding, but there is a great deal of satisfaction in earning a fair wage and knowing that what I have earned is mine and mine alone. I need not answer to anyone or require permission to do as I please, go where I may, and marry whom I choose. My life, sir, is my own, and that is how I prefer it."

Jonathan looked deep into her eyes—eyes that shone vibrantly with stubborn pride and determination. There would be no changing her mind.

"And who will you one day choose to marry?" he asked, not sure he would like her answer. "A footman, perhaps? A butler? A stablehand? Possibly a farmer? Do you not see that housekeepers are limited in their choices? Would you be happy married to someone who was raised so differently than you?"

"I do not care for wealth or position," she defended. "I believe I would be better off married to a footman I respected than a detestable philanderer who's only interest is my father's money."

"Not every gentleman is like that, you know."

She let out a breath and offered him a pained smile that seemed to say, *Let us agree to disagree and be done with this conversation.*

"I do know," she said. "Lord Drayson, Mr. Shepherd, and now you have taught me that there are many good men in society. But I am still determined to make my own way. If you no longer wish to retain me as your housekeeper, I will understand and began my search for employment elsewhere. But Tanglewood holds a special place in my heart, and I would very much like to return."

Jonathan steepled his fingers under his chin. That was not the answer he wanted to hear, and yet he was not surprised. He was coming to learn that once Miss Notley's mind was set, she would not be swayed. It was both a strength and a weakness—one he didn't care for at the moment because it left him with only two options. He could allow her to return as his housekeeper or he must let her go with the knowledge he'd likely never see her again.

Actually, there was only one option.

"If that is how you truly feel—"

"It is, sir," she insisted.

"Then . . . consider yourself welcomed to Tanglewood once again, *Mrs.* Notley."

The smile that beamed from her lips caused Jonathan's heart to pound in an erratic fashion. He felt his world tilt and wobble precariously, and he wondered how he would navigate this new, unchartered situation. She had found her way into his heart and mind, and he knew that something had changed. There would be no returning to the way things were before today.

CORA'S RETURN TO TANGLEWOOD became somewhat of a happy turning point. Instead of being welcomed back with surliness, disdain, or even indifference, the servants greeted her with smiles and warmth. Harry pulled her into a hug, Watts nodded his head in approval, Alice peeked up from the floor long enough to extend a shy smile, and even Mrs. Caddy seemed pleased to see her.

In addition, the household began running smoothly— or, at least as smoothly as it could with Cora still having so much to learn. But true to her word, Sally became an adept teacher, even going so far as to remind Cora to remove yet another attempt at pastries from the oven before they blackened. As a result, Cora finally produced a batch she dared serve, although Harry did tease her about them being dry. But she did not care. They were not too dark or crispy, and for her, that meant progress.

Furthermore, Mr. Ludlow seemed to place more trust in her as well. He began to seek her opinion on menu choices and what she thought of the draperies, linens, or furnishings in various rooms. Every time they encountered one another around the house, which seemed more frequently of late, he had a question ready to ask her. It made her feel quite useful.

One particular day, he requested her presence in his study following luncheon. She found him seated in his favorite wingback chair, a thoughtful expression affixed on his face. As soon as she'd entered, he nodded at the area above the fireplace mantle where a painting hung depicting ocean waves breaking against a rocky coastline.

"What do you think of my recent acquisition, Mrs. Notley?"

Cora considered the painting. The artist obviously had great talent. He had captured the moonlight glistening off the waters in a dramatic, tumultuous way. Most would consider the artwork to be beautiful and romantic, but there was something about it that Cora could not like. Perhaps it was the anger she saw in the churning waves and how they seemed to lash out at the rocks. Or perhaps it was the reminder of a similar painting her father had procured for her family's library not so long ago. She hadn't cared for that painting either. Whatever the reason, Cora wished Mr. Ludlow had not asked her opinion on this particular matter. The piece had obviously captured his interest, and if he had purchased it for his favorite room, he must like it a great deal. She was loathe to disagree.

"You do not care for it." Mr. Ludlow correctly interpreted her thoughts as he watched her closely. A hint of a smile tugged at the corners of his mouth as though challenging her to deny his observation.

Cora cleared her throat and tried to think of something polite to say. "The artist is quite talented."

"I agree," he said. "But did he put his talents to good use in this landscape?"

"Er . . ." Cora did not know how to tactfully respond except to say, "I'm sure he is of the opinion that he did."

"And your opinion?" he pressed.

She clasped her fingers behind her back and shifted her weight from one foot to the other. "If you must know, I think he was in a foul temper when he painted it."

"Ah, so you see the emotion behind the lines."

"It is impossible not to, sir."

"Do you prefer your paintings to be of a more placid nature, then?"

Good grief, the man could be trying at times. Why were they even having this conversation? It seemed silly and inconsequential. If Mr. Ludlow found something to admire in the artwork, then he ought to go on admiring it and leave her to her duties. Cora's opinion did not matter in the slightest.

"Not necessarily," she answered. "I only wonder what a painting by this artist might look like after he'd taken an invigorating stroll through a beautiful garden on a glorious sunny day."

Mr. Ludlow seemed to consider the suggestion before quirking an eyebrow. "Is a stroll through a garden all it takes to improve one's temperament?" His voice held a teasing lilt, and Cora couldn't resist responding in kind.

"Well, perhaps he might spy a lovely and inspiring lady while he was about."

Mr. Ludlow chuckled. He leaned back in his chair and clasped his hands behind his head, shifting his gaze to the painting once more. After studying it a moment longer, he said, "Do you know something, Mrs. Notley? I am now wondering the same thing. Perhaps I should commission another painting from him with the stipulation that he can work only after an excursion with a beautiful lady in the garden."

"Perhaps you should," she said, even though she knew he would never do anything of the sort. The thought merely reaffirmed the silliness of this exchange, and Cora found herself wondering at his reasons for requesting an audience with her.

When he looked at her again, the warmth in his expression caused her heart to bounce and thud in a most unseemly way. Perhaps this was the reason she did not care for conversations such as these with him. The lighthearted nature led to a feeling of camaraderie that she should not be experiencing with her employer. They ought to be discussing the state of his accounts or making arrangements for dinner guests—not talking about how a beautiful woman could inspire a man. What had she been thinking to say such a thing? She hadn't, and that was the problem. When in his presence all coherent thought vanished.

Cora cleared her throat. "If you will excuse me, sir, I really must go. There are sugars waiting to be pounded and herbs needing to be plucked."

"I'm sure you will pound them senseless and pluck them dry," he said. "Good day to you, Mrs. Notley."

"To you too, sir."

Cora practically fled the study, taking deep breaths all the way back to the kitchen. These impromptu meetings with Mr. Ludlow must cease soon, or she would need to dismiss herself and leave Tanglewood once and for all. The man was beginning to invade her thoughts far too often, and she refused to allow that to happen—not now that she was finally feeling at home.

She paused just outside the kitchen, vowing to herself that she would no longer be lulled into any more lighthearted repartees with Mr. Ludlow. From now on, she would only speak to him of household matters and nothing more. She would barricade her heart and keep her mind in the place it belonged.

"Oh, Miss Notley, here you are at last."

Cora's eyes widened to see Sally rushing towards her looking happier than Cora had ever seen. The frizzy, red-haired woman went so far as to clasp Cora's hands and give them a hardy squeeze. Cora blinked in surprise, thinking how dry and frail Sally's fingers felt, as though they might snap with the slightest pressure.

"What is it, Sally?" Cora asked. Although they had been on better terms with one another, Sally had never been nearly this friendly before. The maid's eyes were bright with unshed tears.

"I can scarce believe it, but 'tis real as me standin' here."

"What is real?" Cora asked, perplexed.

"It's me lad. Mr. Ludlow's gone and found 'im a better place with a good woman who's askin' for no more'n I can pay. 'E's also increased my wages so I can put some away as well." She shook her head as the tears trailed down her cheeks. "I don't deserve it after what I done."

Cora's heart swelled instantly. It was a good thing Mr. Ludlow was not standing at her side or she would likely throw her arms around him and do exactly what she'd vowed never to even think, let alone do. Yet how could she not think of it when he'd done something so wonderful?

Cora smiled at Sally and gave her fingers a light squeeze. "You meant to say that the good woman *isn't* asking and you don't deserve it after what *I've* done." Cora had made a point of correcting Sally at every opportunity—hopefully in a helpful way. "And of course you deserve it, Sally. You're a good mother and a hard worker. Your news has made me very happy indeed."

Sally tightened her grip on Cora's fingers one last time before releasing them. "Thank you ever so much, Mrs. Notley. I don't know what else ter say."

Cora shook her head, not deserving of the maid's gratitude. "It is not me you should thank. It is Mr. Ludlow. I had nothing at all to do with it."

Sally's smile became sly. "If you think that, Mrs. Notley, you don't know men at'll. It was you 'e was thinkin' about, not me."

The maid departed with a lightness in her step, and Cora's eyes followed. What a strange thing to say. If Mr. Ludlow had been thinking about anyone, it had been Sally's son. Every child deserved to be cared for in some way, and Mr. Ludlow had done what was necessary to protect a boy who could not protect himself. The only part Cora had played was to retain Sally and make sure Mr. Ludlow understood her circumstances. He had done the rest out of the goodness of his heart.

And his heart was good, Cora thought, feeling hers warm again.

Heavens, she really must stop thinking such things. It would only lead to trouble, and she certainly did not need any more of that. She strode purposefully into the still room, wrapped a large lump of sugar in a cloth, and began to strike it hard with a mallet.

A fortnight following his discussion with Mrs. Notley about the painting titled *Maddening Seas*, Jonathan once again sat in his favorite chair and frowned at the piece. When he had first laid eyes on it, he had thought it commanding and majestic, but after hearing Mrs. Notley's opinion, he now recognized the brooding feeling the dark colors and turbulent seas conveyed. It began to bother him more and more. At one point he'd determined to replace it, but as the days passed and his efforts at furthering his acquaintance with Mrs. Notley met with failure, Jonathan developed a sort of kinship with the painting and no longer wished to part with it.

What had changed? He and Mrs. Notley had been on such good terms once upon a time, and yet she now would not look him in the eye. She answered his teasing questions with either silence or dull and lifeless responses. She made every effort to avoid him, even going so far as to duck down a corridor when she spied him coming her way, even though he had obviously seen her and she had seen him. There were no more cheery hellos or smiles, no more laughter or exchanges that would brighten his day. The only time in the past couple of weeks that he had sensed any warmth at all from her was when she had thanked him for the part he'd played in Sally's improved circumstances. For a brief moment, he'd caught a spark of the woman he'd grown altogether too fond of, but then she bowed her head, stiffened her shoulders, and returned to vague and wooden responses.

He had wanted to take her by the shoulders and demand an explanation, but he'd watched her curtsy and scuttle away instead—not that she'd ever allow that she had.

Loud clucking and hollering sounded from outside his window, and Jonathan pushed himself to his feet so he could investigate the ruckus.

Apparently someone had left the gate of the chicken coop unlatched. The formal gardens contained a mob of pecking birds. Charlie, the stablehand, was attempting to corner one while Harry chased after another with frantic movements. Mrs. Notley had come to the rescue as well. She crouched down, trying to lure a bird to her by holding out a palm filled with seeds. One hen snatched a bite and quickly darted away. It only took her a few more attempts to realize the futility of her plan. She tossed what remained of the seeds near a hedge where Charlie had finally cornered one bird. When it bent to peck at a seed, Charlie nabbed it with both hands. Another bird came to peck, and so he quickly handed the captured one to a surprised Mrs. Notley. She tentatively took hold of the bird, but when it attempted to spread its wings, she squealed and dropped it.

Charlie called out something and pointed while Harry rushed at the recently freed creature, only to scare it right back towards Mrs. Notley, who squealed once again and sought shelter behind Harry, latching onto his shoulders to keep him between her and the now frightened bird.

Harry glanced over his shoulder and said something that made her laugh while Charlie lunged for another bird and missed, landing in a pile of feathers and seeds instead. Mrs. Notley kept one hand on Harry's shoulder as she bent over, her entire frame shaking from uncontrolled laughter. Jonathan couldn't help but notice how comfortable she appeared with the footman. She had even touched him without hesitation.

A memory of Miss Notley's determined voice sprang to Jonathan's mind. *I would be better off married to a footman I respected* she had said firmly. Was Harry such a footman? Jonathan had always thought that being in a position of wealth and power was the preferred life—the one envied by those who could never attain it. But as he looked over the scene in the garden, he found himself envying a footman. It did not sit well with him.

Who had allowed those chickens to escape anyway? They were stirring up dust, leaving a mess of feathers in their wake, and causing utter chaos. He could only imagine what a visitor might make of the scene. Gads, would his household never be able to maintain any sort of decorum?

He turned from the window and stalked out of the room. Down the hall and out the door he went, following the path around to the gardens. Mrs. Notley had progressed to the point where she now clutched her belly as she continued to laugh. Sally had joined the commotion as well, giggling joyfully. They seemed to be having a jolly time watching the hens escape capture.

"What the devil is going on?" Jonathan's voice sounded thunderous, even to his own ears, but he paid it no mind. He wanted the madness to cease so that he might return to his brooding in peace.

His tone had an immediate effect on everyone. They sobered at once, with the exception of Mrs. Notley, whose hand now covered her mouth to muffle her giggles.

Charlie, holding a wriggling chicken, stiffened and stared down at the ground. "I beg your pardon, Mr. Ludlow. The hens . . . well, sir, they—"

"Escaped," Jonathan inserted, having no patience whatsoever. "I can see that. What I'm wondering is who allowed them to escape."

The stablehand, who couldn't be more than sixteen, shuffled his feet, still refusing to meet Mr. Ludlow's eyes. Mrs. Notley, thank heavens, had finally ceased her giggling.

"Well, sir—" The lad began to say but Harry cut him off.

"'Twas me who left the cage unlatched."

Mr. Ludlow lifted an eyebrow, finding that difficult to believe. "What business did you have in the henhouse, Harry?" he asked, challenging the footman to procure a reason Jonathan would believe.

"I . . . er . . ." Harry cast a panicked look at Mrs. Notley, obviously begging her to come to his aid.

She rolled her eyes. "Oh, for pity's sake, Harry, Mr. Ludlow is not a nodcock. He knows very well that it was not your doing. Of course it was Charlie who neglected to replace the latch, but he did not do so on purpose, sir. It was an innocent mistake that we are all attempting to rectify."

Jonathan's jaw hardened. Why was it that Mrs. Notley seemed to be the only person who placed any value in truth? Harry had not hesitated in telling the idiotic fib, nor had he looked the least bit sorry for it, and Charlie had said nothing to correct him. Did integrity mean so little to them that they could overlook it at every opportunity?

Jonathan flicked a glance over the entire scene. Before him stood a lying footman, a cowardly stablehand, an immoral maid, and an incompetent housekeeper who had made her indifference to Jonathan quite clear. They were all surrounded by the most annoying clucking hens. One bird even had the temerity to peck at Jonathan's freshly shined Hessians. He nudged the bird away with his toe as anger simmered inside. Enough was enough.

He directed a cold glare at Harry first and then Charlie. "The two of you are to gather each and every hen, then pack your things and leave Tanglewood this instant. I no longer have need of your services."

Charlie and Harry appeared to accept the verdict without surprise or argument. Jonathan had to give them credit for that. It was Mrs. Notley's eyes that bulged. "But, sir—"

Jonathan turned his glare on her, and she clamped her mouth closed. He knew the effect would only be temporary since the woman could not remain silent for long.

Without further ado, he spun around and walked away. Any onlooker might view it as a powerful exit, but those who really knew him would see it for what it was—a flight to avoid yet another confrontation with his housekeeper.

Unfortunately, he had not taken more than three steps

when rapid footsteps sounded. He knew without looking that she had followed.

"Sir," her voice confirmed. "Please wait."

It took restraint not to break into a run and make his escape, but Jonathan forced his steps to remain purposeful and continued forward, ignoring her plea. He rounded the side of the house and was nearly to the steps when her hand took hold of his arm.

He felt the touch immediately. The power of it moved up his arm and through his body, awakening sensations and desires he had no business feeling. He stopped and stared into her glittering blue eyes, wanting to drag her to him and kiss all arguments from her lips. Why did she feel the need to fight him on this? Why couldn't she understand how much he loathed dishonesty and take his side for once? Why did she not reach out to him because she wanted to? The only reason she touched him now was because she felt the need to come to a footman's defense.

"I already know what you wish to say," said Jonathan. "They both have very good reasons for behaving badly and you would like to tell me what they are."

"Yes."

He stared pointedly at her hand on his arm. "Lest you forget, Mrs. Notley, you promised to never interfere in my decisions again."

She pulled her hand away. "No, I promised to never reinstate a servant that you have sacked. I did not promise to never interfere."

"Perhaps now would be an ideal time to make such a promise, for you are treading on precarious ground, and I am not in the mood to hear your pleas. As I've told you before, I will not tolerate dishonesty of any sort."

She clamped her lips together, her eyes conveying her

obvious disappointment in him. But, as before, she could not keep quiet for long. "And yet you will tolerate a stableboy returning to his drunken father where he will be subjected to a fierce beating because he no longer has a job. Charlie did not mean to leave the gate unlatched, sir."

"He was not dismissed because he left the gate un-latched," said Jonathan, his voice rising. "He was dismissed because he stood by while a footman lied on his behalf and said nothing."

"Of course he said nothing!" she cried. "He believed the consequence of leaving a gate unlatched would result in his immediate dismissal and therefore a severe beating. Don't you see, Mr. Ludlow? Your servants are afraid of you. They believe you to be the most exacting of employers and that one mistake will result in their departure. Why do you think Mrs. Caddy became so unhinged when that dinner went awry? She feared for her job. They all do."

Mrs. Notley paused, biting down on her lower lip as though struggling to rein in her emotions. When she looked at him again, unshed tears filled her eyes. "Your servants are not without integrity, sir. Charlie and Harry are good men. They merely have a lot more at stake than you understand. Please do not send them away for this. It is an unjust punishment."

She blinked, and a tear escaped, making a path down her cheek. Jonathan watched it fall, knowing he had been the cause of it. The knowledge tore at his heart. Only moments before, she had been full of merriment and joy—they all had—and now, because of his quick temper and foul mood there was no joy left to be felt.

Jonathan could not abide to look at her any longer, so he turned and walked away, needing the solace of his study more than ever. At least he would be in good company with his painting.

Once inside, he ran into Watts, who was just emerging from the corridor that led back to the kitchen.

"Good day to you, sir," the butler said cheerfully.

At least someone can still look at me with respect, thought Jonathan. "Good day, Watts," he replied, drawing in a deep breath as he struggled to gain control over his turbulent emotions. It was a battle not easily won. His principles had never accepted an easy defeat, but as with Sally, Jonathan knew Mrs. Notley was in the right of it. Devil take it. How he despised being wrong.

Another deep breath, and Jonathan mustered the ability to say, "Might I beg a favor from you, Watts?"

"Certainly, sir. How may I be of assistance?"

"Would you please inform Charlie and Harry that, following the removal of the hens from my gardens, I would like a word with them in my study?"

The slight lift of the butler's eyebrows was the only indication he was surprised by the request. "Right away, sir."

"Thank you, Watts." Feeling marginally better, Jonathan returned to his study and took one last look at the cursed painting before removing it from the mantle.

Following dinner, Jonathan needed some air and rode into town, stopping by the tavern for a drink and whatever distraction was to be had there. He was in luck. Two drunkards began an argument that quickly escalated into a brawl. Punches were thrown, drinks spilled, and glasses broken, until they were finally shoved out the door by an angry proprietor. Jonathan watched it play out with an inward smile. At least he had not resorted to fisticuffs with Harry and Charlie. Perhaps there was hope for him yet.

In the wee hours of the morning, he swallowed the last of his drink, dropped some coins on the table, and nodded to the proprietor before heading back to Tanglewood. He handed his horse off to a sleepy stablehand and strode inside, where, much to his surprise, he found a sleeping Mrs. Notley at the base of the stairs, her head leaning against the banister with her mouth parted slightly. Jonathan stopped several feet away, watching her.

The moonlight coming through the glass above the door highlighted her dark curls and lovely cheekbones. Her shoulders and chest rose and fell with deep, even breaths, and the smallest of smiles touched her lips. Even in her sleep she appeared content and happy. Goodness seemed to emanate from her, touching him like the warmth from a cozy fire.

Jonathan knew he should bypass her and go straight to his bedchamber. She would awaken on her own eventually, or he could send his valet to rouse her. It was far too late and Jonathan too tired to control the feelings she stirred within him, yet he could not pull his gaze away. She was so very beautiful. He yielded to the impulse to graze his fingers lightly across her cheekbone. How soft and cold her skin felt.

His touched stirred her, and she slowly lifted her head and blinked open her eyes. At first, she appeared confused. Then her gaze traveled from Jonathan's boots up to his face. Her eyes widened, and she immediately pulled herself to her feet, stifling a yawn in the process.

"Forgive me, Mr. Ludlow. I must have dozed off."

Jonathan glanced at the marble steps and lifted a brow. "Surely you could have found a more comfortable place to doze than these steps. Your bed, perhaps?"

"I did not intend to fall asleep, sir."

"And yet you did."

"Yes." She studied her fingers as though they were the most interesting things around. When she said nothing more, Jonathan sighed.

"What are you doing on the stairs, Mrs. Notley? Are you guarding the door against intruders, perhaps?"

"What?" Her eyes flew to his, but when she saw that he was only jesting, her lips lifted a little. "Yes, that is exactly what I am doing, sir. You may rest easy tonight for I have things well in hand." Her lips twitched and quirked, and Jonathan had the greatest desire to kiss them. What would they taste like? Would they feel as soft and supple as they appeared? Would they conform to his or—

What the devil was he thinking? Jonathan closed his eyes and pinched the bridge of his nose, striving to control his emotions. What he needed to do was to leave. At once.

"I shall be sure to rest easy then," he said with a sigh. "Goodnight, Mrs. Notley."

He began to walk past her, but she moved to stop him. When her fingers brushed the front of his shirt, she snatched her hand back as though the mere touch of him had shocked her. Her eyes lingered on the area of exposed skin beneath his collarbone. Hours earlier, Jonathan had discarded his cravat and undone the top two buttons of his shirt.

Her breath hitched and Jonathan felt his own breathing increase as well. Her gaze slowly lifted to his, revealing vulnerability, nervousness, and desire. Jonathan's heart raced, and he had to clench his hands at his sides. He was far too tired for this sort of temptation. What had she been thinking to wait up for him?

"Is there something you needed, Mrs. Notley?" The words came out sounding abrupt and irritated.

She blinked and shook her head. "No, sir. I mean, yes." She paused, biting her lower lip as she searched for the right words. "I merely wanted to say . . . well, thank you, I suppose."

"For what?"

"For retaining Charlie and Harry. For listening and . . ." Her voice trailed off.

"Finally seeing reason?" he finished for her, annoyed that he had to fight off his attraction while she stood there, reminding him of his earlier boorishness. The fact of the matter was that he did not need her thanks or even want it. He only wished to escape her presence, go to bed, and forget this day had ever happened.

Unfortunately, she was making it difficult to do that.

"I was going to say 'understanding,'" she said quietly, her brow furrowed in worry. "And you do understand, do you not?" She paused, looking anxious. "What I mean to say is that the reasons you allowed Charlie and Harry to stay and saw to it that Sally's son received better care was because you were concerned about their welfare, were you not?"

"As opposed to whose welfare, Mrs. Notley?" he asked. "Yours? Do you suppose I did it all for you? That I harbor some . . . special feelings for my housekeeper and *that* is the reason I listened and understood?"

Her cheeks flamed, and she quickly shook her head. "No, of course not. I would never presume such a thing. It's only that . . . oh, never mind." She placed her palms on her burning cheeks. "What was I thinking? I should not have waited up for you. Please, let us forget this whole conversation ever happened."

Jonathan wanted nothing more, but he felt immediate guilt for goading her in such a way. She did not deserve it, not when her worries were justified. The truth of it was that he had thought of her first and foremost in each situation. He thought of her constantly. That was the problem.

He sighed. "You were thinking, Mrs. Notley, that you could not go to bed without expressing your gratitude that I came to my senses long enough to right a wrong. There is nothing so vile in that. Pray forgive me for behaving like a boor. The truth of the matter is that I could not think of them without thinking of you. I suppose you could say that you have helped me to see things more clearly—or, with more compassion, and for that I owe you my thanks as well. I have come to respect and admire your opinion a great deal, and I apologize for making you uncomfortable."

Her mouth opened to say something but no words came out. She stared at him in confusion.

Jonathan could not deny that he enjoyed seeing her speechless for once. It felt rather good. "You no longer need to guard the door, Mrs. Notley. Please go to bed, and let us do as you suggest and forget about today. I should like nothing more, I assure you."

Her answer came as a slow nod, and Jonathan took the opportunity to escape, leaving his tongue-tied housekeeper standing at the base of the stairs. If she had any idea how much she had tested his control tonight, she would flee as well.

As November became December, Cora settled into her role as housekeeper. She now felt confident with the marketing, in the still room, and even in the kitchen as she plated the tasty meals Mrs. Caddy prepared. When Mr. Ludlow entertained, as he was doing more and more, she felt secure in choosing the linens and décor that would be used for the dinner table and even aided Watts a time or two in selecting the wine. Her relationships with the housemaids, especially Sally, improved dramatically, and she grew to adore the timid Alice.

One morning in mid-December, Cora arranged her cap on her head and tightened her apron strings, giving her reflection one last glance before leaving her room and skipping down the stairs. With the house so dark and chilly, it had become more difficult to drag herself from her bed, but once she was up and about she found that she loved the early morning hours. Even amongst the bustle, a peaceful feeling radiated through the house in those precious moments before the sun arose. Cora loved catching glimpses of it cresting the horizon or glowing behind thick layers of clouds. With winter just around the corner, the skies were overcast much of the time.

There were at least six servants clustered around the kitchen window when Cora descended, each of them vying for a view into the murky outdoors.

"Has the Prince Regent come to call?" teased Cora, curious as to the reason for all the fuss.

Sally broke away from the group with a scowl. "It's not so excitin' as all that. Just snowin' like the dickens out there. Haven't seen that much white in ages."

"Truly?" Cora's spirits brightened further as she joined the group, standing on tiptoe to catch a glimpse of the first snowfall of the year. How beautiful it looked, extending light to the dreariness with its untouched brilliance.

"Makes me want ter go build a snow creature," said Harry, looking like a boy who'd just been given a favorite toy.

"Why in Heaven's name are you scowling, Sally?" Cora asked. "It's a lovely sight."

"From 'ere, 'tis lovely," said Sally. "But when I go trompin' about tonight to visit me—I mean, *my*—son, it won't be near so lovely. My boots soak up the snow like a dishrag."

Cora pulled her gaze from the window and smiled at the maid. More and more often, Sally was correcting her own grammar, and Cora loved hearing it.

"If that is the reason you are scowling, you must cease at once. I have a sturdy pair of boots that you are welcome to borrow any time you'd like. And a warm coat as well." Indeed, on Cora's last trip to the Shepherd's, she had returned with a bundle of warm clothing that Mrs. Shepherd had insisted were no longer needed. Cora had accepted them gratefully, for the weather had turned quite blustery the past few weeks, and she had begun to dread venturing outdoors.

Now, however, she couldn't wait for a chance to step outside and lift her face to the heavens. Oh, what a blessed sight.

"Ah, see?" Cora grinned when she saw that Sally's scowl had gone away. "Now you are not so despising of the snow, are you?"

"'Tis . . . lovely, I suppose," Sally allowed, cocking an eyebrow at Cora. "You truly don't mind me borrowin' your boots and coat?"

"Of course not. We can't have you catching a chill, can we? Your son needs a healthy mother, and I need a strong and vigorous housemaid."

Sally smiled. "I thank you, Mrs. Notley."

"It is my pleasure," she responded, thinking how nice it was to finally be at peace with the maid—peace with everyone at Tanglewood, really. At least the servants. Mr. Ludlow was another matter entirely. Cora sometimes wondered if she would ever come to truly understand him and feel comfortable in his presence. Sometimes he looked upon her with unseemly warmth and admiration, sometimes he spoke with a curt air of annoyance, and sometimes he treated her with complete indifference as though she were nothing more than a servant—which was precisely how he should treat her, she told herself firmly. Cora did her best to stay out of his way, but it was impossible to avoid him completely considering he requested an audience with her on an almost daily basis. She suffered through those meetings, attempting to behave as though she felt only respect for her employer.

If only that were true. If only she could make it be true.

"Stop gawkin' at the snow," Mrs. Caddy demanded of the group in her brusque way. "Eat your breakfast and get ter work. No sense in standin' about like a pack of good-for-nothin' goats."

Since Watts was not around, it probably should have been Cora who called everyone to order, but why take on the taxing role of taskmaster when Mrs. Caddy seemed to enjoy it so well?

Cora hid a smile, gazed one last time at the cheery snow, and made her way to the servants' table where Mrs. Caddy had set out a tasty spread. Watts appeared and Cora took her place with the other servants, marveling at the camaraderie she now felt with them. How wonderful it was to finally feel as though she belonged.

As soon as they'd eaten, Cora gestured for Alice to join her in the still room where they set a pot of tea to brewing and began to label and shelve the bottles of preserves they'd made yesterday. After that, she walked into the larder to compile a list of items needed at market, and finally helped Mrs. Caddy prepare Mr. Ludlow's breakfast tray.

"Sally," Mrs. Caddy's voice boomed through the kitchen. "I'll be needin' you ter take this up to Mr. Ludlow at once."

Sally glanced at Cora for affirmation, and Cora nodded. Mr. Ludlow had not requested that his housekeeper bring up the tray, as he often did, and she was grateful for it. She could use a day's respite from the man.

Her gratitude lasted only as long as it took for Harry to bustle into the room. "Mr. Ludlow's askin' that Mrs. Notley bring up his tray," he announced as Sally was leaving the kitchen with it. She promptly stopped and turned around, smiling slyly at Cora in a way she'd come to loathe. Harry's wink did nothing to help matters either. The two of them found great enjoyment in teasing her about Mr. Ludlow's particular attentions, and Cora did not care for it one bit. Why did Mr. Ludlow need to speak with her again so soon? Only last evening, they had discussed the menus for the week, planned the dinner party he would be hosting on

Saturday night, and had even chatted about the state of the storeroom—something he had employed her to worry about so that he would not have to, and yet he found it necessary to continually inquire about it. Why? Perhaps he secretly wanted to be the housekeeper, she decided, refusing to believe it could be for the reasons that Harry and Sally seemed to think.

Or perhaps Mr. Ludlow merely suffered from loneliness and considered her closer in station than anyone else in the household. It made sense like nothing else did, and Cora would be content with such a friendship if not for the fact that she found Mr. Ludlow far too attractive, charming, and intriguing. Not long ago, she had come to the disturbing realization that she would never be able to enjoy any sort of comfortable friendship with him, not if he continued to stir feelings within her that should not be stirred.

Taking his breakfast tray to his bedchamber was the worst summons of all. His room felt far too intimate and caused Cora greater discomfort than usual. If she had chosen to enter society instead of his service, she would never be allowed to even think of going into his bedchamber, yet in her present circumstances, it was a requirement.

Thankfully, he was already dressed and on his way out of his room when she arrived. "Let us adjourn to my study," he said, looking rather stern. Perhaps he did not care for the snow either.

Oddly enough, he took the tray from her hands and carried it himself. Cora felt awkward trailing behind with nothing, but she knew better than to argue with him over such a trivial matter. Once in his study, he set the tray down, closed the door behind her, and sat on the corner of his desk, folding his arms as he stared at the fire. The flames danced in his eyes, and Cora immediately felt the familiar pull he had on her. He looked unaccountably handsome this morning, dressed in a brown coat and buff breeches. She wanted to go to him and touch his freshly shaved jaw, feel of its smoothness, and ease the lines of distress that were etched across his forehead and around his eyes.

What troubled him?

She followed his gaze to a new painting that hung above the mantle. Vibrant red, orange, and yellow desert sands spread across the canvas with interesting ripples and curves. A fierce blue sky watched over from above, providing a stark contrast to the swells and valleys in the sand. Although brighter and less angry than the seascape that had hung in its place before, this new painting did nothing to inspire Cora either. She realized that both paintings felt empty. There had been no ship on the waters, not even a lighthouse on the shore, and the desert looked so barren, devoid of any life whatsoever. What had Mr. Ludlow seen in such a piece?

"What do you think?" he asked, startling her from her thoughts.

Cora knew better than to mince words this time. It would only prolong their meeting. "I think it looks rather lonely. Are you certain the artist is finished with it?"

Her candid assessment did not amuse him this time. He looked at her with brooding, almost haunted eyes. "This painting is my birthday present to myself, but now you have taken all the brightness out of it."

His words made her feel overly critical, and Cora immediately wished her assessment back. What was her problem, anyway? The artist's lines were smooth and skilled, the colors vibrant and beautiful. Why could she not focus on its attributes instead of its deficiencies?

Instead of attempting a fumbled apology, she stepped closer to him, resisting the desire to cover his hand with her own. "Today is your birthday?" she asked quietly.

He seemed annoyed by the question as though she had missed his point entirely, but he answered anyway. "Yes. Which is the reason I wanted to speak with you. I have decided I will be going out tonight and would like you to inform the rest of the staff that they may have the evening off."

Cora blinked in surprise. That was the last thing she had expected him to say. An evening free? How glorious that would be! Her mind whirled with all the possibilities of what she might do with her time. She could go for a long walk in the beautiful snow. Or Harry often spoke of the dances in town. Perhaps there would be one tonight, and they could all go together? Or she could accompany Sally to visit her son or even pay an impromptu visit to the Shepherds. Or—

One glance at Mr. Ludlow and Cora immediately squelched her happy thoughts. Why did he appear so downtrodden? He had said he was going out. Where? He had received no invitations for tonight or the staff would have already known not to plan on him for dinner. Would he be meeting friends or . . . Cora's gaze strayed to the painting, and she suddenly knew the answer. He planned to spend the evening alone somewhere away from his home while his servants celebrated his birthday without him.

Cora refused to allow such a thing to happen. "When will you be leaving, sir?" she asked.

"Five o'clock," came his answer.

Wanting to be sure she had interpreted the state of things correctly, she prodded, "Do you have an appointment of some sort?"

"No." He stared at the fireplace, appearing lost in thought.

She pressed on even though she knew she had no right to do so. "A dinner engagement?"

"No."

"Are you meeting up with some friends, sir?"

"I have no friends here," he said woodenly, his words wrenching her heart.

"You have me," she blurted before she could check herself. Good gracious, why had she said such a thing? She should not be encouraging a friendship or even considering herself his friend.

He was watching her now, his expression one that she could not read, but it still made her heart thump and her body simmer. "*Are* we friends, Mrs. Notley?"

"As good of friends as an employer can be with his housekeeper."

"Yes." He sighed, sounding disappointed in her answer. His gaze drifted back to the painting that Cora suddenly wanted to tear from the wall and toss in the fireplace.

She had never seen him so raw, so obviously aching on the inside. It took all her resolve not to go to him and attempt to coerce a smile back to his lips. It had been far too long since she had seen his dimple. She wanted to see it now, there, just to the left of his mouth.

Forcing her feet to remain where they stood, Cora decided that the servants would not be given the night off after all. In fact, they would work harder today than ever before. Together, they would do whatever it took to see that dimple appear on Mr. Ludlow's face before he became one year older. A person should not be allowed to advance to the next year of his life without at least a smile.

Jonathan tied his cravat with quick movements, not caring that the knot was slightly larger on one side than the other. He had been in a wretched mood all day and had sent his valet away an hour earlier so the man would not be made to tolerate any more of Jonathan's surliness. Now he stood before the mirror, scowling at the grim lines on his face and the dark shadows beneath his eyes. He looked much older than thirty.

Snow had fallen all day without letting up for even a moment. It was a rare thing for Askern to get this much snow—or any snow at all. How interesting it would fall today of all days, as though the heavens thought him befitting of further torment. The road would be a mess, not fit for carriage or beast, but Jonathan would muck his way through regardless. He refused to remain at home.

After one more glance at the mirror, he left his room, grateful to see no servants about. Apparently Mrs. Notley had efficiently spread the word. He could only hope his servants would have a merrier night of it than he would. The echo of his footsteps bounced off the walls of the great hall as he walked down the stairs. The hollow sound of it served to quicken his feet so that he might escape the emptiness. How could a place he'd called home for nearly eighteen months suddenly feel like a foreign, cavernous tomb?

He blamed Mrs. Notley entirely.

Not only had she found fault with the painting of the volatile sea, but when Jonathan had forced himself to choose a work of art that looked brighter and more cheerful, she could not find anything to like in the new piece as well. She had immediately called it lonely, and her eyes had accused him of having the same fault. They had been filled with such pity, and Jonathan hated to be pitied. Initially, he had planned to spend the day holed up in his library, distracting himself with books and brandy. But after Mrs. Notley's sympathetic gaze had landed on him, he had determined that he would not be lonely tonight. He would ride to the tavern and surround himself with crass and surly drunkards, bar maids, and drinks of the most intoxicating variety. He would drink himself into oblivion so he might awake in the morning with no recollection of the day at all.

He paused at the bottom of the stairs to pull on his riding gloves and look for his great coat. His valet had promised to leave it on a chair near the door. Ah, there it was.

"Mr. Ludlow," Mrs. Notley's voice intruded. He twisted his head to see her standing in the shadows of the hallway. How long had she been there and for what purpose?

"Before you go," she said, "I wonder if I might ask your opinion on something."

"Yes?" Jonathan asked testily, not wishing to be detained.

"If you will come with me to the kitchen for a moment, I would be most grateful."

That was the last thing Jonathan wanted. Could she not see that he was in no mood to give an opinion on anything? "Surely whatever it is can wait until tomorrow."

"I'm afraid that is out of the question. Please, sir. It will only take a moment."

Jonathan experienced a surge of annoyance and turned to face her. "What could possibly be so urgent, Mrs. Notley? Has the snow somehow broken its way inside?"

"In a manner of speaking, yes," she said without hesitation. "That is precisely what has happened."

He did not believe her for a second. She appeared far too calm and even amused.

She stepped to the side and gestured down the hallway. "If you will only give us direction on how to proceed, I would be most appreciative."

What the devil was she about? "You cannot be serious."

"But I am, sir," she said. "The kitchen is plastered with snow, I assure you."

Jonathan immediately strode towards the kitchen, brushing past her without so much as a glance. He pushed open the door and immediately halted, his eyes widening at the scene before him. The room was filled with his staff. Even his valet and coachmen stood among the throng. What the devil?

"Happy birthday!" they cried, moving aside to reveal a table piled high with food, along with a large cake coated in white icing.

Who had given them permission to do such a thing? And why? They all stared at him, gawking and looking as though he should be as pleased as punch when Jonathan was anything but. He had no desire to spend the evening here with his servants, feigning a merriment he could never feel. He wanted to be among drunken strangers—people who would not remember him or his misery on the morrow.

What had prompted Mrs. Notley to plan such a celebration when there was nothing to celebrate? Surely, she had perceived that he would not enjoy such festivities—not in his current frame of mind.

He turned to find her at his side, looking as pleased as all the others, though there was a strain about her mouth as though she was worried about his reaction.

She ought to be worried.

"I see no snow, Mrs. Notley," he said, his jaw clenching against the anger building inside of him.

"Then you have not looked hard enough." She pointed at the walls where several decorative snowflakes cut from paper hung from string.

He did not find it at all humorous and glared at her. "I instructed you to give everyone the night off."

"And we chose to spend it preparing a birthday celebration for you," she said. "Mrs. Caddy even allowed me to help frost the cake. Doesn't it look wonderful? I cannot wait to—"

Jonathan grabbed her arm and pulled her from the room, closing the kitchen door between them and the rest of his household. He had a great many things to say to her that he did not want overheard.

"Why is it you always insist on doing the opposite of what I say? Or do you simply choose not to listen to what I have to say? Hear this, Mrs. Notley. I am going to the tavern and that is final. Do you understand?"

"Not at all, sir. Today is your birthday. Why would you want to spend it—"

"My reasons are not your concern, and you are over-stepping yet again. How could you possibly think this would be a good idea?"

"Because it is a good idea, sir. If you would only stop and consider—"

Realizing she would never cease, Jonathan released her arm and walked away. He would deal with Mrs. Notley and her presumptuous ways later. If he lingered a moment longer, her refusal to listen would likely drive him to throttle her.

"Sir!"

Of course she felt the need to follow. Why must she always do that?

Jonathan ignored her as he grabbed his greatcoat and hat and stormed out the door without donning either one. Perhaps he would find peace in the chilly air. Mrs. Notley was not dressed for the weather and would be required to remain indoors.

Unfortunately, he had underestimated her. She rushed

out after him, heedless of the snow, and followed him down the steps in her ridiculous slippers.

"Please do not leave, Mr. Ludlow. This weather is not safe for riding."

"When did my safety become your concern, Mrs. Notley?" He placed his hat on his head as he strode towards the stables.

"When has it not been my concern? Please, do slow down! I cannot keep pace with you."

"I am glad to hear it," he said, not looking back.

A strangled squeal sounded behind him, followed by a thump. Jonathan turned to find her sitting on her backside in the snow, not looking at all happy about it. If he were in any mood to laugh, he might have. She had never appeared more humbled or cantankerous. It was a sight to behold.

He stayed precisely where he was. "Are you all right, Mrs. Notley?"

"Quite," she muttered as she struggled to rise to her feet, only to fall once more.

"Good." He turned again towards the stables.

"Sir!"

Jonathan looked to the heavens before heaving a sigh and turning around again. He strode back to her and held out his hand, which she glared at for only a moment before accepting. He easily pulled her to her feet, feeling the coldness of her bare hands through his gloves. Good gads, the woman could try his patience. Why had she not stayed indoors?

Beyond frustrated, he removed his coat and swept it around her shoulders, then lifted her into his arms so that he might carry her back to the house.

"Sir," she protested, kicking against his hold. "Please put me down. What a scene you are making! I can walk on my own."

"If that is the case, why did I have to pick you up off the ground?"

"I merely slipped on some ice."

"And now you are soaking wet and will catch a chill if you do not get yourself warm and dry soon. I am only helping you on your way so that I can be on mine."

"I do not need your help."

"And I do not need yours."

Jonathan might have tossed her back in the snow if she did not feel so wonderful in his arms or if he did not find the angry sparkle in her eyes and firm set of her lips so alluring. If she continued in this vein, he would have no choice but to silence her with a thorough kissing. Her lips looked far too rosy to do anything else with them. How could he be so drawn to a woman who caused him endless frustration?

He reached the top step and set her down none too gently. "Go inside and warm yourself. We will speak on this matter later, once we have both calmed down."

She wrapped her arms around her chest, refusing to do as he bid. Her body trembled from cold as she looked up at him. "I do not know what past event has brought you such misery on your birthday, but I do know something dreadful has happened to you. But how do you expect to be free from such sadness when you refuse to replace those memories with happier ones? That is all we are trying to do for you, sir. We have not labored this day out of pity. We labored because we care and because we would very much like for you to experience a birthday you can remember with fondness."

She paused, and a slight smile touched her lips. "And besides, what sort of person wishes to walk away from a perfectly wonderful cake? I cannot understand it. I have sampled the icing myself, sir, and it is divine."

Jonathan's heart lurched at her words, and he felt a

spark of something good begin to warm his cold, dark heart. How she managed to do that, he would never know. Standing before him in his too-large coat, her cheeks rosy from the cold, her eyes bright, and her cap askew, with snow falling gently around her, she had never looked more beautiful. He reached out to right her cap before taking her by her trembling shoulders. "Why must you try me so, Mrs. Notley?"

Her body stiffened, but she did not pull away. Wary blue eyes searched his before she swallowed. "Was that not in my job description, sir? To vex you at every opportunity?"

"I'm quite sure it was not."

"Pray forgive me. In the future, I will do my utmost to refrain from causing you further vexation."

He couldn't resist the smile that came to his lips. "Liar."

A victorious light appeared in her eyes, and her mouth transformed into the most radiant of smiles. "Ah, there it is." She lifted a finger to touch his cheek, just to the side of his lips. "I own, I have missed that dimple, sir. It is wonderful to see it again."

Jonathan's breath hitched at her touch. It fanned a fire inside his chest that soon heated his entire body. He captured her frigid hand in his, holding on to it as he gazed at her. Unable to stop himself, he raised his free hand to her cheek and touched it gently.

"You are so beautiful," he murmured.

Her breath caught, and she immediately stepped back. A fierce blush darkened her cheeks as she stared at him in confusion. It was on the tip of Jonathan's tongue to offer an apology, but he swallowed it, knowing it would not be sincere. The only thing he was sorry about was that she had found it necessary to pull away. Did she not feel the almost palpable connection between them?

She removed his coat from her shoulders and handed it back. "I ought to go inside and change into something dry."

"Yes," he said, studying her. "You do look a little . . . unkempt. I can only imagine the conclusions the others will draw once they see you."

She glanced down at her apron and dress with a grimace. "You are correct. This will certainly set the tongues to wagging, won't it?"

He resisted the impulse to pull her into his arms and say, "Let us give them something to wag about, shall we?" Instead, he pushed open the door and gestured for her to go in. "If I precede you into the kitchen, my appearance will most certainly cause a distraction which should allow you a moment or two to sneak by without notice."

Her mouth parted in surprise. "Do you mean to stay then, sir?"

Jonathan did not wish to, but she could be very persuasive. That, and she had made a valid point about replacing bad memories with better ones. But . . . an evening spent with his servants? Did she not realize the awkwardness of the situation?

"I don't make it a habit to socialize with my staff," he said.

She nodded slowly as though trying to come up with a logical reason as to why he should. "I understand it is not the norm, sir, but would you prefer to spend your birthday with interesting and engaging people or blubbering drunkards?"

Snowflakes landed on her nose and her eyelashes, and Jonathan could not tear his gaze away. Nor could he bring himself to disappoint her. She and the rest of his staff had gone to a great deal of trouble for him. Perhaps it would not be so dreadful to stay, especially if it meant spending the evening with his charming housekeeper.

"I believe, as always, that you may be in the right of it, Mrs. Notley. So yes, I suppose I will stay so long as you can promise me an evening filled with merriment."

She clapped her hands together and grinned. "Oh, how glad I am to hear you say that. It will certainly be a birthday worth remembering, I assure you."

"I am glad that you are glad." He gestured inside. "Shall we go in then?"

"Yes, sir."

He had to bite his tongue to keep from telling her to please refrain from calling him sir. It rankled, feeling much too distant and formal. He did not want to be "sir" or even "Mr. Ludlow" to her any longer.

As agreed, Mr. Ludlow returned to the kitchen first and found the servants clustered together, laughing and talking. The food remained untouched as though they had known Mrs. Notley would convince him to remain. And why would they not think that when Mrs. Notley always seemed to have her way of things where he was concerned? At least they had the grace to appear surprised when they spotted him.

It was an awkward moment to say the least. Apparently, they did not know if they should shout "Happy Birthday" again or carry on with whatever festivities they had planned. They looked past him, no doubt wondering where Mrs. Notley had gone, but none dared to inquire.

Not one to enjoy so much attention, Jonathan mustered a cheerful tone and moved through the throng. "I have been told that a person should never walk away from a perfectly wonderful cake, so here I am. Let us celebrate my dreadful birthday and be done with it, shall we?"

Cheers filled the room and everyone surged towards the food. Mrs. Caddy was the first to speak, her brusque voice rising to be heard over the others. "If you think it ain't easy ter reach thirty, sir, only think 'ow I'm nearin' fifty."

Everyone laughed and Jonathan smiled. They seemed to think his foul mood was on account of his advancing age, and he would let them continue to think that. Only Mrs. Notley had perceived that his dislike of this day went deeper than age. She had seen past his disagreeableness and into his heart, and, surprisingly enough, Jonathan found that he did not mind at all.

From the corner of his eye, he spied her hurrying through the room unnoticed by the others. She shared a grateful smile with him right before she disappeared up the stairs. Mrs. Caddy handed Jonathan a plate, which he piled high with the pork roast, potatoes, and a generous slice of cake. He accepted it gratefully and moved to the corner of the room. A few of the others looked his way and wished him a happy birthday, but they did not linger near him, likely because they had no idea how to socialize with their employer. Jonathan understood completely because he had no idea what to say to them either. Apparently he did not know his servants well at all, not even his valet.

At last Mrs. Notley returned, looking much dryer. Her cap was back in place, her cheeks had returned to their usual cream, and her eyes glowed with happiness. Only Sally raised a speculative eyebrow at her, which Mrs. Notley promptly ignored. Everyone else seemed far more interested in their food, which, Jonathan had to admit, was much tastier than the fare he would have been served at the tavern. Mrs. Caddy had outdone herself.

Mrs. Notley filled a plate as well, sampled a bite of cake, and glanced from Jonathan to the rest of the group. He could practically see her mind working, attempting to figure out a way to bridge the distance between the two classes. He could not wait to see how she would manage it, but somehow he knew she would. Once Mrs. Notley set her mind to something, she found a way to make it happen.

She popped another bite of cake into her mouth and walked over to him, raising her voice so that Mrs. Caddy would hear. "Did I not tell you the cake is divine?" She nodded towards the half-eaten cake on his plate. "I do not know how Mrs. Caddy manages to cook such wonderful things, but she does. Every single day. Is she not a wonder?"

Mrs. Caddy's face reddened with pleasure, and she waved a dismissive arm. "Oh, how you do go on, Mrs. Notley."

Jonathan smiled. "You are, indeed, a wonder, Mrs. Caddy. Many thanks for this exceptional meal."

"You're most welcome, sir." She beamed at him before slicing herself a piece of cake.

Mrs. Notley directed her next comment to Sally, "Your boy is quite fond of his new caretaker, is he not?"

She nodded, swallowing the food in her mouth before replying. "'E likes 'er almost as much as me. I can't thank you enough, Mr. Ludlow, for findin' 'er."

Jonathan nodded, accepting her thanks. "How old is your boy?"

"'E be four in two month's time and can't hardly wait till the day. Says 'e wants a pony, a dog, and a cat." She laughed and shook her head. "I told 'im I could manage a cat, but certainly not a pony. Silly boy." Jonathan could see the pride in her eyes when she spoke of her son, and it did her credit.

"You know the small mare in the stables called Tranquil?" asked Jonathan. "Once the weather clears, perhaps on one of your afternoons off, you could bring your son for a ride."

"Oh, 'e would like that very much, sir!" she exclaimed, her smile wide.

Mrs. Notley smiled as well, and Jonathan quite liked the approval he spied in her expression. It inspired him to add,

"Tranquil does not get ridden so much as the other horses and could use more exercise. Please feel free to make use of the beast whenever the opportunity permits."

"Oh, thank you, sir! Jimmy'll like that above anythin'. I cannot wait to tell 'im the news!"

Mrs. Notley did not vocalize her thanks, but the admiring look sent his way was one Jonathan would not forget anytime soon. Like a warm cup of restorative tea, there was a power in her gaze, infusing him with a sense of wonder and goodness. How interesting that only an hour before he had felt the opposite.

Mrs. Notley stayed at his side as they ate and continued to introduce him to the servants that dared to come near or returned for more food. Jonathan discovered that Harry was an avid fisherman, Drew had a knack for cards and recently won a gold pocket watch from a wager, Watts enjoyed flying kites, Charlie was saving every farthing to purchase a race horse, and the timid Alice supposedly had a remarkable voice.

"'Tis true," said Mrs. Notley, causing a rosy blush to appear on Alice's cheeks. "I've caught her singing many times when she believed no one could hear, and she is utterly brilliant. I only wish we could convince you to perform for us now, Alice."

The maid's eyes dropped to the floor, and she shook her head emphatically. "Oh no, ma'am. I could never."

"You could, and you should," said Mrs. Notley firmly. "God did not give you that voice so you could bury it in the still room. Only think of the happiness you could bring to others by simply sharing your talent. It always fills my heart with joy when I hear you sing."

"I'll think on it," was all Alice managed to say before making her escape.

Jonathan watched the girl disappear into the still room, wondering if her voice was as angelic as Mrs. Notley made it out to be. Regardless, it felt good to know something more about his servants than what they did for him. He rather enjoyed spending time with them in this way, when household matters could be put aside and the focus placed on more personal things.

Once everyone had finished with their meal, Mrs. Notley proposed a diverting guessing game and arranged them all around the large table in the servant's hall. She directed them to think of two correct statements and one incorrect statement about themselves—something that no one else in the room might know. The rest of the group would be required to determine which statement was fact and which was fiction.

"As our man of the hour," she said when she had finished with her explanation, "I think Mr. Ludlow should take his turn first."

Jonathan squirmed, not knowing what to say. What facts could he possibly tell his servants about himself? What sort of fiction would be believable? "Since this is your grand idea, Mrs. Notley, I think it should be you who takes the first turn so that you might show us by your example how to play."

"Aye," called Harry from the far end of the table, slapping the table with his hand. "Let's 'ear what you 'ave ter say, Mrs. Notley."

She appeared unperturbed and nodded. "Very well." She pressed her lips together and crinkled her forehead in thought. After a moment or two, her brow cleared, and she said, "Statement one: It has always been my secret wish to perform on the stage at Drury Lane. Statement two: I believe every man ought to know how to dance, and—"

Harry immediately leapt from his chair and raised his arms. "I know 'ow to dance, Mrs. Notley," he declared, gesturing for her to join him. "Come and let me show you."

"Perhaps that can be one of your truths when it is *your* turn, Harry," she teased.

Everyone laughed, and Harry said, "Come now, Mrs. Notley. Won't you be my partner?"

"Oh, do sit down, Harry," she replied, a red hue touching her cheeks.

Jonathan experienced a moment's jealousy at the easy camaraderie the two shared. Had Mrs. Notley been flattered by the invitation? Did she wish to dance with the footman? Did she blush from embarrassment or because she had feelings for the man?

Jonathan suddenly wished Harry to the devil.

"For my third statement," Mrs. Notley continued, returning to the game, "I once caught a field mouse with my skirts."

More laughter was heard, along with comments like, "'Ow can a person catch a mouse with a skirt?" and "'Appen she likes ter watch men dance" followed by Harry's comment of "That's why you wouldn't dance with me, ain't it, Mrs. Notley? You'd rather stand back and admire my 'andsome figure."

Boisterous laughter followed that remark, but Mrs. Notley merely rolled her eyes and shook her head.

Jonathan remained silent while the others continued to joke and speculate. The incorrect statement was obvious. Anyone who knew Mrs. Notley at all would know that she had no desire to perform on any stage—be it at Drury Lane or in a drawing room filled with local society. Her frequent blushes testified to the fact that she was anything but an attention seeker.

"You're all gormless," Sally said to her peers. She lifted her gaze to Mrs. Notley and said firmly, "I'm sayin' it's the one about the mouse."

"What is your opinion, Mr. Ludlow?" Watts asked, drawing him into the debate.

The room fell silent as though the servants had only just recalled their employer was present. Jonathan leaned back in his chair and folded his arms, feeling the desire to tease Mrs. Notley for no other reason than to show Harry that he shared a connection with her as well. He quirked an eyebrow as he answered the question. "I believe Mrs. Notley would rather run through the snow without a coat and in her slippers than seek the stage at Drury Lane."

"Run through the snow in 'er slippers?" Harry said. "She'd 'ave to be daft ter do such a thin'."

"Yes, quite daft," Jonathan agreed, unable to keep the smile from his lips. "And we all know that our housekeeper is anything but daft. Isn't that right, Mrs. Notley?"

Her cheeks became redder still, but her lips began to twitch, showing that she had taken his teasing in stride. "Like any human, I can be daft on occasion," she admitted, neatly side-stepping his teasing. "But when it comes to performing in front of others, especially on stage, Mr. Ludlow is correct. I would never seek for, or even delight in, such an opportunity. I can only pray that Mr. Ludlow will retain my services so that I will not need to resort to the stage for my bread."

"I am tempted to dismiss you just to see you attempt it," said Jonathan. "But alas, I do not know what we should do without our Mrs. Notley. I have become rather fond of dry and crispy pastries and am certain no other housekeeper could make them as you do."

Everyone burst into laughter, and Mrs. Notley glared at

him, or at least attempted to glare. Her eyes brimmed with too much amusement for anyone to believe she was truly offended.

"You are quite the court jester, Mr. Ludlow," she said. "Perhaps you can do better with your statements?" The look in her eyes silently challenged him to come up with something that might fool her and the rest of the group.

Having given the matter more thought, Jonathan was ready to take his turn. "Statement one: I have won a barebacked horserace while riding the animal backwards. Statement two: I once wagered my dignity in a game of cards and lost."

"'Ow can you wager dignity?" one footman asked.

"Rather easily, actually," said Jonathan. "I was required to compose a poem and perform it at a crush of a soirée, and I am no poet."

"I should like to hear that poem," said Mrs. Notley, appearing delighted by the prospect.

"How do you know that is not my incorrect statement?" Jonathan challenged.

"Because it is far too specific."

"As was my first statement. Perhaps my last statement will be specific also."

"Very well, sir. What is your final statement?"

He continued to watch her. "I have quite literally swept a beautiful woman off her feet." There, what would she have to say to that?

Nothing, it seemed. Her cheeks flamed, and she cast a covert glance around the room as though worried the others had deduced that Jonathan had been referring to their recent encounter. He was glad to see that she had been diverted from wanting to hear the dreadful poem he'd written.

"What do you mean by swept?" Sally asked, appearing confused.

"Exactly what it sounds like," answered Jonathan. "I picked her up and carried her off."

"Off ter where?" Harry chortled.

"The destination was not part of my statement," said Jonathan, though he took great delight when Mrs. Notley's face turned a darker hue of red.

"Is your incorrect statement about the horse race, sir?" asked someone.

"I think it's the poem," said another.

"It's got ter be the last," said Mrs. Caddy. "Mr. Ludlow is too well bred ter ever pick up a woman and carry 'er off . . . somewheres." Her cheeks flushed as she finished that thought.

"What do you think, Mrs. Notley?" said Jonathan, noticing she'd been silent throughout the discussion. "She had only to guess between the first and second since she already knew the third was true. Would she guess correctly? He found himself hoping that she would, as though it would somehow prove that she cared for him at least a little.

He didn't realize he'd been holding his breath until she answered.

"I believe that you won a barebacked race, but you did not do so seated backwards."

A slow smile stretched across his face. "You have guessed the incorrect statement correctly, but the facts incorrectly. If you must know, I did race a horse seated backwards, but I did not win. I lost by a large margin to a pretty little girl named Cecily, who rode a pony facing forward. I fear my ego was crushed that day and has not recovered since."

Laughter filled the room once more, and Jonathan shared a smile with Mrs. Notley. It lasted only a moment before she continued with the game and instructed Sally that it was now her turn. As the housemaid gave her statements, Jonathan only half listened. He was too preoccupied with his beautiful housekeeper and the unexpected birthday gift she had given him. This night *had* been a gift, he realized as he relaxed further into his chair, feeling at ease amongst his staff. For the first time in a very long while, he felt a return of his old self—the Jonathan who had not taken things quite so seriously as he did these days. He used to think that part of him was forever lost, but perhaps it had merely been shut away for a while, waiting for the right person to show himself to again.

THE HOUR WAS NEARING midnight, and the house was quiet at last. Sally had only just returned from visiting her son and had given back the coat and boots Cora had let her borrow. Although cold and wet, Cora immediately donned them and crept down the stairs to the kitchen, doing her best not to disturb those who had already taken to their beds. All day long, she had been craving an opportunity to escape into the glistening world of white for a soothing stroll through the snow. She wanted to breathe in its freshness, relish the calm and gentle quiet, and touch the tender snowflakes with the tips of her fingers. Euphoria filled her at the mere thought of it, making it difficult to keep her steps careful.

At the bottom of the stairs, she entered the kitchen and immediately stiffened. Mr. Ludlow was seated at the table with his back to her. He must have heard footsteps for he twisted his head around and lifted a questioning eyebrow when he spied her.

"We must stop meeting this way, Mrs. Notley," he said. "I'm beginning to wonder if you ever sleep."

"Forgive me, sir," she said quickly. "I did not mean to

intrude on your solace. I had thought everyone had gone to bed."

He shrugged and gestured to the plate in front of him containing a partially eaten slice of cake. "As I'm sure you have already surmised, I wanted to sneak another bite of cake with no one the wiser, but alas, you have found me out. I will no longer be able to blame the missing portion on Harry as I had planned to do."

Cora smiled. "Harry is always deserving of a good prank. If you should like to point the finger at him, I will gladly remain silent on the subject."

He chuckled and returned to his cake, taking another bite. "You will join me, won't you Mrs. Notley? I don't believe Mrs. Caddy has ever made a cake quite this flavorful. There is a touch of lemon in it, is there not? I am quite fond of lemon."

Cora remained by the stairs. "So I've noticed. You seem to enjoy the lemon tarts above all others and your favorite dessert is lemon cream."

He glanced back at her. "Was it your idea, then?"

"I merely suggested that Mrs. Caddy try flavoring the cake with a few squeezes of lemon. She was good enough to oblige me."

He did not respond right away, merely continued to gaze at her as though searching for an answer to a question. Cora had no inkling of what he might be thinking and she shifted uncomfortably, wondering if she ought to have escaped out her window and scaled the stone walls instead of coming down the stairs. If she had known he would be here, she would have taken her chances with the window.

He finally spoke. "You seem to know me better than I know myself these days, Mrs. Notley."

"I am certain that is not true." Perhaps it was the dim

lighting, the lateness of the hour, or the romantic, snow-covered landscape in the background. Whatever it was, the comment sounded much too intimate for her comfort. Cora was suddenly most anxious to flee his presence.

She cleared her throat. "This will likely sound childish, but I would very much like to step out of doors for a time and enjoy the snow before it melts away. Forgive me for happening upon you at such an hour, sir. I wish you the happiest of birthdays and will leave you to your cake."

She quickly strode towards the servant's entrance and grabbed hold of the knob, intending to escape as quickly as possible.

"But I *have* seen you, Mrs. Notley. And as your employer and a gentleman, I cannot allow you to venture out at this late hour alone."

What nonsense! Surely he did not mean to deter her. She had been waiting far too long for this treat and refused to allow him to stop her. "Do be serious, sir. You and I both know that I will be quite safe. If it will ease your mind, I will promise not to stray far from the house."

The stool screeched as he stood. Oh dear, what was he doing? He was on his feet and moving towards her. Why? Did he plan to accompany her? Barricade the door? Touch her face in that intimate way as he had earlier? Whatever his reason, it could not possibly bode well for her.

"Truth be told," he said, removing her hand from the knob and placing it in the crook of his arm, "I have been longing to take a jaunt through the snow as well. I do hope you will allow me to accompany you."

The mere touch of him made her feel as though she stood before a roaring fire. She wanted to relish his nearness and draw closer to him, to smell the lemon on his breath and feel the contours of his arms and shoulders beneath the smooth superfine of his coat. He had a mystifying aura that continually bewitched her into a trembling state of longing and confusion.

Good heavens, this would not do at all.

He began leading her in the direction of the great hall, but Cora resisted, pulling her hand free and stepping away from him. "Of course you cannot accompany me, Mr. Ludlow. You have not finished your cake." It was a silly excuse, but Cora's befuddled brain could not conjure up a more substantial reason for him to remain behind.

"Come now, Mrs. Notley. It is still my birthday, and my wishes ought to be granted, don't you agree? You cannot be so cold as to deny me the pleasure of an evening stroll in the presence of your company."

"But, sir—"

"No buts." He reached for her hand again and placed it on his arm, covering it with his own. "I beg you not to sour what has become a surprisingly good birthday for me. Simply agree to let me join you, and allow me to bask in the delight of the day for a while longer."

Cora stared at him, trying to think of some way to extricate herself from this situation. How could he possibly think this a good idea? She could not walk out with him. She would not. And yet how could she refuse him after such a speech—or rather, plea?

Curse the man for being a constant plague on her emotional state. Why had he needed yet another slice of cake? Why could he not keep to his room as he usually did?

"Have I convinced you, Mrs. Notley? Take another look out the window and tell me you do not wish to go out."

Cora opened her mouth to say precisely that, but one glance at the brilliance of the scene melted the words from her tongue. The beauty called to her, telling her she'd be a fool to miss this rare opportunity.

"I . . ." she hesitated, knowing she should not agree and yet unable to say as much.

"Very good then." Mr. Ludlow took her silence as agreement and began leading her through the kitchen. Against her better judgment, she allowed him to take her to the great hall, where he relinquished her hand so that he might he shrug into his greatcoat and pull on some gloves and a hat. His boots, she noticed, were still on his feet.

With a slight creak, he pulled open the large wooden door and stood aside, gesturing through the opening. "After you, Mrs. Notley."

One look outside, and Cora felt the last of her willpower slip away. Her feet began to carry her forward, taking her into the glowing night where chilly air blasted her face and crept through the cracks and crevices of her coat. But Cora did not care. The air felt fresh and clean, rather like a new beginning. Her spirits lifted and soared, and she picked up her skirts to trot down the steps, her smile growing with each crunch of snow.

Mr. Ludlow caught up to her at the bottom and tucked her hand in his arm once again. As they began to stroll towards the gardens Cora tried to remain focused on the serenity of the night and not allow his nearness to unsettle her, but she was having a tricky time of it. The snow became an afterthought as every footstep he took, every movement of his arm that registered beneath her fingers, every smoky breath he exhaled engaged her senses. He rattled her in a way she could not ignore.

"I can now understand why you wished to step out. It is rather enchanting, isn't it?" he said, not sounding nearly as affected as she felt. Curse the man. Why couldn't he have stayed inside and found his enchantment from the window scene?

"I must thank you for tonight," he said quietly. "You have done as promised and managed to turn a dreaded day into a good day, and I am grateful for it. I am grateful for you, Mrs. Notley—you and your unconventional ways."

The tenderness in his voice infused warmth, happiness, and anxiety into Cora's soul. What did he mean, exactly? Was he merely offering a kind compliment—one he would extend to any friend or acquaintance who did him a service? Or did he mean something more by it? She was not well versed in the ways of men and did not know if she ought to be thankful or worried.

Rather than respond, Cora searched her mind for a less dangerous topic—one that would allow her to find at least a little peace during their stroll.

Pulling her hand free from his arm, she stopped walking and mustered a teasing tone. "I have suddenly realized that I have given you the pleasure of my company too freely, sir. It is making me feel like a wanton, and I cannot allow it to continue."

"Indeed?" He appeared both intrigued and confused. "Are you suggesting that I return indoors, or can you propose a remedy?"

"I believe it can be remedied, if you are so inclined," she said. "As it was I who thought to take a stroll through this lovely, wintery night, it is now your turn to contribute something."

His eyes narrowed somewhat. "And what is it you would like me to contribute, madam?"

"Why, the entertainment, of course."

His eyes widened and his lips lifted in amusement. "Shall I dance a jig, Mrs. Notley? Or would you prefer I offer up a riddle of some sort?"

"What I would prefer most—and which also happens to

be the price for remaining in my company—is for you to recount me the poem that caused you to lose your dignity once upon a time. If you refuse me this, I'm afraid you really must go back inside. It is not fair to me otherwise."

"Is it not?" he said, the words sounding a bit like a chuckle.

"No, sir." She strained to keep her expression earnest with incredible difficulty.

He clasped his hands behind his back and nodded. "Very well, Mrs. Notley. If that is the payment you require for the pleasure of your company, I would be a nodcock not to comply. Only let us continue walking so that I need not look you in the eye whilst I relive my downfall. I can only pray you are the forgiving sort and will not hold it against me."

They walked side by side, and after a few steps, he began. "As I said before, it was a crush of a soirée in London, with anyone who was anyone in attendance. My ridiculous friend, Christopher Jamison, was rather adept at landing me in scrapes, and this was no exception. Per the terms of our wager, he put a word in our hostess's ear that I had composed a poem I should like to perform at some point during the evening's entertainment. Not knowing how unskilled I was in the art of poetry, she added my name to the list. I'll never forget Lady Bethany's stirring performance on the harp that preceded my reading. She caused an awed hush to fall over the crowd, followed by the most exuberant applause, and such was the state of expectations when I took the floor. I realized then that I should have insisted on taking my turn first."

Cora laughed, enjoying the tale immensely. "You must not keep me in suspense any longer, sir. I must hear that poem."

"Only if you promise that you will not think less of me once you have. I have never claimed to be a poet of any sort, although I did get the thing to rhyme."

"How could I possibly think less of you then?" Cora teased. "Rhymes are so very difficult to achieve."

He drew in a deep breath and let it out slowly. Then he cleared his throat and began. "The Story of the Calf by Jonathan Ludlow. Once there was a wee calf, and that is half." He paused dramatically. "The poor creature leapt over a wall, and that is all."

Cora waited for him to continue, and when he did not, she said, "That is truly the whole of it?"

"It took me an entire two hours to compose those stanzas. I did not have time to add anything more."

She burst out laughing, attempting to stifle her giggles with the palm of her hand. "I never dreamed it would be that dreadful."

"Yes, that was Jamison's reaction as well," he said dryly. "Lest you forget, you did promise you would not think less of me."

"Of course I do not." She continued to giggle. "I only wish I had been in attendance to see the faces of everyone present. I can only imagine the stir you caused."

"It was more of a stunned silence. The applause was tepid at best, and no one could look me in the eye afterwards. Should I ever learn to draw, I will be happy to sketch out the scene for you. The image is still quite vivid in my mind."

"I'm certain it is." Cora tried her best to stop giggling, but it was of no use. The image that played out in her mind's eye was far too hilarious.

"Did you find my story as entertaining as you thought you might? Am I allowed to continue our stroll?"

"That was most definitely an adequate contribution,"

she said, thinking that she rather liked having him along when he was not touching her or wreaking havoc on her insides.

"Despite being brought so low," he said, "those were indeed happier days. I greatly miss Jamison and his antics."

"Where is he now?" Cora immediately regretted the words when she caught a glimpse of sadness in his expression. What if his friend had met with some horrible demise and her question had caused him to relive the pain of it? Would she never learn to hold her tongue?

"He purchased his colors and joined the navy years ago," he answered. "He was born to a family not so well off as I and needed to earn a living in some way. I suggested that he stay put and marry an heiress here in England, but that was not Jamison's way. He's rather like you in that respect—not wishing to be beholden to anyone for anything. I could only admire him for it, but I was very sorry to see him go. His departure marked the beginning of some difficult years for me."

Mr. Ludlow stared into the distance, his eyes unfocused as though lost to the memory of those years. Cora wanted to reach out and comfort him, but she kept her hands firmly at her side.

"What happened?" she asked quietly.

His eyes refocused on her, and he studied her a moment before he began walking again. Cora stayed at his side, and after several crunches of snow beneath their boots, he said, "About a year after Jamison left for war, I was invited to a house party where I met the most radiant of women, or so I thought at the time. Not only was she a stunning beauty, but she was intelligent, witty, and intriguing. We soon discovered that we had much in common and became quite inseparable. By the end of the month, I felt as though I had found my perfect match—someone with whom I could easily share my life. I returned home and explained as much to my parents, and they promptly extended an invitation for her family to join us at our estate for the entire month of December and through the Christmas festivities.

"It was during that time that my elder brother became caught in her snare as well, unbeknownst to me, and at my birthday celebration a few years ago, I happened upon the two of them in the library, locked in a passionate embrace. They were celebrating her acceptance of his proposal. They wished for my felicitations, if you can believe it, but of course I did not offer them. I slammed the door and walked away."

Cora's heart wrenched at his news and the sound of his voice—so wooden and hollow. Her hands fisted at her side, wanting to plant the woman and his brother a solid facer. How could anyone behave so heartlessly?

"Later," he continued, "when I confronted and demanded an explanation of her, she said that it was I who she desperately loved and not my brother, but surely I knew that love was not enough. Her family's pockets were to let, you see, and my brother was the eldest and therefore heir to the bulk of my family's estate. Though I inherited a great sum from my mother and was quite wealthy in my own right, I also happened to be a younger son who was still beneath my brother. According to her, if she could attract his notice and win his hand, she would be a fool to let her feelings for me get in the way."

He paused, his tone taking a bitter turn. "But all was not lost, she said. Her greatest wish was for us to carry on in secret so that she would not lose me nor I her. She seemed to think it the perfect solution and could not understand my refusal or my outrage. I left Cornwall the following morning and went to London for a time, where I attempted to lose myself in the season. A wedding invitation eventually arrived, which I promptly tossed into the fire, and on the day they were to be married, I left London and eventually found my way to Yorkshire and this property. You should have seen the wretched state Tanglewood was in when I first laid eyes on it—so overgrown and rundown. But I knew it was exactly what I needed at the time and so I purchased it and threw all my energies into restoring it. In many ways, it has saved me."

His jaw clenched and he shook his head. "How I could have ever fancied myself in love with such a woman I cannot fathom. Even now, I feel like an utter fool."

Cora watched him, wondering how anyone could be as unfeeling as that woman and his own brother. It was no wonder Mr. Ludlow did not trust easily and had no tolerance for dishonesty. Perhaps that was also the reason lonely paintings appealed to him, why he had secluded himself at Tanglewood, and why his dimple was so elusive at times.

"You are not a fool, Mr. Ludlow," Cora said. "Merely human. It is a fault we all share, I'm afraid."

"Not you." He stopped walking and peered down at her, his expression raw and vulnerable. A tenderness had replaced the cold sadness from moments before. "Truth be told, I think you rather perfect."

His words caused her insides to flutter, her pulse to race, and her mind to shout out a warning. There he went again, upsetting the precarious balance between them. Why did he feel the need to say such things? And why did his words cause so great a disturbance to her emotions? She needed to be immune to him.

"If you believe that, sir, then I have deceived you as well."

"I believe you incapable of deception," he said quietly,

lifting his hand to her cheek and touching it tenderly. "From the moment I first met you in my study, I felt as though I could trust you as I have not trusted anyone in a very long time. Your eyes were too honest, your expressions too telling, and your smiles too genuine. Add to that your beauty and charm, and is it any wonder my thoughts are consumed by you? You intoxicate me, Mrs. Notley, and I cannot tell you how badly I wish to kiss you right now."

Cora suddenly felt like she had been taken back to her childhood home, when she had stood before the fireplace in her room, transfixed by the flames that burned with such power, color, and vibrancy. She longed to play with them and see what they could do, so she had pushed one end of a dead and lifeless branch into the flames, delighting when the leaves sparked and the branch began to smolder and flame. As the heat crept closer and closer to her hand, she had thought, *One moment longer. I will keep hold only one moment longer.* It wasn't until she felt pain that she had dropped the branch and pulled her hand back, staring at the flames in shock. She had trusted them and they had burned her.

Cora had thought she had learned a valuable lesson that day, but now that she was standing before a man who drew her to him as the flames had done that day, she realized the only thing she had learned was the outcome. She was bound to get burned again and felt powerless to stop it from happening. Only this time, instead of her hand, it would be her heart.

He took her face in his hands, igniting delicious tingles that surged through her body and down her spine. As his mouth neared hers, Cora's heart pounded like a gong in her ears. She should not allow this to continue, and yet she could not move. A whiff of lemon captured her senses right before his mouth brushed across hers in a feather-light touch. His lips were warm and dry and soft. Caught up in the delightful sensations he stirred within her, Cora began to return the kiss, tentatively at first and then with more vigor. It quickly grew in intensity, pulling her into a world that felt far more wondrous and magical than the snow-touched landscape surrounding them. She had always wondered what it would feel like to be thoroughly kissed, but she had never expected it to be this exhilarating or magnificent. Her body had never felt more alive, and she reeled at the power of it. Her hands wound around his back so that she might pull him closer still. She wanted more of this, more of him.

A snowflake landed on her cheek, bringing an unwelcome nudge of awareness. Gradually, outside thoughts began to intrude, weaving their way into the back of her mind. She thought about her position and his, about proprieties, consequences, rules, and reputations. With every thought, the magic subsided until she came to a very real existence where an employer would kiss his housekeeper for only one reason—and it was not because he meant to declare himself.

Feeling suddenly ill, Cora pressed her palms to his chest and pushed him away. Only moments before she had jested about feeling like a wanton and now she had become one. How could she have returned Mr. Ludlow's kiss with such reckless abandon? What must he think of her? Did he believe her open to some sort of proposition now?

She fisted her hands, suddenly angry with him. "I may only be a tradesman's daughter, sir, but I am a respectable one. If we allow this to continue, we will be no better than your brother and the lady who jilted you most abominably. I am your housekeeper and nothing more. You must desist in seeking me out and . . . and . . ."

"Kissing you?" His lips began to twitch, and his dimple emerged. Under normal circumstances, Cora would be thrilled at the sight of it, but she found it most vexing at the moment. How dare he laugh at her? Did he think her silly for having principles and morals? She had told him in the beginning that she was not the sort of woman to cavort with her employer. Surely he had not forgotten that conversation already. The awkward nature of it should have embedded itself in his memory.

"Yes, that is precisely what I mean." She frowned at him, wondering why he continued to smile. Did he think this a great joke? Did he not see how much he had injured her pride and feelings? Cora had never felt more exposed or vulnerable and he did not seem to care at all.

Unbidden tears filled her eyes, and she immediately wished him to the devil. How dare he ruin this perfectly beautiful evening by causing her to cry?

Altogether too late, Mr. Ludlow's smile vanished. He reached for her shoulders but she flinched away from him, turning her face to the side in an attempt to hide her blasted tears. Why did they persist in coming? A person should only cry if he or she wanted to. Tears should never come unbidden, they should not!

"Cora," he said quietly, not attempting to touch her again. "Will you please look at me?"

She shook her head, pressing her eyelids together with the hope of keeping the tears inside. But it only served to squeeze them out. They trailed down her cheeks as a testament of her foolishness.

He took her gently by the shoulders, and when she did not resist he pulled her against him, wrapping his arms tightly around her. She allowed him to hold her because she loved being in his arms. She loved his scent, his strength, the husky timbre of his voice, the rise and fall of his chest beneath her cheek—she loved it all. And yet she should not.

He dropped a kiss on the top of her head. "How could you think that I would ever wish to take your respectability or virtue? I assure you that is the last thing I would ever want. Do you truly not know how dear you have become to me?"

At his words, Cora felt something resembling hope spark in her chest, like an ember on the verge of rekindling. It soothed and comforted her, easing the ache that had throbbed so very badly. She untucked her head from his chest and looked up, wanting to believe him and yet not knowing how she could.

"What is it you want from me?" she asked.

He raised his hand to her brow and slid the back of his fingers down the side of her face, stopping just below her mouth. His thumb grazed her lips, causing them to tingle and yearn for another taste of him.

"More than anything else, I want to dismiss you."

What? Cora blinked, not comprehending. Was he in earnest? His lips were not twitching, his eyes showed no humor, and his forehead had furrowed. If anything, he looked concerned.

"I beg your pardon?"

His tightened his grip on her shoulders and held her firmly. "Do you not understand? Are you so blind to my motives that you cannot see them for what they are? I want to dismiss you because I no longer wish to call you Mrs. Notley. I'd greatly prefer to call you Cora or at the very least, Miss Notley. I would like you to return to the Shepherds and allow them to launch you into local society so that I might see you at dinner parties, luncheons, and balls. I want to play cards with you, dance with you, and be able to pay court to you the way you deserve to be courted. I want to sweep you off your feet with the hope of one day proving to you exactly how much I have come to admire you. You have become so much more than a housekeeper to me. You have become the reason I am out here in this cold, wet night, the reason I arise in the morning and find something to smile about, the reason my birthday has gone from bad to good. I am falling in love with you, and I need for you to not be my housekeeper any longer."

Cora could not breathe. Everything around her seemed to tilt and wobble. Had he really said he was falling in love with her—*her*, the lowly daughter of a tradesman turned housekeeper? How was that even possible? She could scarce believe it and yet he had said those very words. Hadn't he? Had she somehow imagined them? It did not feel real at all. In fact, it felt so very unreal.

Goodness, she needed to sit down. She needed to breathe.

"Have I caught you so unaware?" he asked.

She could only nod in the affirmative. Of course he had caught her unaware! Did he think she had taken on the role of housekeeper with the hope of engaging his affections? Did he have any idea of the struggle it had taken to keep him at a distance and not allow her heart to become too attached? How could she even hope for such an outcome when it had not been in the realm of possibilities?

Cora looked up, imploring him to understand her confusion and uncertainty. She swallowed and forced her voice to speak. "Mr. Ludlow, I need—"

"Please call me Jonathan when we are alone."

"Jonathan," she breathed, rather liking the way it sounded. "I . . . I do not know what to think. I do not even know how I should feel. All I had hoped for today was that you would not be distressed on your birthday, and now . . ." She looked at him, shaking her head once more.

"Now I have asked you to stroll with me, I have taken certain liberties with you, and I have proclaimed my love for you when you had no inclination of my feelings before this moment. Is that what has you in such a stupor?"

Again, all she could do was nod. Could this truly be happening? Her head felt so muddled and cloudy, as though she'd taken a dose of laudanum. Only she was not tired in the least. In fact, she was quite sure she would not sleep a wink this night.

Mr. Ludlow took her cold, limp hands in his and began rubbing life and warmth back into them. "Forgive me for springing this on you so suddenly. I had thought my increased attentions would have prepared you, but I can see they have not. Only tell me this, if you can. Do you care for me enough that you would consider leaving my employ and returning to the Shepherds where you truly belong? You are a lady, my dear. You belong in drawing rooms, not kitchens."

"I assure you, I am no lady, sir. I belong exactly where I am."

"How can you say that when we both know you are a dreadful housekeeper?"

Cora blinked, her eyes widening as his words registered. She pulled her hands free and frowned at him. "How can you say that? I will allow that I was a dreadful housekeeper in the beginning, but I have learned a great deal since that time and am rather proficient at it now."

He pressed his lips together as though attempting to think of a delicate way to refute her words. "I will agree that you are more proficient now than you were, but . . . well, to be quite frank, my dear, your preserves are still lumpy, your pastries remain far too dry and brittle, and your marketing skills leave much to be desired. I will end up in the poorhouse if you continue to be the purchaser of all supplies. You may have a head for numbers, but you certainly do not have a head for bargaining—or rather, the backbone for it. You are far too kind to wrangle over price."

Cora would not have been more stunned if he had slapped her. "I beg your pardon!"

"That was a compliment, Cora, not a criticism."

A compliment? Had the man gone completely mad? "Obviously you have confused the meanings of those two words. A compliment should serve to please and inspire, not make one angry. That was most certainly not a compliment, sir."

"My name is Jonathan."

"And my name is *Mrs.* Notley."

He lifted an eyebrow, watching her closely. "You intend to stay on as housekeeper then?"

"Of course I do!" she said, allowing her frustration to get the better of her. "Apparently I have yet to prove what I am capable of, and until I do, I . . ." She stopped talking, having no idea how to finish that sentence. She would what? Continue to make lumpy preserves? Carry on with her mismanagement of purchasing supplies? Persist in making dry and brittle pastries?

Goodness, he had not painted a very pretty picture of her. No wonder he did not care for paintings with people in them. He'd likely find all sorts of faults with anyone or anything that had the misfortune of being the subject.

"You will what?" he said. "Stubbornly refuse to live up to your potential because I have told you that you were raised to become a lady and not a housekeeper? Is your pride so easily wounded as that?"

Cora glared at him. *Easily* wounded? How could he call

that easy? The man had taken any confidence she had begun to feel these past few weeks and squashed it the way one would a spider. If she had told him that she could manage a fence post better than he managed his staff, would he not also be *easily* offended? Did he truly expect her to dismiss his many criticisms just like that? It felt like he had taken a beautiful moment and turned a bucketful of water over top, leaving her wet, cold, and not at all happy.

"That is precisely what I intend to do," she answered, for no other reason than to spite him.

His jaw tightened, and his lips pressed into a thin line. "Then you will have to prove yourself in someone else's household."

"What are you saying, sir?"

"As of this moment, you are no longer employed at Tanglewood."

Cora opened her mouth to argue, but she immediately snapped it closed when she realized she had no argument to make. As her employer, he could dismiss her or anyone else whenever he wished. It was his right, the power he held as master of Tanglewood. What could an inept housekeeper say to sway him? Nothing. Absolutely nothing. She could only glare, which she did, and stomp her boots, which she also did as she stormed away, fueled by her anger, frustration, and injured pride.

If she could not prove herself at Tanglewood, she would prove herself someplace else.

JONATHAN AWOKE WITH A thundering headache. He groaned and reached over to ring for some restorative tea, only to remember that he had dismissed the person whose duty it was to make it. Had Cora left already? Probably. He flopped back on his pillow and stared at the ceiling, wondering how a night that had begun with such promise could have ended so disastrously.

He could still see the angry set to her shoulders and the way her boots knifed through the snow as she strode away. He would have chased after her if not for the lesson he had learned from his father at a young age. His father had once lost his temper with his mother, and she had quit the room in a huff. Rather than run after her as Jonathan thought his father should, he'd sighed and taken a seat in a large, wingback chair.

"Jonathan," he had said, "if there is one thing I have learned about women, it's that an angry woman is not a reasonable woman. It will do no good to go after her now. Only time and a heartfelt apology has any hope of restoring reason."

The following day, when he saw his parents embracing,

the lesson was sealed in Jonathan's mind as valuable. He thought of it now, hoping the words of wisdom rang true for all women and not just his mother.

With a wince, he rang for his valet. A few moments later, the too-thin man walked in and immediately parted the curtains, allowing bright light to billow into the room. Jonathan groaned and covered his eyes with his forearm. "Deuce take it, Drew, have some compassion!"

The curtains immediately closed and blessed darkness fell over Jonathan once more. "Forgive me sir," said Drew. "I had assumed you were ready to rise. Are you ill?"

"Yes," Jonathan moaned, tossing the pillow aside. "I have the devil of a headache. Would you be so kind as to send for some restorative tea?"

Drew shifted uncomfortably. "Er . . . I believe Mrs. Notley has taken her leave, sir."

"Good," he grumbled. "Her tea tastes like rainwater that has been collected in a tin can and left to bake in the sun for weeks. Please ask Sally to concoct something."

Drew's squinty eyes widened, but he quickly masked his surprise and executed a brief bow. "Very good, sir. I shall pass along the request straightaway. Will there be anything else? Would you like your breakfast tray sent up as well?"

"Only tea at the moment. Then I suppose I ought to dress. I need to call at Knotting Tree this morning."

"Very good, sir. I shall return shortly."

"Thank you, Drew."

His man left, the tea soon arrived, and Jonathan drank the entire cup in a few gulps. Although he had exaggerated the taste of Mrs. Notley's tea, Sally's version was certainly more pleasing to his palate. It also happened to be in the perfect state of warmness, unlike Mrs. Notley's, which never failed to scald his tongue.

When Drew returned again, Jonathan was feeling much more the thing. He allowed for his curtains to be pulled aside without argument, and once his eyes had adjusted to the light, he slowly rose from the bed with only a minor pounding in his head.

Drew helped him to shave and dress, and not thirty minutes later, after Sally informed him that his former housekeeper had indeed taken her leave, Jonathan called for his horse. As he navigated the icy lane and pulled his coat more tightly about him, he cursed himself for not arising earlier to see that his carriage had been made ready for Cora. He hated the thought of her making the journey on foot and prayed she would not fall ill because of his thoughtlessness.

Once he arrived at Knotting Tree, he handed his horse off to a stableboy, jogged up the steps, and pounded the brass knocker against the door. The stodgy Jeffries was slow to answer, and when he finally did, his eyes narrowed as he looked down his angular nose at Jonathan.

"I see you have come to call at an unnaturally early hour again, Mr. Ludlow."

"Forgive the intrusion, Jeffries," said Jonathan. "But I must speak to Miss Notley at once."

"She is taking her breakfast by the fire, sir. She arrived on our doorstep only moments ago, half frozen from the cold. Apparently she has given her coat and boots to one of your maids and ventured out this morning ill-equipped for the weather."

This time, Jonathan cursed Cora. What had she been thinking to give up her coat and boots? If she was so determined to leave them behind, surely she could have worn them here and sent them back later with another servant.

"Perhaps if you return at a more reasonable hour she

will be feeling up to accepting callers." Jeffries began to close the door, but Jonathan's hand on the door stopped him.

"Jeffries, I am truly sorry for any discomfort I might have caused Miss Notley. I have behaved thoughtlessly and am here to make amends. I swear to you that I will only take a few minutes of her time."

Jeffries studied Jonathan for several moments before finally opening the door and allowing him entrance. "If you will wait here, sir, I will make inquiries within."

"Thank you."

The old man turned stiffly and began walking down the hall. Jonathan waited a few moments before divesting himself of his coat, gloves, and hat, then he discreetly followed the butler, leaving some distance between them so he would not be noticed. The butler stopped in front of two large wooden doors, pulled one open, and entered. Jonathan stepped behind the still-closed second door and strained to hear the conversation taking place in the room beyond.

"You may tell him that waiting is futile. I do not wish to see him." Cora's voice was firm and decisive.

Mrs. Shepherd spoke next. "Are you certain, my dear?"

"I've never been more certain of anything."

"Would you like me to have a word with him?" Mr. Shepherd asked.

"If that is your wish. It is of no consequence to me."

Jonathan frowned. Apparently the passage of time had not done its job in restoring reason. Or perhaps the chilly walk to Knotting Tree had served to unrestore it. Regardless, Jonathan still had an apology to make, and he refused to leave this house until Cora listened to what he had to say.

"You may tell Mr. Ludlow that I will see him in the drawing room," said Mr. Shepherd.

Before Jeffries could quit the room, Jonathan entered.

His attention was immediately captured by the library's grandeur. Shelves of books surrounded him, rising from the floor to the top of the walls. One would need a very tall ladder to reach the highest of the shelves and yet some books were askew as though they had recently been read and returned in a haphazard manner. Jonathan had once thought his family's collection impressive, but it had nothing on Mr. Shepherd's. He had never seen so many books in his life.

"Sir, I asked that you wait in the great hall," said Jeffries.

Jonathan's gaze settled on Cora, who sat in a large chair by the fire with a heavy rug draped over her lap. She wore the same white muslin gown she had worn on the day they'd first met. Though her cheeks were ruddy from the cold and she didn't appear at all happy to see him, she looked to be unharmed.

"Ah, Mr. Ludlow. How good of you to announce yourself." Seated beside his wife on the sofa, Mr. Shepherd sounded far too congenial for the present circumstances. "I understand you have dismissed our dear Miss Notley yet again. How interesting. Have you come to sway her into returning as you did before? Is this going to become the thing to do with one's servants? If so, I am not certain I have the temperament for it."

"I have merely come to speak with Cora," said Jonathan, keeping his gaze locked on his former housekeeper.

Her eyes narrowed. "My name is Miss Notley to you, sir."

"I have merely come to speak with Miss Notley then."

Mrs. Shepherd set aside her needlepoint. When she looked at Jonathan, her expression was shrewd and cautious. He could only hope she did not intend to send him packing.

"Tell me, Mr. Ludlow," she said after a time. "Why should our dear Cora be asked to hear what you have to say?" She seemed to be offering him a chance, albeit a small one.

Jonathan considered the question, thinking back on everything that had transpired over the past few weeks. He finally settled on the only answer that had any hope of bringing Cora around. He looked pointedly at her. "A remarkable woman once told me that a person can have a good reason for behaving badly and one should always discover what that reason is before judging him or her too harshly."

Cora frowned and looked away, apparently not happy that he had used her own words as his argument. She stared across the room at a particular shelf of books for a long moment before dragging her gaze back to him. It seemed a struggle for her to say, "Very well, Mr. Ludlow. Let us hear what you have to say."

Jonathan glanced at Mr. and Mr. Shepherd, hoping they did not intend to remain for what was sure to be an awkward conversation. "Would you be so kind as to allow me a private word with Miss Notley?"

Mrs. Shepherd studied him a moment longer before turning to her husband. "I've just realized I need to speak to Cook about something. Will you be so kind as to accompany me?"

Mr. Shepherd cocked an eyebrow at Cora, who nodded her acquiescence, and, as they had before, the Shepherds rose to leave.

"I beg you not to make a habit of this," said Mr. Shepherd quietly as he passed.

"No, sir." Jonathan noticed they did not shut the door but paid it no mind. He strode over to Cora and sat down on the sofa near her. He leaned forward, resting his elbows on his knees, and clasped his fingers under his chin. "I have never seen a library of this magnitude before," he remarked. "It is quite astonishing."

She lifted an eyebrow at him. "Did you come to speak to me about books, sir?"

"No." He sighed. She obviously had no intention of making this easy on him. Perhaps it would be best to get straight to the point. "I have come to beg your forgiveness for the unfeeling way I, er . . . approached you last evening."

She pulled the rug more tightly about her. "Unfeeling? Sir, your words went far beyond unfeeling and I cannot account for it. How can you profess to care for a woman and yet besmirch her character in the next moment?"

"I was not besmirching your character, Cora."

"It's Miss Notley, sir."

"Miss Notley then," he snapped. Before continuing, he forced himself to take a deep breath to calm his frustration. When he spoke again, his tone was much less aggravated. "Please understand that it was not my intention to cause offense. I was merely pointing out that despite what you choose to believe about yourself and your circumstances, you are far more suited to the role of lady than servant."

"There are better ways to make such a point than itemizing a person's flaws, sir. I cannot help but wonder how you can possibly have tender feelings for such an inept creature as I. What is there to like?"

Jonathan raked his fingers through his hair, wondering if he ought to have allowed a bit more time to pass before confronting her. She seemed determined to think the worst of herself *and* him.

"You may not believe this," he said. "But I think your 'flaws,' as you call them, are endearing. If only you could see yourself through my eyes, you would understand. There is an air of gentility about you that you cannot disguise no matter how much you may wish to do so. You comport yourself with confidence, grace, and integrity that, I assure you, does not go unnoticed by others. Please forgive me for saying this, but a servant should never be noticed, and you, my dear, are always noticed. You know how to behave in any given situation and have the unique ability to inspire respect and admiration from all who come to know you. Do you not see this? Who the devil cares if you cannot create a palatable pastry or don't have the heart to haggle for supplies? That does not matter in the least because that is not who you are. You are Miss Coralynn Notley, a beautiful, headstrong, and compassionate heiress. When I look at you, that is the person I see, and I can only be grateful that your father could not wrangle an introduction into society for your family. I am certain that if you had made your debut in London or anywhere else, men would have flocked about you in droves and I would never have stood a chance at winning your affections."

He paused, allowing his words to settle before adding, "Please say you'll forgive my fumbled attempts to explain myself last evening. I cannot imagine finding a more exquisite woman in all the world, and I refuse to lose you because I did not convey my feelings properly."

Cora stared at him, eyes wide, mouth slightly parted. Her hand moved over her heart as tears collected in her eyes. She quickly blinked them away before clearing her throat. "I liked that version much better, sir."

Jonathan relaxed, happy in the knowledge that he had not bungled things this go around. He slowly rose to his feet and held out his hand to her. "Will you not call me Jonathan?"

She nodded and placed her fingers on his, allowing him to pull her to her feet and into his arms. She tucked her hands behind his neck and lifted her face to his. "There is nothing to forgive any longer, Jonathan."

He smiled and wasted no time in kissing her. She tasted like strawberries and felt like heaven, and in that moment, Jonathan determined to never let her go again. This was how his life was meant to be lived.

It wasn't until someone cleared her throat behind him that Jonathan found it necessary to release Cora. They turned to find Mrs. Shepherd standing just inside the door, looking as though she did not know whether to congratulate or scold them.

"Am I to offer you my felicitations?" she asked.

Cora blushed profusely and began shaking her head, obviously mortified that they had been caught in such a compromising position, especially when Jonathan had not officially proposed.

He merely smiled and picked up Cora's hand, bending to place a kiss on it. When he rose again, he turned to Mrs. Shepherd. "Not yet. But soon, I hope. Good day to you, Mrs. Shepherd." He bowed and turned to Cora once more, and with a slight smile, added, "Cora."

Then he strode out of the room and back to the great hall, where he pulled on his hat, gloves, and greatcoat. He wished Jeffries a good day before emerging outside to a scene of slush and melting snow. The crisp air filled his lungs as he sauntered down the steps to his waiting horse. How wonderful it felt to be back in harmony with Cora.

Someday, he would have to thank his father for his sagacious advice.

The moment Mr. Ludlow left the room, Mrs. Shepherd rushed forward in a flurry of lavender muslin to clasp Cora's hands and give them a hearty squeeze. "My dear, you obviously withheld important information from Mr. Shepherd and me. Why did you not tell us that Mr. Ludlow has developed a tendré for you? Is that the true reason for your dismissal?"

"It is one of the reasons." Cora's heart still pounded from Mr. Ludlow's kiss and tender words. How invigorated he had made her feel, as though she could the run the entire length of a meadow without ever tiring even after a wretched night's sleep. Her spirits had never soared so high. It felt like they had been caught up in the clouds and would remain there always, brimming with too much elation to ever come down again.

She shook her head, unable to remove the smile from her lips. "I did not know until last night. He kissed me quite suddenly, claimed to be falling in love with me, and in the same breath informed me that I was the most dreadful of housekeepers. He went on to inventory several reasons as to why I could never hope to become proficient at the job and promptly dismissed me. One moment I was in raptures and the next angry and injured. I am loathe to admit that I stormed off like a spoiled child. I spent all of last night wondering if one or the both of us had gone mad, and by morning, I had arrived at the conclusion that a man such as Mr. Ludlow could never truly love me."

She turned her gaze on Mrs. Shepherd. "Happily, he has proven me wrong, and now I am all aflutter again. Honest to goodness, it feels as though I've been thrown from the fire to the snow and back to the fire again. All I can think is that I am too close to the flames and will likely suffer a burn."

Cora silently pled with Mrs. Shepherd for help in navigating these unchartered waters, but the woman did not seem at all concerned about Cora's distressed state. Rather, her smile widened and she grasped Cora's arms.

"Oh, my dear, that is a perfectly normal way to feel. Love is both thrilling and terrifying, is it not? But you have nothing to fear, I assure you. I have not seen a more besotted man since Lord Drayson looked upon my daughter. I could not be more happy for you."

Mrs. Shepherd's words warmed Cora's heart, but they did not placate her mind. She bit her lower lip and worried over it for a moment. "It is wonderful, but . . ."

"But what?"

Cora suddenly felt weary and laden with a weight that her legs could no longer support. How interesting that a smattering of doubts and concerns could have such a diminishing effect on one's euphoria. She sank down on the sofa and clasped her trembling fingers in her lap.

"Mr. Ludlow wishes for you and Mr. Shepherd to introduce me into society so that he might court me properly."

"That is understandable." Mrs. Shepherd sat beside Cora, eyeing her closely. "Is there something wrong, my dear? Do you not share his feelings?"

"Of course I do." That was the least of Cora's concerns, or perhaps the reason for them. She could not determine which.

"Pray do not say that you are still opposed to entering society," said Mrs. Shepherd. "Mr. Ludlow is in the right of it, I'm afraid. He cannot pay court to you while you are still his housekeeper."

"I realize that," said Cora. "It's only . . ." Oh, how to explain? Her feelings were so confused that words eluded her.

"You once told me," Mrs. Shepherd began carefully, "that you never wished to feel beholden to anyone ever again and sought your own way. But now a very different future lies before you. Do you feel as though you will be giving up your independence if you proceed? Is that the problem?"

Cora could safely say that no, it was not, but Mrs. Shepherd's words gave Cora pause, making her feel rather like a pretender. Only months before she had taken a firm stance on the importance of independence and now she found herself wavering most alarmingly. Or was it wavering? Oddly enough, Cora didn't feel as though pledging herself to Jonathan would require that sacrifice.

"I do not think that is it at all," answered Cora. "Mr. Ludlow respects me. He seeks for my opinions, listens to them, and tries to understand my feelings on various matters. Although I am far beneath him, he has never made me feel unworthy of his notice. Rather, he has made me feel like an equal or partner of sorts, though he found it necessary to remind me of my place many times." Cora smiled at the memories, thinking how they had learned to "manage" each other quite well. "So no, that is not the problem at all. I will happily be beholden to Mr. Ludlow all the rest of my days. He has captured my heart so completely, you see."

A gentle smile lifted Mrs. Shepherd's lips, but her expression remained confused. "Then what is it?"

Cora stifled a groan. If only she had listened to the Shepherds from the outset she would not be in this pickle. Yet here she sat, in a muddled pool of her own making.

"You said it yourself," said Cora. "If I went through with my obstinate notion to enter service, my reputation would suffer in the extreme. The fact of the matter is that I have been Mr. Ludlow's housekeeper for months now. I know how servants talk and how that talk inevitably spreads to polite circles. If people in town do not already know I took a position as a housekeeper, they will eventually learn the truth and discover precisely how far I have fallen. A shadow has been cast on my name and it cannot be undone. What is the likelihood I will be accepted by them now? And will not your good name be tainted by your association with me? I would never dream of injuring you, Mr. Shepherd, or Jonathan in any way."

Mrs. Shepherd released her breath as though relieved that Cora's concerns were not of a more serious nature. "You mustn't worry about that, my dear," she said with a pat on Cora's knee. "Oh, there will be gossip and snide looks, perhaps even a few cutting remarks, but as with all scandals, it will die down in time. Once Mr. Ludlow makes his intentions clear, which I assume will happen very soon, and people see that Mr. Shepherd and I stand behind you completely, all will be forgotten. The only snide looks you will receive will be from those who are green with envy that you have snared the most eligible bachelor in the vicinity. But that is of no consequence. Oh my dear, I cannot tell you how thrilled I am by this turn of events. It is everything I could have hoped for you."

Cora responded with a smile of her own, but she could not calm the disquiet in her heart. It did not seem probable that the situation would play out as seamlessly as Mrs. Shepherd seemed to think it would. Cora had seen firsthand how cruel and vindictive people could be. Every time her fumbling father had attempted to befriend or even approach an elite member of society, the encounter had ended in disaster and humiliation. When a person of influence chose to shun or think less of another, that influence carried a great deal of weight and even went so far as to alter another's opinion. In Cora's experience, there were very few Lady Harrietts or Mr. and Mrs. Shepherds in the world. She couldn't help but wonder at the likelihood of finding more in Askern.

When Mrs. Shepherd began discussing the need for new gowns and fripperies, Cora forced her thoughts back to the present and swallowed any arguments she had on the subject. Mrs. Shepherd radiated enthusiasm, and Cora would be ungrateful indeed if she did not allow the lady her fun.

And why shouldn't they enjoy a shopping excursion? Cora had somehow managed to capture Mr. Jonathan Ludlow's interest—a gentleman who was handsome, charming, kind, wonderful, and good. Was this not what she had always wanted? To have what Lady Drayson and Mrs. Shepherd had—a man at her side who loved her as much as she did him? Cora's future had never looked so glorious. She could one day be mistress of a large and beautiful home. What's more, she could be a mother. Only imagine little boys and girls running amok through the halls of Tanglewood and breathing additional life into the place. It sounded perfectly blissful.

Unfortunately, experience had taught Cora that hopes and dreams were not often realized. Life was filled with disappointments, and Cora had known her fair share of them. It was the reason her smile did not reach into her heart and her enthusiasm did not soar back into the clouds like she wished it would.

THE DAYS BEGAN TO fly by in a flurry of shopping, fittings, and more shopping. Christmas and all it entailed came and went fairly quietly, with Mr. and Mrs. Shepherd attending only a few social events and only for the specific purpose of putting the word about that a close friend of Lady Harriett's had come to stay.

Most evenings the Shepherds preferred to dine *en famille* at Knotting Tree, where they could attend to Jonathan, who visited daily and often returned for dinner or a special event, like lighting the Yule log or collecting greenery to be placed around the house. He even created a kissing bough, which he hung above the drawing room doors and put to use every now and again when Mr. and Mrs. Shepherd were not attending.

They foursome dined a time or two at Tanglewood as well. Upon Cora's arrival, she would sneak away for a few moments to visit her old friends in the kitchen. Sally, with her improved speech, had earned Jonathan's trust once more. He had made her the new housekeeper and Alice one of the housemaids. A new girl had been hired to assist Sally in the still room, and at last, all seemed content at Tanglewood.

Mrs. Caddy and Watts welcomed Cora with smiles of affection, while Harry found it necessary to continue his teasing.

"'Ave you changed your name yet again, Miss Notley?" he said. "Or is it Mrs. Notley now? 'Appen we'll soon be callin' you Mrs. Ludlow, eh? Please say you'll be keepin' that name for at least a time."

Cora tried her best not to blush but failed miserably. She wagged a finger at Harry. "I'll not say anything of the sort and neither should you, Harry. Will you never learn to hold your tongue?"

"Afraid not, Miss—or is it Mrs.? No, it's Miss, but only for now, isn't that so?"

Mrs. Caddy barked out a laugh and the others chuckled as well. Cora stifled her own giggles and attempted to glare at Harry, not that it did much good. He knew all too well that she liked him in spite of his incorrigible nature. She liked them all. They had become very dear to her and would always remain that way.

At the end of her visit, Cora wished everyone well before returning to the drawing room, where Jonathan greeted her with a smile that set her heart to pounding.

He immediately stood and gestured for her to take the vacant spot next to him on the sofa. "Should I be envious that you wished to seek out my servants first and not me?" he teased.

"Very envious," she said with a solemn nod as she sat down. "They are quite a lively bunch in the kitchen."

"I beg your pardon." Mr. Shepherd feigned offense. "Do you mean to say that we are not?"

"Heavens no," said Cora. "I mean to say that you are not *as* lively."

Mrs. Shepherd laughed, and Jonathan arched an

eyebrow at Mr. Shepherd. "I believe Cora has given us a challenge, sir."

"It sounded rather like an insult to me."

"Apparently you do not know her as well as I. Cora is incapable of casting insults. It must therefore be a challenge."

"If you say so," said Mr. Shepherd. "How do you propose we rise to such a challenge, Mr. Ludlow?"

Jonathan pressed his lips together as though giving the matter some thought. "I do know that Cora likes to be entertained. I wonder . . . do you dance, sir?"

"Only when necessary."

"Juggle?"

"Only figuratively."

This earned a laugh from the others. "What about music. Do you sing?"

"Never."

"Recite poetry?"

Mr. Shepherd made a face, and Cora took the opportunity to intervene. "You may not, Mr. Shepherd, but Jonathan has an ingenious way with words when it comes to poetry. Isn't that right? I seem to recall a very entertaining poem you once composed about a goat." She grinned at him, daring him to deny it.

"You are a poet?" Mrs. Shepherd said, clasping her hands together in a show of delight. "How wonderful. Do tell us about this goat."

"Yes, do," added Mr. Shepherd, settling back with a wicked grin on his face. "Something tells me this evening is about to become very lively indeed."

Jonathan directed a look of challenge at Cora. "It *is* an entertaining poem, I will admit. However, I will only agree to recite it if Cora will agree to give us a pastry demonstration. Or perhaps instruct us on what she puts in her tea to make it so . . . restorative."

Cora tried to keep her mouth in a straight line, but she could not contain her laughter for long. "Touché, Jonathan. You have certainly put me in my place yet again."

"If only you were not so quick to leave said place."

His teasing always made her heart glow like a flame on the tip of a candlestick. She liked that he knew her so well and found her weaknesses endearing rather than irritating.

Mr. Shepherd relaxed against the back of the sofa and folded his arms. "I believe we will no longer be privy to a poem about a goat, my dear Mrs. Shepherd. Pray tell, what shall we do now?" He immediately brightened. "What about a reading? Do you have any good books, Mr. Ludlow?"

Mrs. Shepherd placed a hand on her husband's arm and shook her head. "This evening is meant to be a lively one, remember?"

"I propose a game of cards," said Jonathan. "Instead of wagering valuables, we can wager kisses."

"Yes, that would definitely make for a lively evening." Mr. Shepherd grinned at his wife. "What do you say, my dear?"

"I'd say you are both incorrigible wretches," she replied, making everyone laugh. "But a game of whist is always lively, even without a wager."

With no other ideas forthcoming, Jonathan retrieved a deck of cards and the not-so-lively group spent the remainder of the evening pleasantly engaged in a game of whist. They laughed, they talked, they teased, and after the game, when Mr. Shepherd helped Mrs. Shepherd with her coat, Jonathan stole a brief kiss from Cora.

She left with her slippers barely grazing the floor, thinking she could not remember a happier time in all her life. If only it would last forever.

In early January, on an overcast Monday morning, an invitation addressed to Mr. and Mrs. Shepherd *and* Miss Coralynn Notley arrived in the post. Cora was seated in the drawing room with the Shepherds and worried over her lower lip while Mr. Shepherd scanned the missive.

"Mrs. Bidding is hosting a soirée at her home on Friday next and would like for all of us to attend."

Mrs. Shepherd considered the invitation with pursed lips and a thoughtful nod. "I should have liked for Cora to make her debut at a larger event, but Mrs. Bidding is a dear friend and we cannot decline. Perhaps it is for the best." She paused and looked at Cora. "Mrs. Bidding's parties are usually tepid affairs and therefore not very well attended, so we can ease you in slowly. There are likely to be no more than twenty people in attendance, wouldn't you agree, Stephen?"

He nodded as he perused another letter that had arrived.

"What do you say, Cora?" asked Mrs. Shepherd. "Shall I accept for all of us?"

Large party or small, Cora could not muster any excitement about the prospect. She had little experience with social outings and did not know what to say to people who would likely look down their noses at her.

Mr. Shepherd peeked at Cora over the top of his reading glasses before setting his letter down. He leaned forward, taking her hand in his and giving it a light squeeze. "The Biddings are kind and gracious. They will adore you on sight and welcome you into their home. As for the rest, I do not know how they will react or what they might say. But there is no need for you to admit to being a housekeeper, my dear. People will hear what they will hear and think what they will think, but if Julia, Mr. Ludlow, and I remain silent on the subject, no one will ever really know what truly transpired, will they?"

Cora could not argue with that, but she was fairly certain that if asked, she would not be able to hide the truth. Had Jonathan not said that her eyes were too honest and her expressions too telling? As things stood now, Cora was far more likely to add fuel to the gossip than stifle it, but she also knew she could not stay hidden away at Knotting Tree forever. That would be an act of cowardice, and she refused to think of herself as a coward.

She lifted her chin and nodded. "Let us send our acceptance for what is sure to be a delightful evening."

"I would not count on it," said Mr. Shepherd with a small smile. "Julia was being kind when she described the Bidding's parties as tepid. In reality, they are much like reading a dictionary."

Cora decided to take comfort in that. A small party would definitely be the preferable place to begin and she would be grateful for it. But as each day passed, bringing them closer to the day of the soirée, she could not quiet her anxiety. Though she was no stranger to a good snubbing, she had never been able to ignore the sting that came with it. Mr. and Mrs. Bidding had been kind to invite her, but what if all others in attendance only accepted because they wanted to get a look at the woman who'd behaved so scandalously? Once they'd seen for themselves that she was no one of importance, would she be forever ostracized from the community? Would rumors spread about her and Jonathan? Would he come to realize that she was not worth his notice?

By the time the day of the party came, Cora's stomach

had wound itself into the most intricate of knots. She stared at her reflection in the mirror as Katy pushed a few last pins into place, creating a lovely coiffure.

"I'm shaking," Cora said, holding out her quivering hands for inspection.

The maid wasn't overly sympathetic. "What do you expect after eatin' practically nothin' all day? Course you're shakin'!" Katy had brought up a tray earlier and Cora had not touched it. She was certain that if she ate even a single bite, it would come right back up in the most unladylike of ways.

"I am not at all hungry," said Cora.

"'Tis your nerves trickin' your belly into thinkin' that, Miss. You need to eat somethin' or you're like to faint."

Trickery or no trickery, Cora could not even look at the food without feeling queasy. She glanced at her maid, hating that she needed to ask the question she had promised herself she would never voice out loud. But she had to know. "Katy, will you tell me what is being said below stairs about me?"

Katy frowned for a moment, then shrugged. "Not much anymore, Miss. Some used to think you took to bein' a 'ousekeeper so as to catch Mr. Ludlow's eye, but I set 'em straight and told them to stop their tongue-waggin'."

The maid seemed quite pleased with her answer, but it did nothing to settle Cora's nerves. She should have left the question unasked, but it was too late now.

Cora mustered a kind smile. "Thank you for saying so, Katy. And I don't know how, but you've performed a miracle with my hair. It has never looked more lovely."

Katy blushed rosily. "Thank you, Miss, but we both know 'tis you who makes it lovely. Now don't keep Mr. and Mrs. Shepherd waitin' any longer. Off you go now."

Cora picked up her wrap and slowly made her way to the stairs. Mr. and Mrs. Shepherd waited in the great hall below, talking quietly. As soon as they heard Cora's footsteps descending the stairs, Mrs. Shepherd looked up and clapped her hands. "Oh, my dear, it's just as I suspected. That blue is ravishing on you. It puts a sparkle in your eyes and makes you look most angelic. Don't you agree, Stephen?"

"Heartily."

When Cora reached the bottom step, he held out one arm to his wife and the other to Cora. "I shall be the envy of every man in attendance tonight."

"Let us pray there will not be many of them." Cora pressed her palm to her queasy stomach. "I don't think I have ever felt more nervous, not even when I first set off for Yorkshire."

Mr. Shepherd patted her hand. "You have nothing to fear. We are running a bit behind schedule, so you will not be forced to mingle overly long. Then we will partake of the blandest meal you will ever eat and be subjected to the dullest entertainment you could possibly imagine. Our last experience involved listening to an extremely long reading of *Lady of the Lake*. Being an avid reader, you would think I would have enjoyed such a performance, but the man's lifeless and monotone voice put me straight to sleep."

Mrs. Shepherd nodded her agreement. "He is speaking the truth, I'm afraid. Every time Stephen began snoring I had to nudge him awake. It was most taxing, believe me, and I'd never been more relieved for any performance to end."

Cora smiled as they descended to the waiting coach. If she had to make a debut, at least she could make it with Mr. and Mrs. Shepherd at her side and not her own parents. That thought alone gave her some comfort.

The cold air nipped at her nose and whipped across the back of her neck, sending shivers down her spine. She tugged her wrap tighter about her before climbing inside and settling in the seat across from the Shepherds. Her gaze immediately strayed to the small window, where she peered into the darkness. The snow had not lasted more than a day or two and they had seen no more of it since the evening that had changed everything for Cora. There had only been overcast skies, rain, sleet, and fierce winds that had rattled the window panes and woke her up at night.

It all felt like a dark omen now.

While Mr. and Mrs. Shepherd conversed quietly about a book he'd recently read, Cora remained content to watch the shadows play across the landscape, swaying back and forth as the coach rattled onward. Jonathan would be in attendance tonight as well. The thought should have given her some comfort, but Cora did not know what to expect from him either. Would he speak briefly and casually to her, as though they were mere acquaintances, or would he look at her with warmth and tenderness as he did when they were together at Knotting Tree or Tanglewood? It was not the thing to hang on a gentleman's arm all evening, but she hoped he would attend to her for a least a time. She needed to know that he did not regret loving her.

The coach slowed and turned, making its way up the carriage path towards the house. Cora watched the building grow larger and larger as they approached. Light spilled from every window, casting a yellow glow across the stone. It looked warm and welcoming, and Cora could only pray those already inside would be the same.

The coach stopped, and the door creaked open. Mr. Shepherd descended first, followed by Mrs. Shepherd, and then Cora. As before, Mr. Shepherd took both ladies by the arm and led them to the entrance, where a butler ushered the party to where Mr. and Mrs. Bidding waited. Cora had to clench her teeth to keep her jaw from dropping at the sight of their hostess. She was the tallest woman Cora had ever seen and appeared so very grim. Her features were almost more manly than womanly, but her burgundy gown was stunning. It had a delicate silver overskirt that glittered with every movement the woman made. At her side stood a slightly shorter, more portly gentleman with a balding head, a sharp nose, and the same grim expression.

"Mrs. Bidding, Mr. Bidding, what a welcome sight you are," Mrs. Shepherd said brightly, even though their host and hostess looked anything but welcoming. "Please allow me to introduce our dear Miss Notley." She gestured to Cora, and Mr. Bidding managed a pained smile.

Cora forced her lips upwards as well, all the while wondering at the cold reception. Did Mrs. Shepherd not claim them as dear friends? Had Mrs. Bidding not included Cora's name on the invitation, written in her own hand? Why then, did the Biddings seem so displeased to see them? Cora had expected this reaction from others but not her host and hostess.

"Mrs. Bidding, whatever's the matter?" inquired Mrs. Shepherd, apparently unable to ignore the tension any longer.

Mrs. Bidding heaved a sigh and frowned. "I wish I did not have to tell you this, but it appears as though our party will be much smaller than expected. All of the other guests, with the exception of Mr. Ludlow, have been sending their excuses since this morning. We received the last of them not twenty minutes ago."

"What?" breathed Mrs. Shepherd at the same time Mr. Shepherd muttered a few select words that earned him a glare from his wife.

Mrs. Bidding's gaze drifted to Cora for a moment. "Only yesterday, Lord and Lady Pembroke became suspiciously ill and sent a note around saying they would not be able to come after all. Apparently, whatever ails them is quite catching, for today everyone seems to be affected by it, other than us of course."

"How very fortunate that we are still in good health," said Mr. Shepherd dryly.

"Indeed," said Mrs. Bidding, looking at Cora once more. She must have thought Cora required additional enlightenment because she added, "The Pembrokes are the highest ranked family in the province and carry a great deal of influence."

Cora had already surmised as much, but that didn't stop her fingers from tightening around Mr. Shepherd's arm as something resembling anger stirred inside her. What a ninny she had been to worry about making conversation with others. It had never occurred to her that she would not be given the opportunity to speak with them. She felt the cut as keenly as she had felt it numerous times before, only this time it ran deeper because it extended to the Shepherds, Jonathan, and even the Biddings. How could people be so callous and cruel? She would never understand it.

"This is all my doing," said Cora woodenly. "You should not have invited me, Mr. and Mrs. Bidding, or I should not have accepted."

Mrs. Bidding sighed. "Of course we should have. It's just these dratted circumstances. I am beginning to think that Tanglewood inspires scandal in anyone who occupies it."

Mr. Shepherd uttered a mirthless chuckle. "That seems to be the case, doesn't it? And speaking of Tanglewood, has Mr. Ludlow not arrived yet? I had thought we would bring up the tail."

"Oh, yes. He has come and gone, I'm afraid," said Mrs. Bidding with a huff. "Once he heard the news he decided he would pay a visit to the Pembrokes and make certain they are not suffering too greatly. I did my best to discourage him, but of course he would not listen to reason. He will no doubt ring a peel over their heads and be forever ostracized by the family as well."

"It's a sorry business indeed," added Mr. Bidding with a shake of his round head.

"Please tell me you are jesting," said Cora, wide-eyed at the news. Why did Mrs. Bidding wait until now to reveal that bit of information? Why did she not meet them outside and tell them to go after Jonathan with as much haste as possible? Good heavens, what had he been thinking? A confrontation with such an esteemed family would only worsen matters.

Her knees suddenly felt weak and shaky, for she knew what he'd been thinking. He had wanted to defend her honor. No doubt his anger at the situation overcame his good sense, and she could only pray the cold air would chill his temper before he arrived. People like the Pembrokes did not forgive easily.

Mrs. Shepherd shook her head, looking as downtrodden as Cora felt. "What a perfectly wretched thing to have happen. I am truly sorry, Cora. I suppose I should have known better, having experienced a similar situation in my past, but I had hoped more from the people in Askern."

Cora could only swallow and wish that she was anywhere but here. She was well aware of the rules of society and the repercussions that came from breaking or even bending them. Perhaps all would have been forgiven in time had she been born to a genteel family. But that was not the case. She had nothing but the patronage of the Shepherds and the attentions of Jonathan to inspire forgiveness, and though she had held out hope it would be enough, deep down she had known it would not suffice. All she had done was bring the people she cared most about down with her.

"I do hope you will stay," said Mrs. Bidding. "I refuse to tell my cook that she has labored all day for only Mr. Bidding and me."

Mr. Bidding must be a man of few words and even fewer opinions. His nod was almost habitual, as though he was used to agreeing with his wife on any and all matters.

"Of course we will stay," said Mrs. Shepherd firmly.

Cora nodded her acquiescence as well. She was the reason behind this fiasco of an evening and being gracious was the least she could do. She only wished Jonathan had stayed as well.

DURING THE CARRIAGE RIDE home Mr. and Mrs. Shepherd attempted to engage Cora in various topics of conversation, no doubt to distract her. But no matter how hard Cora tried, she could not pry her thoughts away from Jonathan. Had he truly gone to the Pembrokes? Had they convinced him that he was a fool for harboring feelings for Cora? Had his feelings towards her changed? She had no way of knowing what had occurred. He had not returned to the Biddings and would most certainly not visit them at Knotting Tree at this late hour. It would therefore be tomorrow before Cora would know anything more. How dreadfully far away that seemed.

The carriage lurched to a stop and the three occupants exited in a far more somber mood than they'd entered. With a sigh, Cora lifted her beautiful blue skirts and wearily climbed the steps to the house, thinking what a waste of an expense all her new gowns had been. Jeffries held the door as they entered. When Cora passed by, he tucked a letter in her hand. "This missive arrived by courier for you about an hour ago, Miss Notley."

She accepted it with a frown, wondering who might have written. The only letters she had exchanged thus far had been with Lady Harriett, but her replies had always arrived with the regular post, not by courier.

A petrifying worry assailed her. Had her parents finally discovered her whereabouts? Had they written to demand her return?

With shaky hands, she quickly tore open the letter and read the signature before breathing a sigh of relief. "It is only Lady Harriett," she said to no one in particular.

"It must be urgent if it came by way of courier," said Mr. Shepherd with a furrowed brow. "Is everything all right?"

Cora scanned the first paragraph only to shake her head with amusement. Lady Harriett had received an invitation for a ball and could not decide if she should wear the green silk or the blue taffeta. *Which do you suppose would make my eyes sparkle more?* she wrote. *I really must have your opinion because I cannot decide on my own. It is a conundrum of the worst sort.*

Cora sighed and tucked the letter under her arm. "'Tis only a fashion emergency," she said. "Lady Harriett can be dramatic at times."

"Yes," said Mr. Shepherd. "We are well acquainted with Lady Harriett's dramatics. I am glad to hear it is nothing serious."

Mrs. Shepherd laid her hand on Cora's arm and gave it a gentle squeeze. "Enjoy your letter and try to get some rest, my dear. Tomorrow will be a new and better day, I promise."

"Will it?" Cora tried to smile, but she did not feel it. Tomorrow would most certainly bring a new day—there was no way around that—but a better day? How could it, especially if Jonathan came bearing even more distressing news after his visit with the Pembrokes? Did he truly believe he could convince them to have a change of heart?

From where Cora stood, the only person who could

improve the situation for everyone was her, and the only way that she could think to do that was to leave Askern and begin afresh someplace else. Only then could the matter be put to rest.

But that was not the answer either, not when the mere thought of leaving caused her heart to melt into something resembling the muddy slush that came after the snow. She did not have the strength to leave unless Jonathan came as well. Perhaps they could embark on a new life together where no one knew of her folly. Could she ask such of thing of him, or would that mean she did not love him as she should? Which scenario would be better for him? To stay and fight for some sort of life with him or leave quietly on her own and allow him to go on without her?

A mass of dread consumed Cora's already raw stomach. She could not think on this anymore tonight without severe repercussions. Perhaps Mrs. Shepherd was right and the morning would bring a dawning of a different hope—one she could not conceive at the moment.

"Thank you for being so wonderful to me," Cora said, needing to take herself and her sorry disposition off to her room.

Mrs. Shepherd's gaze narrowed. "That sounds rather like the beginning of a goodbye. You are not thinking of leaving, are you, my dear? Because I will not allow it."

Cora managed a smile. "Not when I have nowhere to go at present."

Mrs. Shepherd opened her mouth to say something more, but Mr. Shepherd held up his hand. "Let us not discuss anything more tonight. It would be better to wait and see what tomorrow brings."

Cora nodded in agreement, thankful for his intervention. Her body ached for a soft bed. "I wish you both a good night."

"Goodnight, my dear," said Mrs. Shepherd.

Cora dragged her body up to her room, where she gratefully submitted to Katy's ministrations. Before long, she was tucked under the covers with a warm cup of tea on her bedside table.

Once Katy had slipped out the door, Cora took a sip of the soothing liquid and opened Lady Harriett's letter once more, allowing her head to relax into the pillows. The note could not have arrived at a more timely moment. If anyone could distract Cora from her solemn mood, it was Lady Harriett and her ridiculous fashion woes.

Cora skipped ahead to begin reading where she had left off.

You must think me the most silly and trivial of creatures. While you arise at an inhuman hour and slave away over household duties, I bemoan my fashion troubles. I am beginning to think I need to discover a cause of some sort. If I continue on as I have been for much longer, I will likely become as dull as Lady Rosemont, who can speak intelligently on only two subjects: fashion and the latest on dits. It has been said by some that she has feathers for brains, and I would so hate for people to think the same of me, and yet I do not wish to be considered a bluestocking either. Hmm . . .

Oh goodness, there I go again. Perhaps I do have feathers for brains after all. (You must write immediately and assure me that I do not. I shall not sleep a wink until I hear from you.) Speaking of which, is all well with you? Has Mr. Ludlow found it necessary to dismiss you again, only to ask you back? Oh my dear, how your last letter made me laugh. I have met Mr. Ludlow, you see, and he struck me as being altogether too serious for his own good. You merely solidified that aspect of his character in my mind. I pray you will instruct him, by your own wonderful example, on how to go about smiling more. Life should be an adventure and not a chore, as you and I both know. Despite the many duties and hardships you must endure, I am certain you find something to smile about every day. That is your gift, and it is my greatest wish that Mr. Ludlow will find the emotion infectious. Perhaps he will fall madly in love with you, and the two of you can create a delicious scandal by wedding—or even better, eloping. Oh, how I should love to hear such news! My opinion of Mr. Ludlow would greatly increase if he proves himself such a romantic.

You are likely blushing furiously, so I will stop my teasing, though you must admit it is a lovely notion, is it not? Perhaps that should be my new cause—to put my pen to paper and write a daring romantic novel. I would be very good at it, you have to admit. Of course, it would be necessary to publish incognito, for I could never admit to doing such a scandalous thing, but it would be great fun none-theless.

Sadly, the time has come for me to go down to dinner. I wish you were here to advise me on next week's ball as your taste is always impeccable. But alas, you have gone and left me to my own devices. I miss you greatly, my friend. Please write soon so that I may know you are well.

All my love,
Harriett

At the end, there was an added note, written in what appeared to be great haste. The letters, while still in Harriett's style, were not nearly as neat and composed as the rest of her note.

Oh, my dear, Mama has only just returned from town with the most distressing news. It seems the banns have been posted for Sir Gowen and your sister, Miss Rose Notley. Is she not but sixteen? What could your parents possibly be thinking? I am sending this letter to you directly so that you are made aware as soon as possible. I do not know of the time and place of the wedding, only that it could be as soon as a fortnight away. Please write with haste and tell me what you will have me do. I shall act on it straight-taway.

Cora's entire body went rigid as she stared at the last paragraph. Rose was to be married to Sir Gowen? Could that possibly be true? How could her parents allow such a union to take place? If Cora had known her flight would result in Rose's capture, she would have stayed or taken her sister with her. Rose was too sweet, too timid, too submissive to ever defy their parents as Cora had done. And now, because Cora was not timid or submissive, it was Rose who would sacrifice her life and marry the horrible Sir Gowen.

Why could you not defy them too, Rose, why?

Without another thought, Cora tossed the letter aside and jumped from her bed. She must return home at once to put a stop to the wedding. How she could do that remained a mystery, but Cora would not stand by and do nothing while her young and innocent sister took her place.

After searching through her room, she located her small

portmanteau at the back of her wardrobe and tossed in one of the gowns she had brought with her, along with some underthings. Then she sat at the small secretary's desk and penned two notes: one to Mr. and Mrs. Shepherd and another to Mr. Jonathan Ludlow. If she waited to explain in person, they would insist on accompanying her, which is something she refused to allow them to do. She had burdened them enough.

Her hand shook as she wrote the letter to Jonathan, knowing their future had become even less definitive now. Cora could make no promises or propose any plans. She could only explain what had happened and why she must leave so suddenly, concluding with an apology and "All my love, Cora." Even if Jonathan still wished to marry her, Mr. Notley would never settle for an untitled gentleman when one of his daughters could be wed to a baronet. She signed her name without a flourish and stared at the letter. Her heart had never felt so damaged. It continued to beat on, but with a slow and lifeless cadence. Perhaps she had been right not to expect the blissfulness to last.

Cora crawled back into bed and dosed fitfully until the cloud-coated skies began to lighten. With a yawn, she dragged her weary body from bed once more and dressed in her dependable white muslin gown and matching bonnet. Then she slipped into a warm pelisse, pulled on some gloves, and grasped the handle of her small portmanteau. She gave her lovely room one last glance before leaving it behind and making her way quietly down the stairs and out the door.

The morning air was damp and chilly, but no new rain had fallen, and she was grateful for that. The walk to town would be relatively dry. With any luck she could board the stage and be on her way before the Shepherds discovered her gone.

Jonathan had just finished dressing when Watts knocked and entered his room. "Mr. Shepherd is here to see you, sir. He says the matter is of great urgency and asks that you come at once."

Jonathan frowned and followed his butler out of the room and down to the drawing room where Mr. Shepherd paced in front of the fireplace. He stopped and held out a sealed letter, saying nothing.

Jonathan's frown deepened when he recognized Cora's handwriting. He tore open the seal and quickly read the note before muttering a curse.

"My sentiments exactly," said Mr. Shepherd.

"She's gone then?"

He nodded. "Katy informed Julia as soon as she found an empty bedroom and two notes. While we dressed, I sent a footman to town to delay the stage, but it had already left. I had a feeling the letter she received from Lady Harriett contained some serious news, but Cora looked so frail last night that I thought it best not to meddle and let her rest."

"Why did she not wait? I would have sent her with a maid in one of my carriages and accompanied them," Jonathan said, even though he was not at all surprised. Cora had a mind of her own and would stubbornly behave any way she pleased. It was a quality he found both admirable and frustrating.

"I am certain she did not want to burden us with her problems."

Of course she did not. What Cora failed to realize, however, was that Jonathan would never consider her a burden. She was a bright light in his life, one he did not wish to see diminished. It was the reason he had been so angry with the Pembrokes last night. Cora was the least deserving person of anyone's distain.

"I shall go after her," he said, striding towards the door.

"Would you like me to accompany you?" offered Mr. Shepherd.

Jonathan halted and looked back, wondering why it had taken so long to further his acquaintance with Mr. Shepherd. He was a good man and over the past few weeks had become a good friend. "I thank you, but no. I will go alone."

Mr. Shepherd nodded as though expecting that answer. "As I left, Julia had begun a letter to her daughter, informing Lady Drayson that a Mr. Jonathan Ludlow would likely visit them soon. I hope you do not mind. They are not far from Mooreston and will happily see to your needs while you are there. We will send the letter posthaste so it will arrive before you."

Jonathan swallowed, grateful for their thoughtfulness. "I would like that very much."

Mr. Shepherd walked towards Jonathan and clapped him on the shoulder. "Godspeed, my friend. I hope to see you and Cora back in Askern soon." He placed his beaver on his head and strode out the door.

Less than an hour later, Jonathan did the same.

WHEN CORA FINALLY EXITED the stage coach at the inn in Danbury, she had never felt more weary. She had planned to walk to Mooreston and speak to her parents directly, but Lady Harriett was already in the inn yard, waiting inside her carriage for her friend.

"You are coming first to Langtry Park," Lady Harriett insisted as soon as Cora had climbed inside. "There you will eat, bathe, and change into a fresh gown before I will allow you to face your widgeon parents."

Cora smiled at her frank speech and settled against the cushions. How she had missed Lady Harriett. "You will hear no arguments from me. Thank you, my friend, for writing to me and being here. I will be forever in your debt."

Lady Harriett leaned forward and grasped Cora's hand. In a rare show of earnestness, she said, "Only promise me that you will not offer to take your sister's place."

As the carriage jostled away from the inn and onto the road leading to Langtry Park, Cora looked out the window, wishing she could make such a promise. "You know I cannot. If Father refuses to listen to reason and Rose refuses to cry off, which is highly probable, I don't know what I shall do.

Rose has not yet reached her majority and is not free as I am."

"Only you would consider housekeeping freedom," said Lady Harriett wryly.

Cora breathed in deeply and exhaled slowly, thinking how much more joy she had felt at Tanglewood than all her years at home. "When you are happy you are free, no matter what you are doing or where you are. And for the most part, I was happy at Tanglewood."

Cora had yet to tell her friend about all that had occurred between her and Jonathan. Lady Harriett knew nothing of his declarations, his kisses, or his goodness. She had no inclination that Jonathan was a romantic after all, and Cora could no longer enlighten her. Too much had changed since those wonderful, blessed weeks, and Cora did not know if she would ever know such happiness again.

Lady Harriett sat up straight once more, her body swaying back and forth with the movements of the carriage. "Mark my words," she said. "We shall see you restored to Tanglewood as soon as humanly possible. If it takes kidnapping Rose and tying her up in my cellar to keep her from going through with this wedding, so be it."

Cora chuckled at the image of her sister shackled in Langtry Park's cellar. Perhaps Lady Harriett really should pen a novel. "Tell me of Lady Drayson," said Cora in an attempt to redirect the conversation. "Has your long-awaited niece made an appearance yet? I would love nothing more than to hold a newborn babe at this moment."

Lady Harriett's eyes sparkled with excitement. "Not yet, but soon. She is due to arrive in four week's time and I cannot wait. I'm certain she will be perfect."

"She?" said Cora.

"Of course it's a she. A son would never dare to arrive

first, not when Mother and I have already made the most lovely silk christening gown with flounces and rosebuds and white satin ribbons. It would look utterly ridiculous on a boy."

"What if it is a boy?" said Cora.

"Do stop," said Lady Harriett. "You sound too much like my brother, and I cannot tolerate such impertinence. It is a girl and that is final. Even Lucy agrees with me."

"Very well," Cora said, grateful to have something amusing to think about. She had spent far too many days in a stuffy coach with disgruntled and downcast passengers. Not five minutes after being in Lady Harriett's company, she felt a lifting of her spirits. Perhaps the plan to kidnap Rose was not so outlandish after all. Anything seemed possible with Lady Harriett.

The carriage finally arrived at Langtry Park, and Cora was swept up to a beautiful blue and gold bedchamber, where a petite and kindly maid awaited with a bath already prepared. Cora needed no convincing to slip out of her things and into the warm liquid, closing her eyes and her mind to everything else. But all too soon thoughts of Jonathan intruded, demanding attention. His green eyes, full lips, and that dimple that had not been nearly so elusive as of late. Would it go back into hiding now? Was he angry with her for leaving behind only a note? Would he come after her? Did he plan to wait and see if she returned? Would she return? Or would this time next month find her married to Sir Gowen?

Cora shivered at the thought and sank deeper into the tub, hating that she did not know the answers to any of these questions. She only knew that she ached for Jonathan. She missed him like she had never missed another person. Before meeting him, she had thought she needed nothing more in her life. But now that she had experienced a taste of what it could be like with him, it suddenly felt as though a part of her had gone missing—the happy part.

Knowing she could not dawdle indefinitely, Cora finally pulled her wrinkled body from the wash tub and allowed the maid to help her dress into one of Lady Harriett's gowns. It was a pretty blue dress with a contrasting white waistline and felt wonderfully clean. As the maid wrapped her hair into a lovely knot at the crown of her head, Cora stared at her reflection, wondering if the sadness would eventually fade from her eyes.

Cora thanked the maid for her help and squared her shoulders, ready to move forward so that she could put this day behind her. She felt as refreshed as she possibly could under the circumstances, and the time had come for her to face her parents. Her heart pounded as she walked slowly down the stairs, feeling as though she were about to stand trial. Would her parents even see her? Probably not. They'd likely cut her off after she'd left, and even if they did acknowledge her, Cora's opinion on the subject would not amount to much. Yet she had to try for the sake of her sister.

The butler was waiting in the great hall and led her to the drawing room, where the entire family was already gathered, partaking of afternoon tea. Cora smiled first at Lady Harriett on the sofa, then at the dowager countess at her side. Lord and Lady Drayson sat across from them, and Cora couldn't help but notice the woman's protruding belly. She looked ready to burst at any moment, yet she radiated joy. Cora tried her best not to be envious.

At last, Cora raised her gaze to the gentleman standing beyond the group and next to the fireplace. The moment their eyes locked, her smile froze and her heart began thumping wildly. Jonathan. Could she possibly be dreaming?

Her eyes drank him in as though she had been deprived of him for too long. From his whimsical hair and firm jaw to his strong arms and capable hands, he looked entirely too huggable. She wanted to run to him, throw her arms around his neck, and claim him as hers. But he was not hers and she was not his. Her ruined reputation and Sir Gowen's horrid title had put a division between them.

Yet he was here. He had come.

"You look far lovelier in that frock than I ever have," said Lady Harriett, sipping her tea as though nothing monumental was happening. "Perhaps you ought to keep it."

Cora pried her eyes away from Jonathan and noticed that Lord Drayson was now standing as any gentleman would, obviously waiting for her to cease her gawking of Jonathan and take a seat in one of the chairs. But Cora couldn't move. Her gaze drifted back to Jonathan and his beautiful green eyes. She did not know what to say or do or even how to think. Cora's ears thrummed with every vibration of her pounding heart.

"Do sit down, Cora, so I can tell you how cross I am with you," said Lady Harriett. "I had to find out from Mr. Ludlow himself what a romantic he is. Why did you not write, or at the very least fill me in during our carriage ride home from the inn? I had so hoped you would, and yet you said nothing on the subject. Can you understand now why I am so cross? I had thought we were friends. "

Cora blinked for a few moments, trying to digest it all, only to stare at Jonathan once more. "What are you doing here?" she finally said.

He rolled his eyes as though the question annoyed him. "Did you truly believe I would do nothing while you scuttled recklessly back home? And for what purpose, I wonder? To foolishly offer to marry Sir Gowen in your sister's place?"

Cora frowned at his tone, not liking it at all. "I never scuttle, and if that is what it takes to free her, then yes. As the eldest daughter, it is my duty—"

"Your *duty*?" he said, walking towards her. "To sacrifice your life? To pledge yourself to a man who will only bring you misery?"

Cora pressed her lips together and clenched her jaw. Did he truly not know that a young woman's life was not her own? She had once thought she could make it so, but she had learned otherwise. "I cannot let Rose marry that man." Surely he could understand that.

"Of course you cannot," he said, stopping directly in front of her.

"Pray tell me, what other options exist?"

"I can think of an obvious one." He grasped her hands and held them tight. "Marry me instead."

Cora's breath caught and her heart ceased beating, only to race back to life moments later. She looked down at their clasped fingers, thinking how perfectly they fit together. Oh, how she'd yearned to hear him say those words. How wonderful, thrilling, and exquisitely easy it would be to agree and share the rest of her life with him. She wanted nothing more. And yet it was not so easy as that. Nothing ever was.

"I assure you, sir, I would love that above all things, but—"

"Deuce take it, Cora," he growled. "I can open far more doors to your parents than Sir Gowen ever could. Miss Rose could set her sights a great deal higher than him, I assure you."

She shook her head, wishing it was so. "You overlook my low connections without a thought, but others do not. Mr. and Mrs. Notley will always be my parents, and what they crave most is for one of their daughters to marry into a titled family. Social standing means more to them than good breeding or intelligence or kindness. They will not willingly let this opportunity slip by, not when you cannot guarantee a better match for Rose." Cora's chest began to throb most painfully as she searched his beautiful eyes. "There's also you to consider. Surely you must see that forming an acquaintance with my father, to say nothing of becoming his son-in-law, will bring you nothing but embarrassment. Trust me, sir, you are better off without me in your life."

Jonathan's jaw hardened, and an angry glint appeared in his eyes. "That is for me to decide and not you." He released her hands and turned towards the Draysons, executing a graceful bow. "If you would please excuse us, I believe Cora and I have some business to attend to at her family home. We will return shortly."

"Please do," said Lady Drayson. "I feel as though I am in the middle of a delicious novel and someone is snatching it away."

Jonathan held out his arm to Cora, which she stared at in surprise. "You wish to come with me?"

His eyes widened as though he could not believe she would ask such a thing. "Of course I'm coming with you. How can such an intelligent woman be so thick at the same time? Honestly."

Cora opened her mouth to argue, but Lady Harriett's laughter intruded. "I couldn't have put it better myself, Mr. Ludlow," she said, waving them away with a flick of her wrist. "Now off you go so that my brother may finally sit down. You'll find a carriage waiting just outside."

Cora cast an apologetic look at Lord Drayson, who merely shook his head and smiled. "We wish you well in your endeavors and hope you will return soon with happy news."

"Shall Mother and I begin wedding preparations while you are away?" teased Lady Harriett.

"Yes," answered Jonathan at the same time Cora said, "No."

She glared at him, and he pulled her out the door to the waiting carriage, where the maid who had helped Cora earlier was already waiting inside.

"Lady 'Arriett said I was to accompany you," she said by way of explanation.

Cora nodded and took a seat beside the girl. Jonathan sat opposite them and directed his gaze towards the window, saying nothing the entire drive to Mooreston. When the house finally came into view, Cora looked at it as she would a stranger. She felt no nostalgia or tender feelings or anything of the sort. All she felt was dread.

"HELLO, EVANS." CORA MUSTERED a smile for the butler when his kind eyes widened in shock at the sight of her. He looked older than when she had last seen him, as though he had aged a decade in only a few month's time. She wasn't too surprised by the change. Her father had that effect on people, most particularly his servants.

Evans glanced briefly at Jonathan before he composed himself and bowed. "It is good to see you again, Miss Notley. Are you here to speak with Mr. and Mrs. Notley or shall I summon Miss Rose?"

"My parents, if you please," said Cora, sounding far more confident than she felt. She could not deny that Jonathan's presence at her side comforted and strengthened her.

Moments later, Mr. Notley's voice boomed from the direction of the library. "The audacity of some people! She should know better than to think she'll be welcomed here after what she's done. You may tell the woman at the door to be on her way. She is no longer my daughter."

Cora had expected a reaction such as this, but it did nothing to lessen her embarrassment. What must Jonathan think of her and her family? She strived to appear aloof when Evans returned and was grateful for his expression of sympathy.

"I am sorry, Miss Notley, but your father—"

"Is a fool," inserted Jonathan. "Would you kindly tell Mr. Notley that Lord Jonathan Ludlow, son of the Duke of Rutland, would like a word with him?"

Cora's eyes widened in astonishment, but she said nothing until Evans had retreated once more. Only then did she grab Jonathan's arm. "Sir, you cannot fabricate such things as titles! My father will learn soon enough that you are not who you say and it will only anger him further."

Other than a clenching of his jaw, Jonathan showed no reaction. He simply stared straight ahead. "I did not fabricate anything."

Cora could only gape at him until Evans returned. "Mr. Notley will see you now, my lord."

Jonathan followed the man, and Cora was left to stare after him, unsure what to believe. Could his name really be Lord Jonathan Ludlow? Was he truly the son of the Duke of Rutland? No, impossible. That would mean he had duped her and everyone else in Askern and at Tanglewood. If there was anyone who valued honesty and integrity above Cora, it was Mr. Jonathan Ludlow.

Or was it Lord Ludlow?

Cora felt thoroughly shaken. If he was the son of a duke, what reason could he have for not revealing his true identity? Why hadn't he said as much to her before now? He had only just asked her to marry him, for pity's sake! Surely that was something you would tell your intended!

Her expression became a scowl, and she began to pace the marble floor. Her father would be thrilled by the news that his eldest daughter had snared the son of a duke, if that was indeed the case. This revelation could be the solution to everything—from her ruined reputation to being rid of Sir Gowen once and for all. And yet it would mean he had *fibbed*! To her! Cora could not decide if she should be hopeful or infuriated. She waffled between the two emotions, feeling at odds with herself. What else had he withheld from her?

Feeling lightheaded all of a sudden, Cora sank down on a nearby bench and leaned forward, resting her elbows on her knees and her head in her hands. Her mind reeled, crying out for a break from the highs and lows, twists and turns, jolts and surprises. Would she ever feel at peace again? It did not seem likely.

"Coralynn?" came a quiet and gentle voice.

Cora looked up to see Rose standing on the bottom step, looking like a frightened puppy with her large brown eyes. She had on a lovely pink muslin dress with gray trim, and with her dark blonde hair cascading down from a knot at the crown of her head, she appeared as though the past few months had changed her from a girl to a woman. But her appearance alone did not make her ready to take on the role of a wife or mother, not with the likes of Sir Gowen.

Cora slowly rose to her feet, wondering what to say to her sister. They had never been close. Only four years separated them, but it was their differences that had kept them apart. While Cora had embraced learning, finding enjoyment in everything from numbers and history to needlepoint and the pianoforte, Rose did not seem to take to anything. Her efforts had always been lackluster at best. She did not even enjoy an invigorating stroll through the gardens.

Every now and again, Cora had wanted to give her a good shake and say, "If you like something or do not like something, let it be known. One way or the other, have an opinion! Do not settle for not knowing your own mind. That is worse than anything."

But Cora had never shaken her sister or attempted to understand her. She had merely let her casually wander along life's path with the hope that someday she would learn to embrace it wholeheartedly. But she hadn't. Instead, Rose had allowed her parents to live it for her, and now she was to marry Sir Reginald Gowen who would no doubt take up the reins of her sister's life. Was Rose destined to forever be under the control of another?

Cora was tired of standing by and saying nothing. "Why in Heaven's name did you agree to marry Sir Gowen?" she blurted.

Something akin to panic appeared in Rose's eyes, as though she did not know what to do when someone asked for her opinion. "I . . . I do not know. Mama and Papa—"

"Care only for themselves. They are sentencing you to a life of misery so that they might obtain their own lofty aspirations. Does that not bother you? Do you not find that hurtful and unacceptable in the extreme?"

"I'm not sure how I should feel," she stammered.

"Rose!" cried Cora, irritated by her sister's blind acceptance. "What is it *you* want? If you truly do wish to wed a detestable cur, then by all means, go through with this wedding. But if you have any doubts at all, for goodness sake, speak them!"

Rose's lips began to tremble and tears brimmed in her eyes. Cora would have felt sorry for her outburst if she had not been so glad to see her sister show some emotion for once. Perhaps there was hope after all.

Cora moved forward and took her sister's hands, repeating in a gentler tone, "What is it *you* want?"

Rose shook her head, struggling to fight back her tears. "I . . . I suppose I want to be like you, to care about things and be strong. But you and Father were always at loggerheads with each other, always fighting and disagreeing. I do not have it in me to do the same."

"Even if it means a miserable life for you?"

Rose shrugged, wiping away her tears with the back of her hand. "I have never been truly happy—not like you. I don't even know what it feels like. The way I see it, a life with Sir Gowen would not be much different than the life I have now." She spoke so woodenly and without feeling as she always did. But rather than find it exasperating, the words tore at Cora's heart. Had her sister truly never felt happiness? How could that be?

Cora grasped Rose's arm and held it tightly. "You must trust me, Rose. Happiness does exist and you can have so much more than this if only you choose to want it."

With sad eyes, Rose shook her head. "Even if I do, I have already accepted, the banns have been called, and we are to be married in a week's time."

"You are not married yet," said Cora. "You can still put a stop to it if only you are willing to stand up for yourself. Please, Rose! If nothing else, do it for me. I will stay by you, I promise. All you need to do is tell Father you will not marry that man."

"But—" Rose shook her head, appearing overwhelmed and uncertain.

"Miss Notley." Evans's voice echoed through the great room, startling Rose and making her spin guiltily around as though she had been caught doing something she shouldn't. Which was ridiculous. It was not a crime to speak to one's sister, unless, of course, their father had forbidden it, which was likely the case.

"Yes?" Cora answered.

"Your *father* wishes to speak with you now." His emphasis on the word "father" and the way his eyes sparkled with amusement showed his pleasure in making the announcement. Cora had always liked Evans. While he had never thwarted her father's wishes outwardly, whenever she and her father battled, he had always delighted when she came away victorious.

"How kind of him to acknowledge me now," Cora said dryly, glancing at her sister. "Would you care to join me?"

Rose's eyes widened in fright, and she began to shake her head in the negative, but then she seemed to stop herself and something resembling determination sparked in her eyes. "Yes. I would."

"Good." Cora linked arms with her sister. "I believe both of our lives are about to change for the better in some way, assuming you can stand up for what you want and I can resist strangling Jonath—er, I mean Lord Ludlow." How foreign that name sounded.

The moment they walked into the library, Mrs. Notley flew at Cora in a rustle of orange taffeta. The color clashed with her red hair and painted pink cheeks. "There you are, my dear, dear girl! We have been so worried about you." The embrace was awkward, to say the least. It was obvious motherly affection did not come naturally to her mother, and Cora was grateful when the woman released her.

"Yes, yes," agreed Mr. Notley, smiling fondly at his eldest daughter. He looked the same as he always had—bald and portly, with squinty, distrustful eyes and bushy eyebrows. "How wonderful to have the family back together once more. To think, all this time you have been securing the hand of such an esteemed gentleman! Why did you not tell us where you had gone or what you had planned? I would not have bargained with Sir Gowen had I known."

Cora barely refrained from rolling her eyes. The absurdity of some people. She was certain, now that Jonathan had met the man, he would withdraw his offer of marriage at once. No one in their right mind would willingly enter into an engagement that would tie them to Mr. and Mrs. Notley forever.

"Rose," said Cora. "I believe you have something to say?"

Her sister turned pale and wavered, looking ready to faint at any moment. She stared at the floor, unable to meet her father's eyes. "I . . ." She began weakly, only to clear her throat and speak with a little more force. "I do not wish to marry Sir Gowen, Father."

"Of course you will not marry him," Mr. Notley said. "Lord Ludlow has assured me that you may set your sights much higher than that man."

"To think," gushed Mrs. Notley. "My eldest daughter married to the son of a duke! I would never have thought such a feat possible! But you have proven me so very wrong, Coralynn, and I could not be more pleased."

Cora felt it necessary to intervene before her parents got completely carried away. "I do not know what you're talking about, Mother. I have not consented to marry any man, not even *Lord* Ludlow," she said, making her displeasure with him known. "And I'm not certain I wish to any longer."

"What?" blared her father. "Not consent to marry Lord Ludlow? Are you daft, girl?"

"She is obviously feeling unwell," added Mrs. Notley in a frantic tone. "Now Coralynn, you must calm yourself and think rationally."

Cora ignored her parents and continued to glare at Jonathan, whose lips began to twitch in the most maddening way. How dare he—*the liar*—find this situation humorous!

"Lest you forget, my darling," he said, obviously

unconcerned by her anger. "Sometimes a person has a good reason for behaving badly."

"And sometimes that reason is not good enough," she snapped, her tone making Rose flee to the back corner of the room.

Jonathan glanced at Mr. Notley, whose face had turned quite purple.

"Sir," said Jonathan, "I wonder if you would be so kind as to allow me a moment alone with your daughter? I'm quite certain I can bring her around."

Bring me around? Cora thought angrily. *As though I am a puppy to be led about by a leash? I think not!*

Mr. Notley's mouth opened as though he intended to argue, but Mrs. Notley laced her arm through his and began pulling him towards the door. "Of course you may, my lord. Come along, Mr. Notley, and you too, Rose. Let us give Lord Ludlow and Coralynn a few moments in private."

Cora fisted her hands as Jonathan—no, it was Lord Ludlow now—approached her, stopping a few steps away, no doubt realizing it would not be wise to come any closer at the moment.

"You're quite certain you can bring me around, are you?" she said as anger simmered within her.

Rather than answer the question, he phrased one of his own. "Are you not going to ask about my reasons for withholding my full name?"

"I do not care about your reasons."

His lips quirked into a smile. "Ah, so the tables have turned, have they? I recall saying as much to you not so long ago, and yet you saw to it that I listened."

"You lied to me!" she cried.

"Not precisely," he said. "My name *is* Jonathan Ludlow."

"Are you even from Cornwall?"

"Yes."

"Do you have an elder brother?"

"Two, actually. Peter and Oliver. It is Peter who shall one day become His Grace, the Duke of Rutland, and his new wife Her Grace, the Duchess of Rutland. Perhaps now you can understand better why Peter was much more appealing than me."

At the reminder of his loss, Cora felt her anger weaken, dwindling into something far more pitiful. "Why did you come to Askern as Mr. Ludlow, and why did you not tell me the truth before now?"

Jonathan reached for her hand, touching it tentatively and causing an outbreak of sensations to whip up her arms and through her body. Oh, how she delighted in his touch. She could not muster the willpower to pull away, which he seemed to take as a positive sign, for he tightened his grip and stepped closer, his thumb tracing intoxicating circles across her palm.

"The day I was jilted for my older brother, I realized the only reason Miss Baxter had focused her attentions on me in the first place was because of my title, wealth, and family name. Once she met my brother and discovered she could set her sights much higher, she did so without so much as a twinge of conscience. I knew then that she had never loved me as I had her. The anger I felt at their betrayal made me hate titles and standings and social positions. I knew I could never trust in another woman's love if my name was Lord Jonathan Ludlow, and so I came to Yorkshire wanting a new, untainted beginning as Mr. Ludlow. I know it was a deception in a way, but it was something I had to do for myself, just as you found it necessary to flee your home and become a housekeeper, even though that is not who you are."

He gingerly touched her cheek with his hand, his eyes

pleading with her to understand. "Can you forgive me, my darling? I had planned to tell you—truly, I did. I was merely waiting for the right moment, which never seemed to come. When the Pembrokes slighted you in such a cruel manner, I knew the only way to convince them to look past your faux pas was to go to them as the son of a duke, which I have done. The Pembrokes have chosen to think of you as an original, by the by, and will be sending you an invitation to their ball in a fortnight."

Cora felt slightly mollified, but only a little. Why had he not bothered to explain all this before now? "I wish you would have told me."

"And I wish you would not have left without a proper goodbye. I would have accompanied you, you know."

"I did not want you to feel any obligation towards me."

He chuckled, moving his thumb to her soft, plush lips and tracing them gently. "It is not an obligation, it is an honor. Can you not understand that? I love and adore you, Miss Coralynn Notley, and I want nothing more than to take your worries as my own. Will you please make me the happiest of men by accepting my hand and becoming Lady Coralynn Ludlow?"

Cora's heart began to pound like the thunderous sound one hears at a racetrack. How had it come to this? She wanted so badly to say yes, but did he truly know what he was asking and what her acceptance would mean for him?

"Are you certain you want my relations to become yours?" she asked. Now that he had met her parents, he couldn't possibly wish for such a fate.

"If they remain in Danbury, I believe we will get along fine," he teased.

"And if they should move to Askern to be nearer their esteemed son-in-law?"

Jonathan already had an answer at the ready. "Then we shall find them a suitable house on the other side of town as near to the Pembrokes as possible. But let us pray that it will never come to that."

Cora smiled as happy tears wet her eyes. Goodness, she was an emotional mess today.

Ever so gently, he framed her face with his palms before lowering his mouth in what became a delightful kiss. Cora melted against him, winding her arms around his back and returning his kiss with a zeal that he probably found quite brazen. But he didn't seem to mind.

He eventually drew back and pressed his forehead to hers. "Say you'll marry me," he murmured.

"I will," she said with absolute certainty, her mind and heart in complete agreement.

He drew back and grinned, his expression one of triumph. "I knew I could bring you around."

And he had, quite proficiently, she conceded with a shrug. "You are rather good at putting me in my place."

"And you are rather good at not staying put."

She rose to her toes and wrapped her arms around his neck, dropping her voice to a whisper. "It is one of the things you adore most about me, is it not?"

"Indubitably." He moved in for another kiss, but she turned her face to the side, and he kissed her cheek instead.

"Would you like to know what it is I adore about *you*?" she asked, twirling a lock of his hair with her finger.

He drew back and peered down at her, his expression intrigued. "Very much."

She moved her finger to his left cheek, near his lips, and touched it lightly. "Your dimple." Her finger moved to the tip of his nose as she added, "Your slightly crooked nose." After that, she touched the top of his head and trailed her finger slowly back down to his lips, saying, "Your unruly hair, striking eyes, and kissable lips." Her hands settled on his shoulders. "But most of all, I love that you have deplorable taste in paintings."

His lips twitched, and he raised an eyebrow. "Is that so?"

She nodded. "You've made it clear that you think my housekeeping skills leave much to be desired, so it is only fair that you should be deplorable at something as well. Otherwise we would not suit in the least."

"Ah," he said, as though he found her reasoning very sound.

She smiled and fiddled with the lapels on his coat, thinking how handsome he looked in dark colors. "I adore everything else about you, you know." She peeked up at him, not sure how to say what was in her heart. "I . . ." Her voice trailed off as words failed her. The joy, love, and hope she felt could not be described adequately, not without sacrificing some of its power. And yet she wanted him to understand and somehow share in the glory of it all.

He clasped her hands to his heart and captured her gaze. "I know exactly how you feel," was all he said, and in that exquisite, most memorable of moments, she knew that he did.

THE MORNING OF THE fifteenth of February, the wind whirled outside Jonathan's bedchamber window, vibrating the pane of glass not far from where he stood. While his valet finished tying his neckcloth, Jonathan glanced at his reflection in the looking glass. He was dressed in buff-colored breeches, a white shirt, a light blue waistcoat, and a navy tailcoat. It was a fairly simple ensemble for a groom to wear to his wedding, and yet it suited the event perfectly. It was to be a small affair at his parish with only close friends and family attending, including all of Tanglewood's servants. In only two hours, Jonathan would make Cora his wife, and the only question that remained was whether or not her parents would grace them with their presence.

Mr. and Mrs. Notley had insisted on returning to Askern with their daughter to help plan the wedding, but during the past several weeks they had done nothing but brew tension. They had made their temporary home at Knotting Tree and had immediately begun plans for an extravagant June wedding in London, paying no heed to their daughter and future son-in-law who were both opposed to extravagance and waiting until summer. When Cora had insisted the wedding would be held on Friday, the fifteenth of February in the small parish in Askern, her father had dismissed the notion with a wave of his hand while her mother said, "Please, Coralynn, do be serious. Not only is the parish church far too small and simple, but it is too far from London. We must make the location as convenient as possible for all who will wish to attend." From the looks of her invitation list, she wanted to invite the entire United Kingdom, probably so that everyone who was anyone would know their daughter was to marry the son of a duke.

Jonathan and Mr. Shepherd had attempted to reason with them, but they seemed determined to make their eldest daughter's wedding a grand event and rode roughshod over anyone who attempted to negate them. They would not listen when Jonathan had told them they'd engaged a rector. They rolled their eyes when Cora informed them that plans were underway for the wedding breakfast. And Mrs. Notley actually laughed when her daughter showed her the simple, yet elegant wedding gown she had ordered from a seamstress in town.

"That looks more like a nightdress than a wedding gown," Mrs. Notley had scoffed. "Of course you will not be wearing something so plain as that. Your wedding clothes must come from Madam Lanchester in London and no other. Why must you insist on being so difficult?"

Jonathan was grateful he had not been present for that conversation or he might have attempted to slap some sense into the woman. Instead, he had merely fumed when Cora had told him about it later. Apparently, she could feel his anger, for she found it necessary to lay a hand on his arm and say, "Calm yourself, my love. No good will come from arguing with them. Our wedding will go on as *we* have planned, and if they continue to think it will not, they will not come. I fail to see that as a disadvantage."

She spoke with flippancy, but she could not fool Jonathan. He saw the hurt in her eyes and knew that even though she did not look upon her parents with much affection, she did want them at her wedding.

A knock sounded on Jonathan's door, and a footman entered bearing a missive of some sort. He picked it up and frowned at the smudges and creases. From the looks of things, the letter had traveled some distance. Had his family already responded to the announcement Cora had insisted on sending them? Jonathan had made her wait to send any correspondence until a week before the wedding so they would not have time to come. He knew he would eventually need to make amends with his brother, but he did not want any family drama clouding his wedding day.

He fingered the missive for several minutes before breaking the seal and opening it. He immediately looked at the signature and breathed a sigh of relief. It was only Christopher Jamison, his good-for-nothing friend from a lifetime ago.

Jonathan began to read the letter, attempting to decipher the dreadful handwriting, which seemed to have worsened over the past couple of years.

Ludlow, old chap,

It has been an age—or possibly two. Have you begun to wrinkle? Has your hair thinned, your skin spotted, and have your teeth fallen from your mouth? I picture you quite elderly now. It seems that long since last we met and, try as I might, I cannot imagine you young any longer. I, on the other hand, have aged quite handsomely. I have become devilishly robust and dashing, and though my skin has darkened to an alarming shade of brown, the ladies do not seem to mind. I declare, as an injured war hero, I have become quite popular among them. I would consider it a nuisance if I did not enjoy the attention so very much. Lest you are concerned for my well-being, I escaped the war with barely a limp, though I confess to making it a little more pronounced when the ladies are present. Surely you cannot blame me for that.

As you've no doubt concluded, I am back in England, a naval sea captain no longer. I have lived through many adventures, thought my days were numbered a time or two, and my skin, as mentioned above, has been tried and tested. I visited our families in Cornwall for a fortnight (your family is well, by the by) and have spent another fortnight in London. But it lacks the luster it once had. I thought I might write and encourage you to meet me here, but only last night the most intriguing news has reached my ears that you are to be married.

Married!

Could it possibly be true? If so, I must come at once so that I might meet the woman who has finally captured the heart of the great Lord Jonathan Ludlow. Please say you will have me (not that you have any choice in the matter). By the time you receive this letter, I will already be en route.

I shall see you very soon, my friend.

Capt. Christopher Jamison

Jonathan fingered the letter with a frown. It would be wonderful to see Jamison again, but his timing was dreadful.

Immediately following the ceremony, Jonathan had arranged to take his new bride on a wedding trip to the coast, which meant that Jamison would arrive at an empty house with only the servants to keep him company. Perhaps the Shepherds could be prevailed upon to invite him to dinner. If only his friend had bothered to wait for a reply. All Jonathan could do at this point was write a note of apology and leave it with Watts.

He went immediately to his study and penned a brief note to his friend. Watts entered the room just as he finished.

"Lady Harriett is here to see you, my lord."

Jonathan looked up from his desk in surprise. "Who?" Surely, he had heard wrong.

"Lady Harriett. Were you not expecting her?"

"Not at all." Jonathan quickly scribbled his signature to the end of the letter and sealed it, blowing it dry as he stood. He handed the note to Watts with a brief explanation about what to do with it and went directly to the drawing room where, sure enough, Lady Harriett sat waiting for him.

When had she arrived? "Lady Harriett, what a happy surprise this is. What with the recent arrival of your nephew, we did not expect you to make the journey."

She scowled, as though not appreciating his lack of faith in her. "Of course I have come. I would not miss your wedding for the world, though I should have liked a little more notice. Must you have been so quick about it? I hardly had time to forgive my nephew for not being a girl and remake his christening gown into something more masculine."

Jonathan flipped up his coat tails and took a seat across from her. "Does Cora know you are here?"

Lady Harriett shook her head. "I thought it would be fun to surprise her. I arrived only last night and stayed at the inn."

"Not at Knotting Tree? Surely the Shepherd's home would have been more comfortable."

"I seriously doubt it," said Lady Harriett. "Or am I wrong in assuming they are housing Mr. and Mr. Notley?"

Jonathan chuckled, settling back in his chair. "Yes, I can see why you preferred the inn. I realize the wedding has come about rather rushed, but Cora does not wish to inflict her parents on the Shepherds for long, as I'm sure you understand. It is for that reason she wanted the wedding to take place as soon as possible."

Lady Harriett nodded, causing the feathers in her large peach bonnet to sway back and forth. "I understand completely," she said. "I can only imagine what a trial they have been to the Shepherds and to you."

"You have no idea," muttered Jonathan. He went on to explain how ridiculous Mr. and Mrs. Notley had been over the past few weeks. "At first they would not accept that we were to be married today, and when they finally realized that our minds were set, they refused to attend, saying they cannot support a daughter who so willfully defies them."

Lady Harriett gaped at him. "Surely you are jesting. They truly do not intend to come to their own daughter's wedding?"

He shook his head. "I seriously doubt it. No one of importance will be in attendance, other than me, of course, so why should they? It would be a concession for them, and they do not like conceding anything."

"Imbeciles," Lady Harriett muttered, and Jonathan couldn't agree more.

He leaned forward, resting his elbows on his knees. He must leave very soon for the church but did not want to sound rude. "Is there a reason you have called upon me this morning?"

With a sigh, she rearranged her skirts before placing her palms in her lap once more. "I wanted a private word with you before the wedding. After making such a long journey, I would prefer to remain in Askern until Mother is ready to meet me in London for the season. But I would go mad living under the same roof as the Notleys for even a day, so Knotting Tree is, of course, out of the question. And I don't wish to stay at the inn for more than a day or two either. I heard in town this morning that there is to be a wedding trip, so I came to you with the hope that you would allow me to stay here at Tanglewood while you and your new bride are away."

Jonathan considered her request, thinking it rather providential. Instead of Jamison arriving at an empty house, Lady Harriett could be here to welcome him.

"Of course you may stay for as long as you wish," he said. "But there is one slight complication."

Lady Harriett cocked her head at him, swishing the feathers in her bonnet once more. "Complication?"

"Only this morning a letter arrived from a close friend of mine, a former captain in the navy, informing me that he is on his way to Tanglewood for a visit. He believes he will find me at home, but, as you are aware, I will not be here. Would you consider receiving him in my place? I'm certain he will wish to return to London directly. All he will require is a meal and a bed for the night."

She blinked at him, eyes wide. "You wish for me, who has only my maid to act as chaperone, to receive a gentleman into a house that is not my own and keep him overnight? Surely you must know how improper that would be."

"You're right," agreed Jonathan with a frown. "Perhaps the Shepherds can be prevailed upon to act as chaperones."

"I'm afraid they will be unable," said Lady Harriett. "According to Lucy, Mr. and Mrs. Shepherd have plans to travel to Danbury following the wedding. They are most anxious to see their new grandbaby, you know."

"Of course," said Jonathan. "How could I have forgotten? Well, I suppose all I can ask is for you to explain the situation to Jamison and direct him to the local inn for the night. You will get no argument from him, I am certain."

Lady Harriett nodded slowly, considering the plan. "Very well, In that case I shall be glad to receive your friend." Her lips puckered into a frown. "You mentioned he's a former captain in the navy. Please tell me he is a gentleman and not some scoundrel."

Jonathan thought about all the pranks and scrapes Jamison had dragged him into over the years and smiled. "He is a gentleman, but only in the loosest of terms, I'm afraid. Let us hope the navy has subdued him somewhat."

Lady Harriett blinked in surprise. "You mean to say that I am to receive a man who may or may not behave as a gentleman?"

Jonathan chuckled, wondering what his friend would think of Lady Harriett and what she would think of him. "He is a gentleman, I assure you. He's merely a bit of a loose cannon at times. But if anyone is equipped to manage him, it is you, Lady Harriett. You strike me as a very persuasive sort of person, and I have complete confidence in your abilities." Jonathan's brow furrowed as a new idea struck him. "Come to think of it, I wonder if you might be able to convince a certain Mr. and Mrs. Notley to attend their eldest daughter's wedding."

Her scowl faded, and she pursed her lips, considering his words. After a moment, she smoothed her peach skirts once more and picked up her reticule. "You are quite right, Lord Ludlow. I can be most persuasive when I wish to be, and I suddenly find that I am in a very persuasive mood this morning. Pray forgive me for detaining you on such an important day."

Jonathan rose to his feet and extended his arm to Lady Harriett, walking her to the door. Then he bowed over her hand and said, "I shall inform Watts that you will be arriving this afternoon, and we shall hold the wedding until you arrive."

"You had better," she said. "I would so hate to travel all this way and not witness the marriage of two of my dearest friends."

Jonathan straightened, slightly taken aback by the compliment. "I am honored to be called such, Lady Harriett."

"As you should be," she said. "I do not have many dear friends, after all. But how can I possibly think of you as anything else when you have made Cora the happiest creature in all of England? So long as you keep her happy, you will always be dear in my book. Please accept my felicitations. I shall see you both shortly."

With a parting smile, she swept from the house, her peach skirts swishing about her as she descended the stairs. Jonathan watched her go with a smile. He could see now why Cora thought so highly of Lady Harriett. One could not help but admire the woman. He rather pitied the Notleys for what was to come, but only a little. They deserved whatever lecture she planned to read them.

The grandfather clock behind him chimed the hour, reminding Jonathan that he must be on his way as well. He couldn't very well arrive late to his own wedding.

"I believe it's time." Mr. Shepherd looked at Cora with something akin to fatherly pride and held out his arm. They were standing in a small cloakroom just outside the chapel doors, waiting for the wedding to begin.

Not long ago, she had entered the church as Miss Coralynn Notley and would soon leave as Lady Coralynn Ludlow. How strange that the mere span of one hour could change one's life so drastically. It both thrilled and petrified her. Was she truly ready for this?

She drew in a deep breath and closed her eyes, conjuring Jonathan's face in her mind. In his eyes, she saw the familiar warmth and tenderness and an immediate peace settled around her heart.

Yes, she was definitely ready.

With renewed confidence, Cora took hold of Mr. Shepherd's elbow, grateful that it was he who would be giving her away. In the short amount of time she had known the Shepherds, they felt more like a mother and father to her than her own. Perhaps it was good that Mr. and Mrs. Notley had chosen not to come. The wedding could proceed without arguments or dramatics or any other embarrassments. Deep down, however, Cora was injured by their unwillingness to care about her at all.

The cloak room door opened, and in walked Harry. He was not dressed in his usual livery but in brown trousers and a matching coat. He looked handsome and confident in his lanky way, and Cora found herself wondering if Sally had noticed as much. If they would ever cease goading each other, the two would make a pretty pair.

"Lord Ludlow is expectin' a few more guests to arrive and 'as asked that you wait a bit longer," said Harry, for once not teasing her about committing herself ter a man who changed his name almost as much as she. "A match made in 'eaven, it is," he'd said with a chuckle.

Cora had to agree.

She glanced past Harry, wondering which guests were still missing. Rose was here, along with the Shepherds and all of Tanglewood's servants. Even the Biddings had come. Lord Ludlow couldn't possibly be expecting her parents to have a change of heart, could he? But who else could he be waiting for?

A commotion sounded at the doors, and to Cora's astonishment, in walked her parents, appearing red-faced and disgruntled. What in the world?

Mr. Notley looked at Cora and Mr. Shepherd, frowned at their linked arms, and took a determined step in their direction.

"Mr. Notley, where are you going? The chapel is this way. We must make haste for the service is about to begin." Lady Harriett stepped into view, and Cora squealed in delight, rushing forward to grasp her friend's hands.

"What a wonderful surprise! I cannot believe that you are here!"

Lady Harriett directed a stern look at Cora. "Why must you and Lord Ludlow insist on being shocked by my appearance? Of course I am here. I would not dream of missing such an important occasion. It is not every day one's dearest friend marries, after all."

Cora had never known the blessing of friendship before, but now she felt it keenly. Wondrous and good, it felt almost like a hug to her heart. She did not realize tears had come to her eyes until Lady Harriett looked at her in alarm.

"Good heavens, you cannot become a watering pot yet, not before you have been given away!"

"Get a hold of yourself, girl," hissed Mr. Notley, reminding Cora of his presence.

She quickly dried her eyes and composed herself, turning to face her parents. "Mother, Father, I know this is not the wedding you desired for me, but I am glad you have come nonetheless. I hope you can one day come to understand, as I have, that there are more important things than titles, pomp, and pageantry."

Mrs. Notley frowned and looked away while Mr. Notley ignored Cora completely, turning his glare on Mr. Shepherd instead. "I shall be giving my daughter away, sir."

Mr. Shepherd nodded graciously, ready to concede the role, but Cora would not allow it. She had asked Mr. Shepherd to give her away and give her away he would. She returned to his side and took his arm once more.

"No, Father," she said firmly. "It is Mr. Shepherd who will be giving me away."

Mr. Notley's face became redder still. He spun on his heel to leave the church, but one glance at Lady Harriett's stern expression, and he turned stiffly towards the chapel and strode inside, leaving his wife to rush after him.

Cora stared at Lady Harriett in wonder. How had she convinced them to come? They certainly did not appear happy to be here.

As though reading her thoughts, Lady Harriett flashed a smile and dropped her voice. "I merely reminded them that the Cavendish family has a great deal of influence in Danbury—influence that not even the parents-in-law of Lord Ludlow could overcome. It did the trick nicely. You look ravishing, by the way." With a wink she continued on into the chapel, leaving Cora alone with Mr. Shepherd once more.

Mr. Shepherd smiled, giving her arm a pat. "You have honored me, my dear. I'm feeling quite puffed up at the moment and couldn't be more proud to give you away."

Cora returned his smile, detaining him a moment longer. "Before we go in, I must explain my decision. When Lady Drayson first proposed that I come to Knotting Tree, I was anxious at the prospect of traveling so far and putting myself at the mercy of strangers. She assured me that as soon as I met you and Mrs. Shepherd, I would feel more like a daughter than a stranger. And she was right. I can think of no one else I'd prefer to give me away than you."

Mr. Shepherd smiled, his eyes glistening with unshed tears. "I will most happily claim you as a daughter, my dear. Shall we go in?"

She drew in a deep, fortifying breath before nodding. Together they walked into the chapel, where Cora immediately sought out Jonathan. His eyes were already fixed on her, warm and tender, his lips lifting into a small smile. As she slowly approached, Cora marveled at how a simple look could make her feel so loved and treasured. How had she come to find such a man? She would never understand it, but she didn't have to. She merely needed to embrace the feeling—and him—with her entire body and soul, thanking God every day for placing people and circumstances in her life that had brought her to this point and to him.

Cora arrived at Jonathan's side, where Mr. Shepherd left her with a kiss on her forehead. She turned to face the man she was about to marry, and the ceremony began.

"Dearly beloved, we are gathered together here . . ."

Cora didn't even attempt to listen. In that moment, no one existed but Jonathan. She smelled his familiar clean scent and noted his freshly shaved face, his smooth lips, and the way his dimple teased her, not quite there and yet not quite gone. His eyes glowed a vivid green, capturing hers with a look that promised her the world and then some.

At some point, she must have said "I will" because Lord Ludlow was taking her right hand in his and repeating after the rector.

"I, Lord Jonathan Benjamin Ludlow, take thee, Miss Coralynn Eliza Notley, to be my wedded wife, to have and to hold from this day forward, for better for worse, for richer for poorer, in sickness and in health, to love and to cherish, till death us do part, according to God's holy ordinance; and thereto I plight thee my troth."

Cora managed to repeat the words as well, even though her heart thudded loudly in her ears and her voice wavered and trembled.

Jonathan lifted her left hand and slid a cool, gold band onto her fourth finger, keeping both of her hands locked in his. She felt the warmth of his body and his breath on her face as he spoke. "With this ring I thee wed, with my body I thee worship, and with all my worldly goods I thee endow: In the Name of the Father, and of the Son, and of the Holy Ghost. Amen."

More beautiful words had never been spoken. The rest of the ceremony became a blur with the rector's voice droning on in the background. Once it ended, they were ushered outside into a windy and cold February morning. A smiling crowd flanked them on both sides, cheering, extending felicitations, and tossing handfuls of rice and seeds over them. How foreign it all felt, like a beautiful dream.

The couple waved as they climbed into the carriage, at last alone. As soon as the door had been secured, Jonathan leaned in close, murmuring, "Hello, my wife," before he kissed her soundly. The carriage began to move, breaking them apart, so he released her and dropped his voice to a conspiratorial whisper. "Lady Ludlow, if I were to suggest that we forget our wedding breakfast and depart immediately for our honeymoon instead, what would you say?"

She grinned, liking the idea immensely while knowing they could not. "I would say that I should have broken my

fast before the ceremony. Though beautiful and unforget-
table, I own I did not expect it to last so long. I'm afraid the
experience has left me quite famished. Are you not as well?
Surely we cannot leave without at least tasting a bite of the
lemon cake Mrs. Caddy has prepared just for you."

He chuckled and relaxed against the cushions. "Very
well, you have convinced me. We shall go to our wedding
breakfast, but we will stay only as long as it takes for me to
eat some cake and you to have your fill."

"Agreed." She snuggled against him and laid her head
on his shoulder, only to be jostled away when the coach hit a
rut in the road. Lord Ludlow's arm snaked around her,
pulling her tight against him once more.

"Good gads, woman, must I always be putting you back
in your rightful place?"

"What place is that, sir?"

He dropped a kiss on her forehead and glanced out the
window. "Precisely where you are, my love. At my side,
within the circle of my arms, and always in my heart."

Cora warmed at his words, loving them and him. "Why
Lord Ludlow, that sounded almost poetic."

"It did, didn't it?" He grinned down at her. "Perhaps
there is hope for me yet."

"Perhaps there is."

She kissed him again and continued to do so until they
came to an unwelcome stop. The door opened altogether too
soon, revealing a large stone house that Cora had seen only
once before. The Biddings had kindly offered to host the
wedding breakfast, and from the number of carriages that
lined the path ahead of them, this particular event, as
opposed to the one before, was not lacking in attendance. It
appeared as though all of Askern had come.

Jonathan surveyed the scene only to look back at his

wife. "It seems the town is ready to embrace the new Lady Ludlow. Are you certain you wish to go in?"

Cora watched the house, feeling a twinge of nervousness. The last time she had walked through those doors, her hopes had been trampled upon most cruelly. But things had since changed, her hope had been restored, and Cora could now say that she had no ill feelings for anyone inside that house, not even the Pembrokes. If they could look past her offenses, she could look past theirs. Tanglewood was to be her home now, and she would do everything she could to make friends of the people of Askern. With some it would come easier, as it had with the Biddings. With others, it may never come. But if there was one thing her experience as a housekeeper had taught her, it was to never give up regardless of the obstacles. She had learned that if she pressed forward, everything would right itself in the end.

Cora no longer believed in dreary destinies or unalterable lives. She believed in bumps and lumps, twists and turns, highs and lows. Life was a muddle of happy and sad and always would be. But if a person surrounded themselves with love, friendship, and as much happiness as they could muster, all the bumps, lumps, and lows became slight setbacks on a road leading to exquisite vistas. Cora was on her way there now, she could feel it in her soul, and she could not wait to begin her journey.

Dear Reader,

Thanks so much for reading and supporting my efforts! I hope this story provided you with a break from the daily grind and rejuvenated you in some way. If you're enjoying the Tanglewood series, stay tuned for *The Splash of Lady Harriett* (Tanglewood 3), coming August 2017.

If you're interested in being notified of new releases, feel free to sign up for my New Release mailing list on my website at RachaelReneeAnderson.com. I will keep you in the loop and notify you when books and audiobooks are available.

Also, if you can spare a few minutes, I'd be incredibly grateful for a review from you on Goodreads or Amazon. They make a huge difference in every aspect of publishing, and I'm always so thankful when readers take a few minutes to review a book.

Thanks again for your support. Best wishes!
Rachael

TANGLEWOOD SERIES

Book 1   Book 2   Book 3 - coming Aug 2017

ACKNOWLEDGEMENTS

I have several people I must thank for assisting me with this book. My awesome sister, Letha, for aiding me in the plotting/outlining process. Sarah and Samuel Adams, a husband and wife who served as a housekeeper and butler during the regency time period, for writing a book called *The Complete Servant* that helping me immensely. Many thanks to Braden Bell, Andrea Pearson, Karey White, and Karen Porter, for being my first readers and for giving me the sort of valuable feedback that makes a book so much better. My dear friend, Kathy Habel, for reading all my books and assisting me with marketing (my least favorite part of this business). I would never dare release a book without her help. I'm also grateful for my newfound friend in the UK, Helen Taylor, for proofreading and narrating the audiobook so beautifully. And of course Kathy Hart, for nudging me to write this series.

Lastly, I must thank my family for their continued encouragement, my readers for their support, and my Heavenly Father, for challenging and blessing me throughout this journey.

ABOUT THE AUTHOR

RACHAEL ANDERSON is a *USA Today* bestselling author and mother of four crazy and awesome kids. Over the years she's gotten pretty good at breaking up fights or at least sending guilty parties to their rooms. She can't sing, doesn't dance, and despises tragedies, but she recently figured out how yeast works and can now make homemade bread, which she is really good at eating. You can read more about her and her books online at RachaelReneeAnderson.com.

46165482R00152

Made in the USA
San Bernardino, CA
27 February 2017